IRISH MAGIC

A SECOND CHANCE ROMANCE

BOOK 3

SUSAN B. JAMES

DREAMS R US PUBLISHING

PRAISE FOR SUSAN B. JAMES

"A quirky tale of love where and when you least expect it, but exactly when you need it most."

— TOMETENDER BOOK BLOG

"A lovely cross of contemporary with a touch of fantasy. I'd definitely pick up more books like this one from Ms. James."

— TRISH ON GOODREADS

This charming and highly enigmatic tale uses a little fantasy fun and plenty of bright and breezy Irish culture to whisk its readers away.

— K.C. FINN FOR READERS' FAVORITE

To Arlene and Don

who told me about Ireland's Matchmaking Festival.

To Jane and James Dunning
who journeyed with me to Ireland,
to the Matchmaking festival and beyond.
We traveled by bus and stayed at the hostels Jane found for us in her own inimitable way.
You are grand traveling companions.

Ireland is a marvelous adventure.

I hope I've captured a wee bit of it's magic for you.

ACKNOWLEDGMENTS

Books require lots of birthing.

Thank you, Debby Gilbert for taking a chance on me. Thanks to Cheryl Yeko, editor extraordinaire.

Thanks to my critique partners, Kelly Hartog, Therese Gilardi, Tema Merback, and Alison Morse. They make me a better writer.

Thanks to Gail Ruggles and Allison Morse for their Beta reads and their wonderful comments.

A note to my readers: I knew Leprechauns best from *Finian's Rainbow* and *Darby O'Gill and the Little People*. Neither the films nor my extensive internet research answered the questions. Where do Leprechauns come from? How do they reproduce? That left me free to make my own lore and to add in Ireland's fairies. I hope you enjoy the result.

Second edition

978-1-7370751-8-9

Irish Magic KDP and D2D

978-1-7370751-9-6

Irish Magic Print version

Original edition August 2019 By Soul Mate Publishing

Published November 2024

Dreams R Us Publishing

To Arlene and Don

who told me about Ireland's Matchmaking Festival.

To Jane and James Dunning
who journeyed with me to Ireland, to the Matchmaking festival and
beyond. We traveled by bus and stayed at the hostels Jane found for
us in her own inimitable way.
You are grand traveling companions.

Ireland is a marvelous adventure.

I hope I've captured a wee bit of it's magic for you.

1

Madison Square Park, New York City

Hanford House wants its advance back.

Kate's author mind edited her agent's six-word text down to two. *Panic now.*

Blowing the last of her book advance on a ticket to Ireland to do research might be her worst idea to date. If you didn't count getting engaged to Eric and using him as a model for her hero. Or quitting her day job before turning in the revisions on her second book. Did bad luck come in threes?

From her seat on the grass, she focused on the barely visible triangular point of the Flatiron Building. She was supposed to leave for Ireland next week. She was pretty sure her trip insurance wouldn't accept needing a new job as a reason for a refund. The brownie she'd bought to celebrate her last day as a bookkeeper tasted like ashes. What was she going to do now?

Batten Barton and Dunston had already replaced her. Her savings would take her through the next two months, but she'd been counting on the second part of the book advance to tide her over till she finished her next book. And now they wanted the first part back?

She fisted a handful of grass for comfort, praying for an answer to stop this disaster. None came.

Advance spent, Kate texted back. **Stall them.**

You broke contract. Revisions due last month.

Almost done. Just one thing to fix.

One major thing. The ghost of her ex-fiancé tainted her hero's every word. Physically Eric had been the perfect inspiration for dashing, mysterious Lord Rotherham, but . . . Kate's throat constricted. She was no Jane Austen, turning the real-life man who broke her heart into a hero that haunted readers' dreams. Her Lord R was a complete ass.

Why did she have to be the kind of writer who needed a real person to hang her fictional character on? Her thoughts raced till they crashed into the wall blocking her creative mind.

Traveling to Ireland had seemed reasonable when she bought the ticket. She'd kill two birds with one trip. Find a new model for Lord Rotherham and research her next book, *Perfect Match,* on the Bus Eireann tour she'd spent the last month planning. The plot had already bloomed in her head. All she needed was the bus tour to nail down the details.

Kate twiddled broken blades of grass between her thumb and forefinger. One fell free. No. Not grass. It was a four-leaf clover. Her first ever. In the middle of New York City?

Kate picked it up carefully. True love might be a dead issue, but there was still the hope of magic. She closed her eyes and made a wish. "Please. Send me the perfect hero."

BRADLEY FLYNN, CEO of Abbey Public Relations propped his feet on the windowsill of his fortieth-floor office, feeling lord of all he surveyed. He loved New York. In seven years, he'd achieved more than he thought possible. The only thing he needed now was . . .

The intercom buzzed. "Brad, a Mr. McPhee is on line two. He says he has a contract with you."

Brad's size-eight Ferragamo's hit the floor with a bang. He swiveled his chair to face the desk. Icicles clog-danced on his spine. "Tell him I'm out."

The Wearing of the Green blared from his cell phone. McPhee's signature ring with McPhee's own lyrics meant to entice errant half-Leprechauns back to the auld sod. *Oh, there is a little island and our people love it well. A place by Nature gifted with a most endearing spell—* Brad switched off the phone.

The picture on his monitor pixilated; re-forming into the face he least wanted to see. Damn the Leprechaun Guild and especially the Guild Master.

McPhee smirked at him. "You're up."

"I can't be. It hasn't been—"

"The woman used a clover."

The monitor view reformed again, revealing a woman with closed eyes speaking into her cupped hands. Her mass of auburn hair was wound into a granny bun. She might have a nice figure. Impossible to tell because of the oversized NYU hoodie she had on over . . . a business suit? Seriously?

"She wants a real hero."

"I suppose I could manage that." At least, he could teach her how to dress.

"You're not what she has in mind. Find her a hero." McPhee's smirk got nastier. "And remember. No magic."

"No magic? Why?"

"Because you're dealing with a heart wish. You can't use magic to make someone fall in love. Find another way. And remember, if you don't succeed, you're mine for the next seven years." The screen went dark.

Brad glared at the two pages his printer spat out. Kate Carnahan. His wish client. Name, address, and pertinent history. He scanned them rapidly. Hah. She was going to Ireland next week. Score one for The McPhee.

Well, forcing him back to Ireland wasn't going to work. He'd find a way to accompany her, see to her wish and be back in New York in a fortnight. But how in the name of Finn was he supposed to provide her with a hero without magic?

Perhaps a bit of help? Asking a favor didn't count as magic. He scrolled through his contact list till he found the name he wanted and punched in a call. The vibrant voice he remembered sounded much older now. Humans aged so fast. "Essie, how would you feel about an all-expenses-paid trip home to Ireland?"

CHAPTER 2 MICHAEL

Parsonville, California

Dr. Michael Walshe looked at the golden leaves blowing past his office window, wondering if he could get in a run before sunset. The intercom buzzed. "Michael, you have a call from Mrs. O'Brian on line one."

Michael picked up the phone. "Essie, what's wrong?"

Essie's voice had more spring in it than he'd heard in months. "And can't a body call you without being sick? I was wondering if you could drop by today, Michael, I've got to go home to Ireland and I'm not sure I can do it by myself."

Couldn't be a funeral. She sounded too perky. "Somebody getting married?"

"More than one, dear boy. I've got a mission to fulfill."

Not good. That sounded delusional. "Of course I'll come. How bout I make dinner. Spaghetti okay?"

"That will be grand." Essie's voice dropped to a whisper. "It's not just the trip. I don't know what to do about Chloe."

"Relax. We'll figure it out. See you soon." He flicked the intercom. "Lynne, how many more patients?"

His nurse poked her head through the door. "Prissy was the last one. She told me she's got a date with you for Saturday. Where was your running pass formation?"

"I zoned out after about fifteen minutes and she slipped it in sideways."

"Doctor Adorable bites the dust again." Lynne lounged against the door frame, her rocker-punk hairstyle contrasting oddly with her broad moon face. Her daughter must have been playing hairdresser again. "You know they wouldn't try so hard if you weren't hot."

"Stuff it, Lynne."

"I'm serious. You look exactly like the new doctor on *As She Turns*. Tall dark and dreamy."

Michael turned on the faucets in the small office sink. Lynne needed a new hobby. "Watching soaps will rot your brain."

"That hint of beard on your strong, manly chin. And that aloof but rumbly look in your eyes and . . ."

He took the last paper towel out of the dispenser. "We need more towels."

"Your only fault is you don't have a romantic bone in your body." Lynne clasped her plump hands over her Hello Kitty scrub top. "I'm having a fantasy here. Don't ruin it."

He would never understand women. "What do you need a fantasy for? You're in love with your husband."

"So? Tom has fantasies too. Part of being happily married. His is Tracy Jay."

Michael winced. Growing up with a well-known actress for a godmother meant he'd met lots of A-list stars, but his heart had been immune until Lorena introduced him to Tracy Jay at the wrap party for *Just the Girls* two years ago.

"Come on, Michael. Don't you have fantasies?"

"None that I care to tell you about." His relationship with Tracy was classified. Tracy had wanted it that way. He exchanged his white coat for the tan windbreaker he kept in the small closet. "I'm off to check on Essie. We have a dinner date. I'm making her my secret-recipe spaghetti sauce."

"Big deal. I know you use Ragu."

"What is it with this town? You know my grocery list?"

Lynne patted his cheek. "I think there's a town website devoted to your every move."

"Go home and annoy your children. We're done for the day."

Lynne blew him a kiss and shut the door behind her.

A quick stop at the market, and off to Essie's. What kind of secret mission could she be fantasizing? His phone buzzed. Another phone call from Tracy. They'd been coming like clockwork all day. He pushed delete without answering.

Lynne's question echoed in his mind. Don't you have fantasies? His heart twisted, remembering his last sight of Tracy.

Not anymore.

CHAPTER 3 KATE

Kate strode down 3rd street, barely registering the huge plastic bags of garbage piled up along the curbsides. The age-ravaged brownstones on her side of the block were some of the last rent-controlled buildings left in the East Village. She loved their worn stone steps and the plaster lintels carved with eroded gargoyles.

Enrique and his cronies sat in their usual place, the dented metal chairs next to Habibi's Deli. "*Hola. Katarina? Como esta?*" Enrique shouted over the noise of construction from the new apartment building across the street.

"*Bien.*" Kate smiled and hurried past. If she said anything more, there'd be a twenty-minute recap of neighborhood news.

The building next to hers had a Chinese dragon's head carved into its gray stone banister. Kate touched it for luck. Her grandmother Carnahan taught her to look for luck everywhere. That was Grandma Rainbow's gift to her.

That and the bequest of her rent-controlled apartment. Kate knew she was lucky. A struggling writer, even one with a good bookkeeping job couldn't afford to live in Manhattan.

Her apartment was probably what attracted Eric to her in the first place. When he moved in, he'd persuaded her to replace her grandmother's eclectic furniture with Ikea modern. She'd put Rainbow's huge loom, her woven walls hangings, and her furniture in storage, and allowed Eric to hang his cherished Klee and Picasso prints.

When Eric left, he took the prints with him. She'd put the Ikea living room suite on the street.

Kate climbed the five steps to the graffiti-decorated door of her apartment building. A blast of rap from a passing car tangling with the love song floating out of Lupita's Mexican Bodega followed her inside.

Lily poked her head out of apartment 1A. "Someone broke 5B's mail slot." Her voice was scratchy from years of shouting at possible government spies. "I ran him off before he got to yours. I think he was from the IRS."

"Thanks, Lily. The building is lucky to have you watching out for all of us."

Kat waited for Lily to go back inside before unlocking her mailbox. Flyers from Duane Reed and Trader Joes spilled out, followed by a legal-looking envelope and a heavily embossed invitation.

She cringed when she saw the return address. An invitation from her mother meant one thing. She was getting married again. Oh, joy. Another stepfather. She'd fake bubonic plague rather than go to her Mom's fifth attempt at happy ever after. How could she keep thinking there was a Mr. Right when all her marriages ended in disaster? Mom could give Pollyanna lessons in optimism.

Kate ripped open the legal notice. And the good news kept coming. The building was going cooperative, and the landlord wanted to offer her the opportunity to buy her apartment.

She surveyed the narrow hallway leading to the battered staircase. The shabby wall paneling was decorated with more scratched-in aphorisms than her old high school bathroom. The once-white linoleum flooring was now the color of an antique treasure map. Condo? How much was it going to cost?

"Don't kid yourself, Kate," she muttered. "This is New York. It will probably sell for a million dollars a floor."

Kate climbed the four flights of stairs to her apartment, unlocked the three locks, flipped the light switch and surveyed her kingdom.

The plain wooden desk holding her huge computer monitor, and her lucky glass bluebird, sat between the room's two narrow windows. She drew the red woven curtains across them, shutting out the night.

The gentle glow from the track lighting reflected the patchwork of colors on the floor to ceiling bookshelves. Childhood and adult favorites jostled in happy abandon. They were her most precious possession. Books never failed her.

The latest Andrea St. Claire novel sat on a Chinese red end table begging for her attention. Toeing off her heels, she sank into the squishy cushions of the blue velour sofa and propped her feet on Grandma Rainbow's hand-painted coffee table.

Her grandmother's woven tapestry made a joyous splash of color on the wall between her bedroom and the bathroom. The ever-present sound of traffic was a far-off hum. Her computer was silent. She knew she ought to boot it up and make another stab at fixing Lord Rotherham, but —.

Her phone whistled. A text from her office mate, Dee.

Don't forget. 7:30 Got a surprise for you.

Kate winced. She'd promised to meet her co-workers at Masterson's to celebrate her last day at the company.

The last thing she wanted to do was spend the evening in a bar. She'd met Eric in a bar. That was when she was young and stupid and still believed in the possibility of true love.

And he *had* looked like the perfect Prince Charming.

Lesson? Prince Charming types who hang out in bars are toads in disguise.

"Stop it, Kate. You're feeling sorry for yourself. Dee and Brandi were nice enough to invite you. The least you can do is show up."

She swung her feet off the table and dragged herself to the bedroom. The suit she'd worn to work had grass stains on the pants. She slipped it off and scrolled through her closet for a pair of dressy pants. The bronze maxi skirt Carrie gave her for her birthday glowed in the dim light from the overhead bulb. She paired it with a black scooped necked T-shirt and surveyed the result in the dresser mirror.

Strands of hair flew around her face making her look like a demented schoolteacher. She tried to smooth them back in, but the ancient scrunchy snapped in her hand. Muttering a curse, she bundled the unruly mass into a rough twist and fastened it with the flamboyant jeweled hair clip Brandi and Dee had given her as a good-bye present.

Moaning slightly, she squirmed her feet back into her work high heels. "This is a terrible way to spend a Friday night."

MASTERSON'S WAS her idea of Hell. The lights were dim, the sports screens bright, and the buzz of conversation bounced off the walls. It was hard to hear above the gritty throb of music. Whoever made the playlist had terrible taste.

Kate spied Brandi immediately. The rose-colored bar lights spotlighted the magenta stripes in her Afro. Brandi shoved her way through the crowd and grabbed her arm. "About time. We were beginning to think you stood us up."

She pushed Kate toward the bar where Dee stood holding an umbrella-topped drink. Dee had removed the pinstriped jacket of her Armani power suit and unbuttoned the top two buttons on her cream chiffon blouse, allowing the world a glimpse of her impressive cleavage.

"My treat." Dee handed her a large martini glass full of something pink.

"Looks lethal." Kate sniffed and caught a heady whiff of grapefruit and lime.

"It's Jake's special. He muddles some stuff with pink vodka. I think it's got raspberry in it." Brandi nudged her. "Take a look at Jake. He's definitely hot."

Kate ignored the invitation to check out Jake and tasted the drink. Tart with a thread of sweet. "Not bad."

A burst of laughter turned her head to the far end of the bar. No. It wasn't possible. Eric stood there, arm around a gorgeous blonde. The woman raised her hand to stroke Eric's hair. Light sparkled off her ring finger.

A wave of hurt and inadequacy washed over her. She turned back to Dee and Brandi. "I have to leave."

Dee barred her way. "You are not going to run from that asshole. Brandi, emergency makeover time. Kate, forward march." Brandi and Dee flanked her, guiding her to the ladies' room.

The mirror reflected Kate's shell shocked face. She set her drink on the counter and tried to smile. "Trust Eric to find the newest 'in' bar in the city. It's okay, really. I'm over him."

"He's an idiot." Dee removed the jeweled clip holding up Kate's hair. "And you are going back out there and show the world what he gave up." She whipped out her hairbrush and arranged Kate's hair in sexy swirls. "Here, use my lipstick. It's a good color for you."

"No. I don't wear lipstick."

"You do tonight."

Muttering, Kate complied. "This is not me."

"Open your eyes." Brandi lengthened Kate's already thick eyelashes with a swipe of mascara. "Now close them."

Kate obediently shut them and felt the feather light touch of a brush on her lids. "You know there is a reason I don't wear makeup."

"Yeah. You don't want to look like the hottest girl in the room," Brandi said. "Tonight that's who you need to be."

Kate opened her eyes and cringed. The fire-red lipstick and sultry eye makeup made her look like a Playboy cover model.

Brandi handed Kate back her drink. "Straighten your shoulders, girlfriend. Pretend you're the heroine in your book—Miss Minerva wouldn't let the world see her crying."

'I'm *not* crying." Kate knocked back the rest of her drink.

The door opened and the blonde who had been twined around Eric walked in. Her mouth dropped open. "You look just like Rita Hayworth in *Cover Girl*. Are you an actress?"

"No. And I'm not dead either." Kate stalked back into the bar, feeling a little floaty. Summoning up the memory of her favorite cartoon vamp, Jessica Rabbit, she walked seductively to the bar. "Pour me another special, Jake."

The men facing her way stopped talking. Someone whistled.

Eric looked up from his phone and his mouth dropped open like some stupid fish. "Kate. You look—"

"Taken." A short redheaded man with the face of a prize-fighter smiled up at her. "Hi, Kate. I'm Brad."

"You're late," Dee said. "Kate, this is Brad Flynn, an old friend of mine. He's the surprise I texted you about. He's—"

Eric pushed in. "You're Brad Flynn from Abbey PR. I've been trying to get an appointment with you."

"Call my secretary. I'm busy right now. Come along, Kate."

Brad's hand covered hers. A tingle shot up her arm and straight to her brain. It didn't make any sense, but she felt comfortable and safe. He didn't feel like a possible Prince Charming. More like a friend she hadn't seen in a long time.

Dee followed them to the door. "All right, then. Mission

accomplished. Take good care of her, Brad, or you'll answer to me." She hugged Kate, whispering in her ear. "You should see Eric's face. Definite score for the good guys."

Kate let Brad guide her out. The cool air felt like a blessing on her burning cheeks. Her head still buzzed from the drink. "How do you know Dee?"

He smiled at her again. "I'll tell you about it over dinner."

Her stomach leaped in response to the word dinner. Food sounded heavenly. She needed something to sop up the alcohol. "That's nice of you, but I don't—"

"Talk to strangers? Quite right. But I'm not a stranger." He touched his fingers to the back of her hand.

There it was. That tingle again. A sense of comfort infused her. He really had the most wonderful smile.

"Dee and I go way back. Let me be the new friend who's taking you to dinner." Brad raised his arm and a yellow cab screeched to a halt in front of the bar.

"You're pretty good at that," Kate said enviously. Cabs never came when she beckoned. Not that she often beckoned.

Brad opened the taxi door for her. "I perfected the skill a few years ago. It's all in the hand." He showed her the five-dollar bill he'd palmed.

She choked back a laugh.

Brad slid in next to her and gave the bill to the driver. "Sardi's please." He turned to Kate. "Ever been there?"

"No. I've heard of it, of course."

"They make amazing cannelloni. And we'll beat the after-theatre crowd by about an hour."

The cab pulled up to a red awning on 44th street just across from Shubert's Alley in the heart of the theatre district. The Shubert and the Majestic Theatres' marquee lights blazed across the street. The St James Theatre, two doors down from Sardi's, was home to Kate's current favorite show on Broadway.

Kate pointed at the sign. "I've seen it twice once by myself and once with . . ."

"With whom?"

"It doesn't matter. He's out of my life and soon he'll be out of my book and . . ." She was *not* crying.

Brad whipped out a white handkerchief. "Wipe your eyes. You'll be better once you get some food inside you. And you can tell me all about it."

Kate blotted the tears. The handkerchief came away smeared with black. "I've ruined it."

"Keep it. I've others." Brad held the door open for her. Heat from the restaurant blew out to welcome them.

The maître d' beamed at Brad. "Good evening. Mr. Flynn. Your usual table?"

"Thanks, Eduardo, but tonight I want a more private setting. The back corner?"

"As you wish." He led them past a score of empty tables to the far corner. Brad held out a chair for her, facing the red upholstered banquette against the wall. Kate shook her head. "I'd like to use the ladies' room first."

"Of course." Eduardo pointed her in the right direction.

Stepping inside, Kate stared at her reflection in the mirror. Black mascara ran down her cheeks like a bad Pierrot drawing. A mime face gone wrong. She turned on the water which ran delightfully hot, used the scented soap and scrubbed away every trace of Dee and Brandi's handiwork.

Feeling marginally better, thoughts still a bit muzzy, she returned to the main dining room. She'd seen photographs of Sardi's but it was more impressive in person. Above the red upholstered banquettes, lining the Chinese red walls, were rows of framed caricatures three deep.

Brad rose to seat her. "I thought you'd enjoy looking at the portraits rather than the room."

Kate nodded. Most of the portraits were unfamiliar. She

recognized Helen Mirren and Katherine Hepburn and a few other actors, but . . .

"Vincent Sardi opened this restaurant in 1927," Brad said. "He needed a drawing card to attract people, so he paid a Russian immigrant to draw the famous theatre people of the day. For twenty years, the artist got one meal a day in return for his drawings. Then he died and someone else took over. Sardi's has over thirteen hundred caricatures. Many have been donated to a museum."

"How do you know that?"

"I'm a publicist. It's my business to get some of my clients up on these walls."

The waiter handed them each a large leather bound menu. Kate used hers to hide behind. She felt teary again. She never cried. It had to be the drink. Or seeing Eric. Or the text from her agent. Or the landlord. Or her mother's wedding invitation.

Kate cleared her throat. "I'll have a cup of tea."

Brad took the menu from her. "We'll have the cannelloni au gratin and a bottle of Chianti."

"No. No more alcohol."

"Cannelloni's not the same without Chianti, but have it your way." Brad turned to the waiter. "The lady will have a pot of Earl Grey and I'll have the Chianti."

Brad folded his hands in front of him on the table and looked into her eyes as if she was the only person in the room. "Tell me about your book."

Kate's breath hiccupped. She willed back the tears. "The one that's published or the one I can't finish?"

"Both."

Kate stared past Brad to the caricature of Katherine Hepburn. Now there was a woman who'd loved and moved on. "My first book was published this year."

Brad smiled and waited. There was something about him

that made her want to talk. "It's called *Miss Minerva Takes a Dare*."

"Where can I get it?"

"You won't like it. It's a romance. A Regency romance."

Brad took out his phone and tapped busily. "I see it. Interesting cover." A few more clicks and he put his phone away. "I'll read it tomorrow."

Kate cringed. "You don't have to." She'd never thought about a man reading her book.

"But I want to, Kate. It will be my great pleasure."

The waiter returned with a silver pot, a white cup and saucer, a small milk pitcher, and a basket of bread sticks. A second waiter came and placed a bottle of Chianti and two wineglasses on the table. He uncorked the Chianti and poured two glasses.

Brad handed one to Kate. "Perhaps a sip while you're waiting for your tea to steep? Tell me about your latest book."

She needed something strong if she was going to talk about *Chasing Cressida*. Taking a small sip, she let the tart flavor roll across her tongue, swallowed. Delicious. "I was halfway through it and . . ." Kate took another sip. "My writer brain has a quirk. It needs to model my fictional characters on real people. I based my hero on my fiancé, and when he broke our engagement, Lord Rotherham turned ugly. The publisher sent it back to me for revision. But I haven't been able . . . I can't find . . . Everything dried up." Kate's fingers curled tightly on the stem of her glass. "The publisher wants the advance back."

"I see. Your hero disappointed you, and now you need a new one."

Kate blinked. Brad made her hang-up sound normal. "A kind of magic happens when I find a person with a face that fits the story in my head. When I see the face, everything comes more easily."

"I'll be happy to loan you my face." Brad's lips twisted wryly.

"That was a joke. I'm not anyone's idea of a hero. I'm the buddy type. They never get the girl."

"That's not true," Kate protested. "Spencer Tracy used to play buddies and he ended up with Katherine Hepburn."

"Yes, he did, didn't he?" Brad's eyes twinkled. "Maybe I'll get lucky."

The waiter placed their cannelloni in front of them. Kate's mouth watered at the creamy, slightly cheesy scent.

"It tastes even better than it looks. Eat up, Kate Carnahan. You'll need your strength."

Kate took a forkful of the beef and sausage filled crepe and gave herself over to bliss. Then the import of what he'd said struck home. *She'd need her strength?* Was he going to hit on her?

Brad refilled his glass. "The look on your face is priceless. Either the cannelloni startled you or you're worried I'm going to make a pass."

Was he psychic? And why hadn't she noticed that hint of Irish brogue before? "It crossed my mind. You're being awfully nice to a friend of a friend."

"What if I told you I was gay?"

"You are?" There was nothing effeminate in his tough, streetwise face. "Are you sure?"

Brad cleared his throat. "I am completely sure I'm not interested in you as a sexual partner."

Oh. He was gay. Excellent. She could like him and not be worried about the result. She turned her attention back to the cannelloni. "Where is your boyfriend?"

"Ah . . ." Brad's eyes slid sideways. "I'm between friends. Tell me, Kate, the writer, what kind of hero are you looking for?"

"Actually, you might have made the cut. I like your looks. Sort of angel turned prizefighter."

Brad snorted. "Now I have to read your book. That's a hell of a description. Would you like to come to work for me? I could use a copywriter with your talent."

Copywriting? Wonder if it paid better than bookkeeping? The Chianti was as tempting as the cannelloni. But she'd had enough. Any more and she'd stagger home. She poured herself a cup of tea. "I might take you up on that. After I get back."

"Back? Where are you off to, then?"

"Ireland." She dropped two cubes of sugar into her tea. "I haven't seen sugar cubes in years. Reminds me of my teens when my best friend Carrie and I tried to build a castle with them. We were seduced by a picture in a magazine. It was a disaster." She lifted the cup to her lips to stop her inane babbling. *Definitely too much wine.*

"Ireland? Let me guess. You're going on a quest for a new hero."

Kate savored the tea. Perfect. "Well, I haven't found one in New York."

Brad refilled her wine glass. "If you're going on a hero journey, you require a faithful companion. I'd be happy to offer my services. You like castles? How would you like to stay in one?"

And if that wasn't a pass, what was it? She pushed back her chair. "It was nice talking with you, Brad. How much do I owe you for the meal?"

Brad rose when she did. "Not a thing. My treat. Can I not convince you to stay?"

"No." She tried to smile, but her lips felt funny. "I need to go home and sober up."

"About the castle—"

"Sounds lovely. Thanks for dinner. Nice meeting you." Kate turned and concentrated on walking a straight line.

Outside, an Uber driver leaned out his passenger window holding out his phone which displayed her picture. "Right here, Ms. Carnahan."

How? She hadn't called Uber. She pulled out her phone. Staring up at her was a picture of the Uber driver accompanied by a text. **Thank you for your company. Anwar will see you**

safely home. Brad. At the bottom of the text was a form signature. **Bradley Flynn. CEO Abbey Public Relations.**

Kate's good sense surrendered. She stepped inside and gave him her address. She tapped out Anwar's driver's license number in a text to Carrie. If she was murdered, she wanted to leave a clue.

She shook her head, trying to clear it. Abbey Public Relations? What had Eric said at the bar? A memory of an article in last week's *New York Magazine* popped up.

Kate leaned back and let the world spin behind her closed eyes. She'd quit her job, spent the advance her publisher now wanted back, and told the owner of the hottest publicity firm in New York to get lost.

What next?

4

CHAPTER 4 MICHAEL

Michael walked up the two stone steps to Essie's craftsman cottage with a grocery bag in each arm. He set down one bag on the stone banister support and rang the little bell dangling from the china shamrock next to the door. "Essie, open up."

Essie opened the door, her wrinkled face lit with pleasure. "Michael, me darling, I was beginning to think you weren't coming."

He indicated the bag in his arms. "I had to stop at the store for my secret ingredients. Now, what's all this about a mission?"

Essie stepped aside. "Come away in. Set your bags down." Her eyes held a glimmer of mischief. "You might want to pour us both a wee dram of whiskey."

"Essie, you're a bad influence on me. Let me get the dinner started before we begin carousing."

He set the bags on the shelf under the arched window framing the wall which opened into the combined living room and dining room, and surveyed the space for any new hazards Essie might have acquired. On his last visit, he'd removed the rickety old ladder she used to change the ceiling light.

He locked eyes with the biggest hazard, Essie's cherished calico cat. "Hi, Chloe."

The cat's amber eyes stared back at him unblinking. She slowly rose from her sprawled position on the padded rocking chair, stretched and turned her back on him.

"Don't keep your feelings to yourself, Chloe. Let them all out." Michael turned back to the sunny kitchen. The flowered dinnerware was now displayed on the counter. Easier for Essie to reach. Earthenware pots of herbs occupied the windowsill. The white curtains were tied back with yellow ribbons. A copper kettle sat on the small four-burner stove.

"And it's a dear man you are to remember a cat has feelings. Some people think animals are dumb."

"Animals aren't dumb." He took a large pot and a frying pan out of the lower cupboard. When I was a kid, my best friend was a red setter named Doggie."

"Doggie?" Essie sounded amused.

"I was three when we got him. My brother John wanted to name him Krypto, after Superman's dog, but he stayed Doggie." He filled the large pot with water and turned on the gas. "Doggie was my hero. He took the blame for the stolen pizza slices and snitched cookies. And he was always ready to listen to my problems. What's more, he never interrupted. How many friends can you say that about?"

Michael unwrapped the packages of ground meat and ready-chopped onions, spreading them out in the frying pan; then reached into the second bag for his special secret sauce. The bag crackled. He pulled out a tabloid newspaper. "I didn't buy this." He looked at the pile of gossip magazines on the low table beside Essie's rocker. "That's why Doreen was snickering when she bagged my stuff. She must have put it in here for you."

"Doreen is a lovely woman. She knows I like to keep up."

Essie unfolded the paper and gasped. "Michael, there's a man who looks just like you hugging Tracy Jay."

His heart nose-dived into his stomach. "Let me see that."

Essie handed it to him, her face the picture of tragedy. "I didn't know you were seeing someone. Now what will I do?"

A picture of him and Tracy Jay was topped by a headline, *No Wedding Bells for Tracy. Her Fame Tore Them Apart.* Outrage warred with fury. That's what everyone in the store was giggling about. He handed the paper back to Essie, resisting the impulse to tear it to shreds. "Excuse me, Essie. I have to make a call."

He strode out to the porch, taking care not to bang the door behind him and punched in Tracy's number. The call went immediately to voice mail.

His phone buzzed. Another call. His godmother. "Have you seen *The Star*? That bitch! Michael, I'm so sorry. I wish I'd never introduced you."

"Not your fault, Lorena." He loosened his death grip on the phone. "I didn't read the story. How bad is it?"

"She makes you sound like a jealous, self-important ass. Stay away from Twitter. Her fans want you crucified."

His phone buzzed again. "Lorena, I've got another call."

"If it isn't a number you recognize, don't take it," she warned. "They've already called your mom trying to find you. Sherry says there are paparazzi camping in front of the store. She says some of the older customers who remember you from when you worked at the store are giving interviews about you to the hungry hoard."

Michael's lips curved into a reluctant smile. Of course, they were. Half of his mom's clientele were in show business. To them, all publicity was good publicity. "Tracy insisted our relationship be a secret. Why would she announce it now?"

"Don't you watch the news? Tracy got pulled in again for a DUI. She spun it by telling Entertainment Tonight a sob story about how you'd broken her heart and she'd had one drink too many trying to forget you."

His phone buzzed again. He didn't recognize the number. "Lorena, I've got to go. I'm burning dinner."

"New girlfriend?" Lorena's voice sounded hopeful. "I hope she's the understanding type."

"She's not. Bye."

He retried Tracy's number. Voicemail again. "Tracy, I don't know what you're playing at, but I want it to stop. Now."

The phone buzzed again. Michael shut it down. Any emergency calls would be routed to his answering service and they'd contact him by pager. He went back into the house. "Sorry about that, Essie."

She looked up from the magazine. Bright flags stained her cheeks. "What a terrible woman, saying things like that about you. It's good riddance to bad rubbish with that one."

Michael gritted his teeth. He supposed everyone in town had read it. "Close your eyes, now, Essie. I don't want you peeping at my secret ingredients." He removed the jar of Ragu and a package of Mozzarella from the bag, emptied both into the simmering meat, and added spaghetti to the boiling water.

"I think it's time for that dram of whiskey." Essie offered him her cherished Jamieson's.

He'd rather have a water glass full, but that wouldn't solve anything. He poured the thimble full of Irish whiskey Essie was allowed into a small crystal liqueur glass, then poured himself one slightly larger. Raising his glass to hers, he repeated the toast she'd taught him. "Slainte."

"And to you, Michael." She patted his hand. "I never trusted that one on the telly. She looked sugar sweet, but I caught a spark of mean in the corner of her eye."

Michael smiled wryly. "Would that I'd been as wise as you."

"Well you don't have the gift, do ya? It takes a trained eye to weed out the wrong ones." Essie took another small sip. "It would be good for you to get away for a bit. It's fine to read gossip about people when you don't know them. But it's another thing altogether when it's someone you know."

Especially if that someone is your doctor. Michael shuddered at the thought of paparazzi descending on his office.

Essie set down the little crystal glass and clasped her hands together. "As it happens, I've a need of you. Would you come with me to Ireland?"

The whiskey burned a fiery trail down his throat. "Ireland?" The thought was a cool green rain to his senses. He'd always wanted to visit Ireland.

The timer dinged. Michael set down his glass. "Dinner first. Discussion after." He put a small portion of pasta and sauce on one of her flowered plates and added a piece of garlic bread. Too much food killed her tiny appetite.

"It looks delicious." She sat down and waited for him to serve himself. She'd set the table with a lace cloth and matching embroidered napkins.

Michael brought his own plate and took a seat.

Essie sampled the spaghetti. "It's a grand cook you are, Michael. You'll make some lucky woman a wonderful husband."

"I mistrust that look in your eyes, Essie O'Callaghan O'Brian. You're plotting."

"I was thinking that you could use a bit of help in the female department." Essie's eyes crinkled at the corners. "You're altogether too trusting."

"Don't worry. I'm off females for the time being. Except for you. Tell me about this mission of yours?"

"I owe a debt to an old friend and tis time to pay it."

"What kind of debt?"

"The most important of all. A life favor." Essie pushed her plate away. "Here's the way of it. When I was a girl, I was a bit of a wild one. Ripe for any mischief. One Samhain my brother,

Fiercra, dared me to go with him to Ballyban Hill. Ballyban Hill was a forbidden place because everyone knew it was sacred to the Fae."

Michael raised a questioning eyebrow. "Samhain? The Fae?"

"Samhain is a harvest festival. Your Halloween derives from it. And the Fae are the fair folk of Ireland," Essie explained. "Ballyban Hill was sacred to all of them. The good and the bad. Fiercra and I wanted to find a leprechaun, but . . ."

"But?" Michael prompted. Essie told the best stories.

Essie shook her head. "I wasn't feeling so brave when we got there. Twas a wanchancy place to be near anytime, but being there at Samhain made it spookier. The mists were high that night and somehow Fiercra and I got separated. He called out that he heard music and for me to catch up. But that's not what found me." Essie shivered. "I'd never heard a banshee before, but I could hardly mistake it. The banshee would have had me for sure, had it not been for a boy who belonged to the fair folk. He pulled me inside the hill with him."

"He pulled you inside a hill," Michael repeated, trying to keep a straight face. "Did he say 'open sesame' or something?"

"Ah, you don't believe me. Well. No matter. If you were raised as I was, you would know the superstitions are true. The boy saved me from a terrible fate and I owed him a boon. That's the way of these things. And now he wants my help and I have to be in Ireland to give it."

"What does he want you to do?"

Essie's eyes slid away from his. "Well I can't be telling his secrets, can I? Once I get there I can stay with my brother and his wife. I used that fine new phone you got me to give them a call."

The thought of Essie traveling on her own telling her fantastical imaginings as truths to strangers made his blood run cold. Someone had to deliver her to her family. "I'll be happy to escort you, Essie."

Essie beamed. "I was hoping you'd say that. You're exactly what I need. And it will do you good to get away from the stramashing."

Stramashing. A nice descriptive word for the uproar that article was going to cause among his patients. "I'll call the service for a backup doctor."

"That's grand, Michael. Now all I have to do is find a place for the cat."

5

CHAPTER 5 KATE

The tinny sound of her cell's ringtone jarred Kate out of her dream. She struggled up through a haze of sleep. Eyes at half-mast, she spotted her phone on the narrow bedside table, wedged between the open Andrea St Claire book and the blue ceramic base of her reading lamp.

"Lo." She yawned.

"*Miss Minerva* is terrific. All your book needs is the right kind of publicity."

Her eyes flew open. "Who is this?"

"It's Brad Flynn. I finished it last night, but I didn't think you'd appreciate a call at three AM."

Kate squinted at the gray light coming through the tie-dyed curtains and tried to clear her head. "Either it's the crack of dawn or it's raining."

"A bit of both actually." Brad's voice sounded way too cheery. "I come bearing coffee and bagels. You didn't think I'd wake you at the ungodly hour of eight o'clock on a Sunday morning unless I brought breakfast, did you? I want to talk about your book."

Her face cracked into a huge yawn. The import of what he said struck her. "You liked it? But it's so girly."

"Jane Austen was girly, too. You have a stunning comedy of manners here. Are you dressed?"

"Huh?"

"Your obliging neighbor in 1-A buzzed me in. You have three more flights before I knock at your door."

The queen of paranoia buzzed him in? "What did you do to her? Lily never opens the door for anyone. She thinks everyone is a drug dealer or the IRS in disguise."

"Nonsense. She's a lovely woman."

Kate ran to the front door and unlocked it. The sound of footsteps echoed up the stairwell. He couldn't be a stalker. Dee vouched for him. Even Lily succumbed to his charm. And he said nice things about her book. Maybe he had more nice things to say.

"Door's unlocked," she called down. "I need to change."

She sped to the bathroom. A fast shower made her feel slightly more awake. Wrapping her hair in a towel, she pulled on jeans and a sweatshirt. She slipped her cold feet into fuzzy slippers and hurried to the living room.

Brad sat there sipping coffee. He looked up from the newspaper. "I hope you like mocha." He held out a venti Starbucks. "Your book's great. I think with a little help, you'd have a bestseller on your hands."

Bestseller. Kate savored the word. It was a perfect accompaniment to warmth of the strong chocolate flavor traveling down her throat. Why did he have to be gay? He liked her book and brought her coffee. What more could a girl want except sex? She took another sip of coffee. Maybe sex was overrated. "I have a website and a blog."

"Good. After the crossword, we'll take a look at them. I know I can up your traffic a thousand percent."

"The crossword?" The Times Sunday crossword was her secret addiction. How could he possibly . . .

"Yes. The Sunday Crossword is sacred. Crossword first. Work after. I brought you your own paper." When his hand touched hers, a bubbly warmth shot through her. Suddenly it seemed like gorgeous fun to breakfast with her new friend and race him with the crossword.

She chose a bagel and slathered it with the veggie cream cheese he'd brought. Brad took the bagel with murmured thanks.

"Hey, that was my bagel."

"Always serve the guests first," he said reprovingly. He took a bite out of the bagel mumbling, "I learned that from Miss Manners."

She gave up and fixed a second bagel. A few more sips of coffee cleared her head enough to open the paper. After an envious peek at the Sunday bestseller list, she looked up at Brad. Could he really do that for her?

He'd already turned to the crossword. Kate grabbed a pen and started filling in her own.

Brad finished first and walked into the kitchen. He poked his head out. "Mind if I make some more coffee?"

"Go right ahead. Coffee's in the right-hand cupboard." Her pen raced through seventeen and eighteen down. She heard the sound of coffee beans grinding. Yeah, sex was overrated. He made coffee and beat her at the crossword puzzle. Wonder how he'd feel about a roommate?

"You're awfully slow," he commented.

She raised her head and glared at him. "Not all of us are speed demons."

Brad walked over to her computer and fingered the mouse. The screen lit up. "Point me to your blog and let me see what's going on."

Grumbling under her breath, Kate typed in the password to her blog software.

"Move," Brad ordered. He scanned a couple of posts. "You're a fine writer but you don't know diddly-squat about promotion. Do you have a Facebook author page?"

"No. It's a time-sink. I have to focus on my writing."

"Fine. I'll do the time-sink for you."

"Why are you doing this? I can't pay you. Good marketing help isn't in my budget."

Brad swung round. "Kate, I'll make you a deal. I need to pay a visit to Ireland and I'd prefer not to go alone. Let me go with you to Ireland and I will be your unpaid marketing consultant."

"But why? Why do you want to go to Ireland, and why with me?"

Brad's eyes shifted to her lucky bluebird. He picked it up and turned it round in his hand. "I've always meant to go back, but . . ."

"Back?"

He shrugged. "My family is from Ireland. When I was ten, my parents split, and my mom left me with my father and moved back to Ireland. I always meant to go back and try to find her. It's not the kind of trip you want to make alone."

"That's horrible. How could she leave you?"

Brad shrugged. "I guess I didn't mean enough for her to stay. I was kind of an ugly, awkward kid."

Kate studied his face. His eyes, the green of a frog pond, reflected sincerity and sorrow. Her mouth dropped open. "You're such a liar. That's a total lie. You're really bad at it for someone who's in public relations."

Brad sighed. "Maybe I didn't believe it hard enough. Belief's the key to a good story. Do you want to hear my version of The Wizard of Oz? You'd totally believe that."

"Someday I'll listen to it, but right now I want to know why you want to go with me to Ireland."

Brad turned back to the computer. His hands moved so fast she couldn't follow what he was doing. He was like freaking Superman. "What you need is a review or two from recognizable people. Do you mind if I open up my email?"

She tried to put just the right amount of sarcasm in her tone. "Be my guest." She headed to the kitchen for a coffee refill.

"Do you have an eCopy of Miss Minerva?"

"It's on the desktop."

"Excellent." He attached the file, hit send and swiveled around to smile at her. "Is that coffee for me?"

"No."

Brad gave her a pitiful orphan stare. Kate relented and fixed him a cup. After all, he'd made the coffee. "Who'd you send it to?"

"Andrea St. Claire."

Kate felt for the armchair and slid bonelessly into its worn cushion. "Andrea St. Claire is going to read my book?"

"Yes. She's a client of mine. And a good friend."

She couldn't believe it. This man was her own personal leprechaun. "You can come with me to Ireland. I don't know why you want to, but I don't care. Anyone who can get my book read by Andrea St. Claire can have anything they want."

Brad's face lit up. "Excellent. Have you already got your itinerary?"

"I said you could come. I didn't say you could run it." Doubt reared its ugly head. What if he wasn't her leprechaun but a personable serial killer?

Brad sighed. "You have a very readable face, Kate. What can I do to prove to you that I am a perfectly safe traveling companion?"

Kate looked at his smile, radiating sincerity and innocence. There was no way she trusted her own judgment anymore. But Carrie? Her best friend had a sense about people. Carrie had warned her about Eric, but she'd been too dizzy in love to listen. "I'm supposed to have Sunday dinner at my best friend's house. Would you like to come?"

"In a heartbeat." Brad pulled her out of the chair. "Come on."

6

CHAPTER 6 BRAD

Brad maneuvered his precious Jag through the snarl of traffic on FDR drive. Kate had more prickles than a hedgehog. He'd never had to jump through this many hoops with a wish client. Did she even remember she'd made a wish? Humans could be so careless with their wishing. He sped up when they got onto the Major Deegan Expressway.

He glanced at Kate. Eyes wide. One hand on her seat belt. The other on the dashboard. "Slow down," she said through clenched teeth. "This isn't the Indy 500."

"Relax. I'm a whiz on Grand Theft Auto. Tell me about your friend." Brad cut in front of a BMW with barely an inch to spare.

Kate gasped at the squeal of brakes and the heavy hand on the horn from the SUV behind them. "Slow down or let me out. You're not my kind of driver."

He gave an exaggerated sigh but pulled onto Saw Mill River Parkway at a more moderate speed. If he could win over the friend, the rest should be smooth sailing. He'd introduce her to Essie, and whatever candidate Essie picked out for her and let nature take its course. One perfect hero and back to his beloved company. "This friend of yours, what's she like?"

Kate loosened her death-grip on her seatbelt. "Carrie and I made friends in second grade when she beaned Heather Milbank for calling me a freakazoid. When she asked me over to play, I fell in love with her mom and dad. They were so welcoming. They made me feel like part of their family. Carrie and I decided we were secret sisters separated at birth by an evil witch. Her parents went along with it. Mine didn't care. I managed to spend almost every weekend at Carrie's house."

Brad drove down the long winding dirt driveway, praying for the safety of the Jag. The dirt was hard-packed, but it only took one stray pebble to ruin the finish.

The white clapboard two-story house at the end of the drive had a Colonial look to it. White spindle wraparound porch. Black shutters on the upper story windows. The front lawn was surrounded by forest on two sides. Dogwood, he surmised from the slenderness of the trees. He cracked the windows before switching off the Jag. It sounded a bit like home. Birdsong and the distant sound of a river. "Nice. Very nice, indeed."

A cacophony of barking broke the peace. A herd of Great Danes rounded the corner of the house. One clutched a ragged teddy bear in his mouth.

Brad cringed back against his seat. "I hope he didn't kill a child to get it."

"No. He might have kidnapped one, but he would never kill." Kate stepped out of the car and was instantly surrounded.

"They look more like ponies than dogs. Are you all right with them?" Brad got out to help Kate. The dogs turned from Kate and pressed up against him, inviting caresses.

"Ah," he crooned." You're beauties, all of you."

The front door banged open and a diminutive gray headed woman burst out. "Damon, Affleck, Downey, Clooney, Griffith, Destiny, *down*."

"It's all right, Anne." Kate extricated Brad from the pack. "I'll put them away." She reached into her purse and took out a bag of liver treats. "Come on guys, back to the pen." She looked at Anne. "Who left their gate open?"

"Danny. Ethan lost track of him for a moment and found him freeing the dogs." The woman smiled at him. "Hi, I'm Anne."

"This is Brad, possibly the new love of my life," Kate tossed over her shoulder.

Anne looked confused but hopeful.

"She's a terrible liar." Brad extended his hand. "She's not interested in me that way. In fact ..."

"In fact?" Anne asked.

Kate joined them, her jeans and black jacket dusted with a fine film of dog hair. "He rescued me from a bar, read my novel, and brought me bagels this morning. Now he wants to go to Ireland with me. I need Carrie to interrogate him. What's for dinner?" She turned to Brad. "Sunday dinner's at three."

The door opened and Morgan Freeman's double appeared. Grizzled gray hair, chocolate skin, and hooded hawk eyes. "Anne, where's the mint jelly?"

Kate hugged him. "Hi, Ethan. What's new?"

Ethan's eyes shot a laser look at Kate. "You're late. I've had to deal with Danny all morning."

"Where's Carrie?"

"She's upstairs trying to finish her thesis. Matt's at a conference in Atlanta. Minding Danny is like trying to follow one of those snake firecrackers."

Brad heard a clatter of falling pans, followed by a toddler chortle.

Ethan sagged against the door frame. "I don't want to look."

"I'll handle it." Kate sprinted inside.

A voice from an upstairs window yelled, "Dad, I thought you were going to watch him."

"Your sister has arrived. She can take over," her father yelled back. Ethan straightened to his full five-foot-ten and glared at his wife. "I'm going to the garage to build something. Anything. Call me when dinner's ready."

"I understand, dear," Anne said. "You deserve a break. How about another bird house?"

Ethan's only answer was a growl.

"Ethan builds lovely bird houses." Anne led Brad inside. "The only problem is that the birds don't seem happy with them. I think they fail to appreciate the dogs as neighbors."

A cappuccino-skinned goddess clattered down the stairs, her wildly curling hair held in place with two pencils. "What's Danny done now?"

Kate appeared with a giggling Danny upside down in front of her. "I've caught the rabbit. Shall we sacrifice him, or wait till after dinner?"

"Sack flies. Sack flies." Danny chanted.

Kate turned Danny right-side-up and handed him to Carrie. "Carrie, meet Brad. He wants to go to Ireland with me."

The toddler reached out to Brad, trying to grab a fistful of his hair. "Sack flies. Sack flies."

Anne frowned. "Sacrifice? Where did he get *that* word? Have you been reading him your theses?"

"No. I think it was Dad roaring about sacrifice bunts in yesterday's baseball game. Although," Carrie added, "the Mayans used to play a ball game where they sacrificed humans. They could have been watching PBS."

Anne sighed. "I meant for them to watch *Sesame Street*. Come on, Carrie. Help me get dinner on the table. We'll let Brad and Kate entertain Danny."

"No," Kate said. "I want Carrie to vet Brad for me. Let *them* watch Danny."

"She doesn't trust me," Brad explained. "Or herself, for that matter." Brad did his best to look like a trustworthy harmless companion.

Carrie's expression reminded him of the look his third grade teacher used to give him right before she sent him to the headmaster. "Come with me."

Brad followed Carrie and Danny into the living room where the TV blared out a baseball game.

"Fight. Sack flies." Ignoring the baseball game, Danny raced for a box of hero figures.

Too bad. Brad hoped he'd been talking about the game. The Yankees were up by one.

"You can watch the game if you like," Carrie said. "Danny and I will battle."

"No. Battles first." Brad switched off the TV to avoid temptation and surveyed the jumble of action figures. "What side do you want to be? Star Wars, Superman, or The Avengers?"

Carrie's lips curved slightly.

Progress. At least that cool queen look was gone. The intelligence he saw in her eyes was formidable. He shuddered to think what she would do if she detected a lie in him. Fortunately, his intentions were pure.

"I think I'll be Harry Potter." Carrie chose a Quidditch-cloaked Harry Potter complete with broom.

"Excellent choice. It always helps to have a bit of magic on one's side."

"You want to go to Ireland with Kate? Why?" Carrie had the inquisitor look down pat. It probably came with being a mother.

"I've a need to be in Ireland and I prefer to travel with a friend." Carrie's expression was not encouraging. "Truth?" Or part of it, at any rate. "I don't like the idea of Kate journeying by herself. A beautiful woman traveling on her own is vulnerable to attentions she may not want."

He could see from her expression that Carrie agreed with

him. "Think of me as a human mastiff. I have no amorous intentions toward Kate. I'm looking for a friendly companion with no romantic complications."

Danny grabbed a plastic sword from under the coffee table. "I am He-Man. I sack flies you." He hacked at Luke Skywalker till he fell over.

"He may not be able to pronounce it, but he's got the meaning right," Brad said. "Where did all these figures come from?"

Carrie removed the sword from Danny's grasp and substituted Superman. "Mom kept all my stuff. Matt's mom kept all of his, and when Danny was born, we all added to it. For the moment, I've taken the Barbies out of the mix. They have a height advantage and that doesn't seem fair."

Brad righted Luke Skywalker and slipped him into his pocket. "I'll keep Luke out of the fight. Danny isn't old enough to appreciate the finer points of Star Wars."

Danny tossed Superman over his shoulder, grabbed Mickey Mouse and kissed him on the nose.

"Dinner's ready," Anne called from the dining room. "Kate's gone to get Ethan."

Carrie picked up Danny, popped him into the high chair, and fastened a bib around his chubby neck.

"Sack flies. Sack flies." Danny pounded on the table with the Mickey Mouse figure he'd grabbed from the melee.

"Rule seven-hundred and five," Anne said, placing a roast of lamb on the table. "Never say anything in front of a child you don't want them to repeat. Because they will, and at the worst possible time."

"Amen," Ethan said. He moved Danny's highchair closer to Carrie. "Guard yourselves. Danny is ambivalent about food. Sometimes he thinks it's ammunition."

Carrie cut lamb into small pieces and added a dab of mint jelly and a spoonful each of potatoes and peas to a plastic

Winnie the Pooh plate. "Do you remember when I told the minister that daddy was being mean to you, 'cause he was on top of you?"

Anne laughed. "I remember the minister's face, certainly. That's exactly the kind of thing I'm talking about. Ethan, pass the rolls please."

Ethan passed the rolls to Brad. "Young man, what are your intentions toward Kate?"

"Dad, stop it!" Carrie looked at Brad. "The next question is how much money do you make? I still can't believe Matt stuck around long enough to propose."

"Kate's looking for a hero," Brad said.

They all looked at Brad.

Ethan looked thoughtful. "Interesting concept. The romantic anti-hero. Break stereotype."

"No," Kate said forcefully. Her face flamed. "I mean Lord Rotherham—"

"Doesn't have red hair and freckles." Brad grinned. "Kate's looking for someone of heroic stature and fair of face. That's how all the heroes in romances are," he informed them piously. "I can be but the noble sidekick or possibly the Duenna."

Carrie smiled at him. "I think you should reconsider, Kate. He seems like a lovely man."

Danny offered Brad his mashed -potato dotted Mickey Mouse. "Sack flies?"

"Jury's in," Carrie said. "You'll do. When do you leave for Ireland?"

THE FAMILY SAW them off with hugs and foil-sealed leftovers. The first part of the drive passed in satiated silence. Kate replayed the afternoon in her mind, watching the telephone poles flash by.

It was almost magical the way Brad charmed them all. He had this relaxed feeling about him, and he was funny and kind. In some ways, he was perfect hero material. Except for the fact that he was shorter than her. And gay. She closed her eyes and leaned back. In her mind's eye, she grew him two inches, erased the freckles, straightened his nose and changed his tousled curls to perfectly ordered auburn waves. She kept Brad's smile and that lurking amusement in his eyes. She sent him toward Cressida and had him pick her up in a sweeping embrace.

The picture twisted in her brain. Brad-slash-Lord Rotherham and Cressida started dancing a jig. Kate giggled.

"What's so funny?" Brad asked.

"I was trying you out as my hero. But you wouldn't cooperate."

"Wait till we get to Ireland. I'll be a perfect lamb."

Kate shook her head. She didn't think Brad had a lamb bone in his body. "Remember, this is my trip and we're going to do it my way."

"Of course."

Why didn't she believe him?

7

Dublin Airport. One week later.

Kate stared up at the huge banner posted at the customs entrance.

Attention arriving passengers. Due to a national bus strike there is no bus transportation available into Dublin. Bus Eireann would like to apologize for any inconvenience caused to customers due to this industrial action.

A bus strike? Her vision of the perfect bus tour with like-minded strangers, including, of course, her new hero, shattered.

"Now we'll *have* to rent a car." Brad's *I-told-you-so* smirk flicked her last nerve.

"What part of budget don't you understand? No. Car." Did Ireland have subways? She didn't think so. "Maybe there's a train."

"I'll check." Brad strolled toward the uniformed officer at the customs entrance.

Kate willed back tears of frustration. They'd probably have to hike into Dublin. "She hummed her grandmother's favorite song under her breath. "After every storm, there is a rainbow." The lyrics flaked away like day-old confetti. There'd been too darn many storms lately. She stepped forward to the next open customs window.

Where was the rainbow the song promised?

~

MICHAEL HANDED Essie back her passport, using the opportunity to unobtrusively check his friend's pulse. Still a bit rapid. "Bus strike, huh?" He turned the wheelchair he'd bullied her into using for the trip toward the crowded concourse. "It's a good thing I reserved a car."

Essie's blue-veined hands gripped her purse as a child might grip a teddy bear. "Indeed, it is. I have a promise to keep and no way to do it without transport."

"I'm going to find a place to park your chair while I deal with the luggage." Michael followed the signs promoting *The Loop*, Dublin Airport's shopping area.

"You're a dear man to come with me. I don't know how I'd have managed on my own."

"I'm grateful to you for the excuse to get away." The tabloid picture sparked a storm of media attention. Once the paparazzi found his address, they camped outside his office.

The series of glass-walled stores looked like a high-end shopping mall. Outside of the Starbucks were floor to ceiling windows looking out at the landing field, and a cluster of upholstered armchairs meant for enjoying the view. He transferred her to one, lifting her swollen feet onto his duffle bag. It made a perfect footstool. Michael felt the tension in Essie's slight body lessen. He watched her eyes dart from side to side, trying, no doubt, to absorb everything at once.

"They've fancied the place up since I left Ireland. I never thought to see a Starbucks in Dublin. It's kind of them to provide such comfortable seating."

"I'll get you a cup of tea. And you can finish the romance I see sticking out of your purse."

"I wouldn't mind a drop of tea," Essie admitted.

The musical Irish cadence of the baristas' voices kept him entertained as the line inched forward. Essie was doing much better than he expected after a twelve-hour flight. He'd made her get up and walk around every few hours. That helped. Michael added a scone to the order since she'd barely touched the meal they served on the plane.

He set the cardboard tray down on the table next to her. "I put an extra spoonful of sugar in the tea. I'll be back for you as soon as I've got the luggage."

"I'll be fine, Michael. Take your time."

He strode toward the baggage claim. Turning for one more look at Essie, he bumped into a couple arguing in low voices. Something clattered to the floor. A hair clip thingy.

"Well, drat." The woman bent down to retrieve it, and tripped over his foot.

"I'm sorry." Michael reached out to steady her. The woman looked like a cranky mermaid. She stared up at him through a tangle of auburn hair with eyes as green as the North Sea.

His heart lurched. It felt like energy was flowing between them. Obviously, too little sleep was catching up with him. Why was she staring at him like that? She looked like someone had hit her in the head.

Her short red-headed companion's face reminded him of someone. Oh yeah. Ron Weasley. He'd always had a soft spot for Harry Potter's sidekick.

The man's appraising stare would have been insulting except for the twinkle in his eyes. He turned to his companion. "Is this what you were looking for, Kate? Want me to round him up for you?"

"Shut up, Brad." The woman certainly could blush.

"You said you wanted a hero. He looks just the type. Dark brown hair, a bit longer than fashionable, dangerous brown eyes. I can picture him on your cover." The man's eyes narrowed. "Wait. I think I have seen him on a cover. Aren't you . . .?"

"No. I'm not." Michael strode on. That damned picture. He didn't think it would haunt him in Ireland. His eyes felt gritty from lack of sleep. A couple more hours and he'd have Essie safely settled. He moved his shoulders trying to unkink the knots of tension that were always with him.

He retrieved Essie's three large bags from the carousel and loaded them onto a luggage cart. It felt as if she'd packed the fruit cakes she baked for her brother and sister into cast iron pots. What other goodies were in there?

The line for Europcar snaked halfway around the terminal. A harried man wearing a Europcar blazer walked down the line. "We are sorry for the inconvenience, I am afraid we will not be able to accommodate all of you. We're having cars transferred from other sites. Will all those with reservations please step to the left?"

Michael joined the line to the left, averting his eyes from the envious stares of those in the longer queue. Once he had the keys, he trundled the luggage back to Essie. She'd fallen asleep in the comfortable chair. He hated to wake her . . .

"Need a hand?"

Ron Weasley, sans mermaid.

Michael looked from Essie to the luggage. "I could use one."

"You take care of her, and I'll wheel the luggage." The man eyed the three large cases dwarfing the duffle bag and Michael's backpack. "I'm betting those are hers," he said. "Reminds me of my grandmother's luggage. She always traveled as though she were on procession with the queen." He stuck out his hand. "Brad Flynn."

"Michael Walshe. My sleeping friend here is Essie O'Brian. Where's your companion?"

Brad nodded toward the bookstore. "Kate wanted to check out the books. Couldn't wait for town. I opted for coffee."

Michael shook Essie gently.

Her eyes fluttered open and fastened on Brad. "Saint's preserve us. You found the leprechaun."

Brad bowed to her. "Indeed, he has, and it's happy I am to be of service to you both."

Essie looked like a guilty child. "It's sorry I am to have called you a leprechaun. I was dreaming of . . . of Ballyban Hill."

"Brad, look what I found." The mermaid raced toward Brad, waving a book. "The Legends of Ballmorag Castle." When she noticed Michael, she froze.

"Ah look," Essie said. "The leprechaun's brought you the Queen of the Fairies."

The mermaid smiled down at Essie. "You believe in the wee folk? I do, too."

Michael lifted Essie into the wheelchair. "This gentleman offered to help me get our things to the car."

"You've got a car? Fortune smiled on you then," Brad said. "I don't suppose you'd give us a lift into Dublin?"

"No. We don't want to impose." The mermaid glared at her companion. A very imperious glare. Maybe Queen of the Fairies was a better term for her.

"There's no train, Kate. I checked. There are taxis, but it will be a long wait."

"I'll be happy to give you a ride." Michael looked at their two modest suitcases. "I got a wagon because I thought I'd need it for Essie's luggage. With the overhead rack, I think we can make it."

"Great," Brad added their suitcases to the luggage cart. He turned to Essie. "I'm Bradley Flynn and this is my friend, Kate Carnahan. We're both pleased to meet you, Essie O'Callaghan.

Michael blinked. Had he zoned out and missed part of a

conversation? O'Callaghan was Essie's maiden name. How had Brad known it?

KATE FORCED her expression into a polite smile. Michael was too good looking. He made the back of her neck prickle. "Thank you. It's very kind of you." She hated being beholden to a stranger. Especially one who walked like he owned the earth.

His grandmother was a different story. Essie. What a lovely name. She looked like she'd stepped out of one of the Arthur Rackham fairy tale illustrations she'd cherished as a child. Kate quickened her steps to keep up with the wheelchair. "This is my first trip to Ireland. Do you live here?"

"Ah no. Not for forty-five years. I wouldn't be here now, were it not for . . ." Essie glanced at Brad. She cleared her throat. "Michael, my darling boy, is taking me to see my family."

Michael had hero material written all over him, from the lurking smile in his eyes for his grandmother, to his unconscious aura of command. Bet if he said "jump", people hopped. Her writer brain engaged.

Lord Rotherham's whiskey brown eyes promised retribution. "You have no right to be alone with me in my chambers. Society dictates a young woman must never be unaccompanied."

"I am accompanied," replied Cressida, her dimpled chin held high. "I have Parsley with me." The tiny dog bared his teeth. "Parsley would never let anyone harm me. Especially such a cad as you."

"Earth to Kate. Come in Kate." Brad tapped her on the shoulder.

Her steps slowed. She had no trouble envisioning Michael picking up Cressida, slinging her over his shoulder and taking her to the bedroom to have his wicked way with her.

A strong hand jerked her back from the curb. She looked

up into Michael's frowning face. "Traffic comes the other way here. You've got to be careful."

"Sorry." Kate shook off his arm and hurried after Brad and the luggage cart.

"Don't write while you walk," Brad said. "Save it for the B and B, which we still have to find, by the way." He palmed his iPhone. "I found a great app. Why don't you let me call ahead and book?"

"No. I want to see it first. The sales clerk at the bookstore said to try Abbey Court on Bachelors Walk. I love the sound of that."

"Fine." He shoved his phone back in his pocket. "But for the record, this is a damned crazy way to do things."

"No one asked you to come on this trip." Kate knew she sounded like a cranky twelve-year-old, but she didn't care.

Brad had the good sense not to reply.

Michael stopped in front of a gray four-door Audi. "This is it." He opened the passenger door and came back for Essie.

Essie waved him off. "I can walk."

He slid an arm under her legs. "Your legs are swollen from the plane trip and I don't want to take any chances. You'll be better tomorrow."

"Slide in, Kate." Brad hefted the first of the large suitcases. "Plenty of room in the back seat for these. Kate doesn't take up much space. Your duffle bag and our cases will fit in the boot."

He laid the first one lengthwise and somehow managed to fit the next two on top of it. He shoehorned himself in, pushing the suitcases toward Kate. "See? We didn't need the roof rack after all."

Kate, scrunched into the corner by the pile of bags, thought the roof rack would have been a better idea. Men. Why did they constantly have to re-invent the wheel? Oh well, at least she could see out the window.

Michael pulled a GPS out of his backpack and plugged it in.

The screen brightened. A sultry Marilyn Monroe voice issued from it. "Good morning, Michael. Where do you want to go?"

"Nice touch," Brad commented.

Michael half turned. "Where shall I drop you?"

"The clerk told me Bachelors Walk was across from the statue near the O'Connell Street Bridge," Kate said.

Michael shrugged. "Lola's good, but she's not up to finding an unnamed statue." "O'Connell Street Bridge, Lola." He adjusted his mirrors and pulled smoothly away from the curb.

Kate pressed her nose against the window, unwilling to miss a thing. Everything was different. The cars. The gas stations. No, she reminded herself. Petrol stations. "Look. Gas is the same price it is in New York."

Michael chuckled. "Not quite. In the US, they sell gas in gallons. Here they do it in liters."

Kate's bookkeeper mind did the math. "That's four times the price of American gas. No wonder people drive smaller cars."

Brad leaned forward and tapped Michael on the shoulder. "Is this your first trip to Ireland?"

"Yes," Michael said. "It's . . ."

Kate shut out their conversation, absorbing the scenery. Small stone and brick houses. Not a lot of wood. Neat, green lawns. As they neared Dublin, the houses got closer together. Ahead she saw a brick castle set back on a huge expanse of lawn. They drew parallel to it. Oh. Not a castle. A college campus and . . . "It's for sale. The college is for sale."

"Who sells a college?" Michael sounded amused. "More to the point, who buys one?"

Kate swiveled to keep the building in sight, noting the copper domes with their green patina. The color of the Statue of Liberty. "I'd like to buy it," she said wistfully. "It would make a wonderful summer home." She caught Michael's eyes assessing her in the rear-view mirror. He must think she was a nutcase.

"It would be rather expensive to keep up," Michael remarked. "The gardening would be prohibitive, not to mention the land tax. Perhaps you should think about something smaller. Possibly, a cottage in the Lake District? I hear they have some lovely ten bedrooms for sale."

Kate suppressed a grin. Michael was playing her game. "But the grounds are so important. I do want the children, all eight of them—"

Michael quirked an eyebrow.

"—to have plenty of space to roam. But perhaps you're right. A smaller property, with one or two acres of forest attached. And a folly."

Michael's serious expression belied the twinkle she could see in his eyes. "I feel sure you'll find the ideal place, but for now, perhaps a small pied-à-terre in Dublin?" He pointed at a three-story edifice in gray stone with white trimmed bow windows. It had a flight of stone steps leading up to a porch. Small trees in planters, and flower boxes, bright with impatiens, flanked the pillared entranceway.

"Yes, that will do nicely," Kate said. "I'll wire my business manager to arrange it."

The car turned down O'Connell Street. Massive stone buildings vied with smaller storefronts. An island lined with trees and huge statues ran between the two lanes of traffic.

Which statue had the salesclerk meant near the O'Connell Street Bridge? "I didn't think there'd be so many statues," Kate said.

Michael pulled into the right-hand turn lane. "I imagine she meant this one."

A larger than life figure of a man stood on a pedestal adorned with a three-dimensional frieze of figures. Below the frieze, four full sized, seated angels guarded the base. Between the angels were ledges, one currently occupied by a man playing the guitar, the case open at his feet.

Michael pulled over in front of the statue. "I'll have to leave you here. Lola says Bachelors Walk is a one-way street. Will you be all right?"

"We'll be fine." Brad got out and retrieved their cases from the boot.

Kate leaned over to Essie. "It was nice meeting you. I hope you have a wonderful visit."

Essie cocked her head and smiled at her. "Ireland's a small country. I've no doubt we'll meet again."

Kate's eyes met Michael's. She wanted to say something, but she didn't know what. He'd followed her imagination game. No man had ever done that before.

Brad opened Kate's door. "Hurry up woman. You're holding up traffic. Don't want to see you killed on your first day."

Kate stepped out, smiling a 'thank you' to Michael.

Brad clapped Michael on the shoulder. "Thanks for the ride. Have a good trip."

She watched Michael shift into gear and drive off. She really should have said something.

MICHAEL WATCHED Kate disappear from view.

Essie tapped him on the shoulder. "You'd do well with the Fairy Queen, Michael."

"I don't need a girlfriend."

"Of course, you don't. You need a wife. I dreamed I found the perfect wife for you, Michael."

"*Turn right at the fork*," Lola's voice intoned.

Michael almost swerved into the turn lane. "Essie, I told you I'm not interested in a wife. I want a nice uncomplicated vacation with no women at all."

"That terrible Jay woman soured your outlook. Not all women are nasty grasping strumpets."

"*Your destination is on the right.*"

It seemed nothing in Dublin was very far from the town's center. Michael pulled up in front of a gray stone house with windows framed in green shutters. Geraniums bloomed brightly in the window box.

Essie peeped around him. "It's a fine house, indeed."

"Wait here. I'll knock and get some help with the bags"

A short wiry man with a shock of white hair opened the door.

"I'm Michael Walshe and I've a gift for you in the car."

The man's face lit up. "Declan O'Callaghan." He pumped Michael's hand and called over his shoulder, "Shauna, they've come." He bounded down the steps.

Essie was already out of the car and limping toward them.

Declan caught Essie around the waist and drew her into his arms. Tears ran down their faces.

"Oh, Declan, look at you. Your hair got white."

"Forty-five years, Essie. Forty-five years."

A dumpling of a woman, who looked like the baker's wife in a picture book from Michael's childhood, appeared in the doorway. Her green apron bore traces of flour as did the smudge on her cheek. "Don't be standing out here in the chill. Come away in."

Declan helped Essie up the steps.

Shauna enfolded her in a gentle hug. "You look exactly like your pictures. It's good to have you under our roof."

Michael turned to deal with the bags.

Declan joined him, wiping his eyes. "We always planned to go to the United States for a visit, but first there were the children, and then their university fees. We never had the wherewithal." Declan grunted at the weight of the suitcase.

Michael took the bag from him. "You take the red one with the wheels. The two plaid monsters balance each other out."

Declan snapped up the handle on the red case. "That's our Essie. When she left for the United States, she wanted to bring everything, including the fireplace. She had to settle for a small trunk."

Michael followed him up the steps through a narrow hallway filled with framed photos.

"We've put Essie on the ground floor so she won't have to worry with stairs." Declan opened the door to a sunny yellow room. "Pop those bags in here and I'll show you where you'll be staying."

"Thanks, but I've booked a room at a hotel."

"But Shauna's already made you up a room," Declan protested.

"And I am more than grateful, but I want to give you some time to yourselves. You have a lot to catch up on."

"Shauna's made Irish bacon and mashed potatoes and peas," Declan said. "A traditional Irish meal to welcome you. Surely you'll stay for lunch?"

Irish bacon? That wonderful aroma didn't smell like any bacon he'd ever tasted. His stomach would never forgive him if he didn't stay. "I'd be delighted."

The dining room table was covered with a cloth, trimmed two inches deep in crocheted lace. A padded tea cozy sat at one end. A basket of steaming bread, a blue china plate filled with curls of butter, and a cut-glass dish of jam occupied the center.

Essie held the kitchen door for Shauna, who came in bearing a platter of what looked like a roast. "Sit yourselves down," Shauna commanded. "I won't be a minute."

Michael pulled out a chair for Essie and sat down beside her.

Shauna came back with a bowl piled high with creamy mashed potatoes and an oval dish of green peas. She plopped into her chair and folded her hands in her lap. "Declan, will you say the blessing?"

Michael let the words of the blessing roll over his head and concentrated on not drooling.

"Amen." Declan took up the carving knife and fork and sliced the roast.

Shauna poured the tea. "Serve yourselves potatoes, Michael. That way, you'll not be getting too little or too much."

The Irish bacon tasted like corned beef to Michael. The best corned beef he'd ever had. And the warm bread was unlike any he'd ever eaten. He became an instant fan.

"Ah, you're a dab hand at the soda bread, Shauna." Essie added a second curl of butter to her slice. "I'm fine with pies, but I could never master the soda bread. I gave up trying. Is this Mam's recipe?"

Shauna nodded. "She gave it to me on our wedding day. I reckon that's why we're still married. Will you have some more bacon, Michael?"

He shook his head. Declan had well and truly filled his plate.

"We know about California," Shauna said. "We see it on the telly. Do you see a lot of film stars there, Essie?"

Essie chuckled. "Not a one. Michael, though, he's got a connection."

Shauna looked expectantly at Michael.

"My godmother is Lorena Anderson," he said. "I spent some time on film sets."

Shauna's face lit up. "I know her. She's on that series, *Looking for Love*. We got it over here two years ago. It's one of my favorites. Who else do you know?"

Michael hoped his expression didn't look as hunted as he felt. He had no intention of bringing up everyone's favorite starlet, Tracy Jay.

Mercifully Essie intervened. "When do I get to meet your children?"

"Brenna gets off work early today." Shauna beamed. "She's that excited to meet you."

Michael excused himself shortly after Brenna arrived. He left them talking and reminiscing. He saw the love there. It must have been hard being far away from each other with no cheap way to communicate until cell phones and computers came along.

His mom had told him stories of times when long distance rates were prohibitive. She said when she went away to college, she called her parents collect to let them know she'd arrived. They would refuse the call. That way it didn't cost them anything to know she was safe.

Essie had been limited to sending letters and pictures. No wonder she had wanted to bring big suitcases.

It was a five-minute drive to The Cormorant. The small hotel was just off Temple Bar, not far from O'Connell Street. Nice room. Dark green walls. The queen-sized bed took up most of the room's space. The bedspread looked uncomfortable. Some sort of gold tapestry. A puffy white quilt was folded across the foot of the bed.

Michael pulled back the curtains. Gray clouds swirled and reformed and reflected in the river. The light rain falling soothed him. The tension slid off his shoulders as though the rain washed it away. For the first time in two years, he had no responsibilities. He'd seen Essie to her family. Trevor Pinnock was covering his practice. A yawn welled up; it felt like his jaw was cracking. He kicked off his shoes and stretched out on the bed, pulling the quilt over himself. A vision of green eyes looking at him in the rear-view mirror played behind his eyelids. He blinked it away.

No. No women. A short nap and he'd . . .

8

"Do you often do that kind of thing?" Brad asked.

"What?" Kate watched the Audi pull away and join the stream of traffic over O'Connell Street Bridge. Michael definitely had hero possibilities. She wished she'd snapped a picture of him.

"It was like you were improvising a scene with him. The two of you could have been in a play." Brad pulled up the handles on the suitcases.

"We were joking." Kate grabbed her bag out of his hand. "You should have slept more on the plane. You need a nap."

"Yeah, I do. In a good bed." He followed her up Bachelors' Walk to a narrow entryway where a purple sign on the second story read *Abbey Court*. "This place looks small. If they don't have a two-person room, I'm taking you to a hotel."

"Go right ahead. I'm sure you'll be much happier. I'm staying here."

Brad opened his mouth to protest.

Kate cut him off. "I'm on a budget. I can't afford hotels." It was one thing to accept his companionship. But no money.

Brad frowned. "I'll wait for you at the bakery next door. I'm hungry."

∼

THE WINDOW of the brightly lit bakery had a sign advertising free Wi-Fi.

Brad strolled in with a sense of being let out of school. Alone at last.

Not that Kate wasn't a delightful companion. She had a childlike sense of wonder and a loving heart underneath her prickly exterior. That, more than the stunning beauty she insisted on hiding, almost tempted him to offer himself as her answer. Wonder what his family would say if he brought home a fully human bride?

No. Look at the problems Mum and Da went through. Kate deserved better than the kind of life she'd lead with him.

The girl behind the counter wore a pink striped cap and matching apron. "What will it be, Luv?"

"I'll have a couple of sausage rolls and a cup of tea." He eyed the chocolate croissants. Surely a *drop* of magic wouldn't hurt? "And a croissant to go, please."

Her smile was as wide as the River Liffey. "Sit yourself down. I'll bring them to your table."

It was good to be home, as long as he didn't have to stay too long. Tuning out his fellow patrons, he joined his iPhone to the Wi-Fi network. First problem, get a decent room. He was damned if he was going to spend time in a dormitory.

"Here you go, love." The server set a plate of flaky sausage rolls and a thick white china cup and saucer in front of him. "I'll be back with the tea and your carry-out."

Brad's fingers tapped busily. Hacking into the Abbey Court reservation system didn't count as magic. It was simple technology. Marvelous what you could do with iPhones these days. He'd always wondered if Apple had a little help from the Fae.

The server set down a brown china pot and a crisp white bag smelling of chocolate.

"You're a darling." Brad poured a dark rich stream of tea into his cup and sniffed appreciatively. "Tea is one thing they don't do properly in New York."

The server's smile glowed. "You're from New York? I've an uncle there. Donal Cleary. I don't suppose you know him?"

Brad shook his head, regretfully. "The loss is mine, I am sure." How do you explain to a Dubliner the insane size of New York City?

"I'm planning to go visit him next year. If you give me your phone number, perhaps we could meet up?"

Brad reached into his wallet for a business card. "Call me when you get to the city. I'll stand you a drink."

She ran her fingers over the raised lettering. "Flynn Public Relations. Bradley Flynn CEO. You've got your own company then?"

"For now." Brad eyed the paper bag. He couldn't love-spell a croissant with someone watching. "But if I don't catch up my email, I won't have a company to come back to."

"I'll leave you to it then." She started away and turned back. "I'm Meghan. Meghan Cleary. Don't forget now."

* * *

Kate joined the small line leading to the desk. She was actually here. Her mind fizzed with excitement, jumping from her dratted hero to the new book whose plot was already fully formed in her head. Buses or not, she had to get to Cluhalaugh.

The line inched forward. Someone jostled her from behind, snapping her back to her current problem. She couldn't write

Perfect Match till she turned in *Chasing Cressida* with a re-fashioned Lord Rotherham. She winced at the memory of Eric. Why on earth had she even tried to find her own happy ending? After her parents' string of debacles, she should have known better.

"Can I help you?"

The lanky man behind the desk reminded her of her favorite incarnation of Dr. Who, Matt Smith. After Eric, she'd tried using Matt Smith as Lord Rotherham, but he kept talking about Time Lords.

"Yes, I need a room for two. Separate beds."

"I have just the thing if you don't mind a bit of a walk."

KATE JOINED Brad with a smug expression and two sets of keys. "Wait till you see what they gave us."

Brad looked up from his email. "About time. I got you a snack." He handed Kate the bakery bag.

Kate looked inside. One lone chocolate croissant with the end missing. "You nibbled on my snack."

Brad peered into the bag. "Oops. That's what comes of multitasking." A fine film of sweat beaded his face.

"Are you all right, Brad?"

"I'm fine. It's just I'm allergic to . . . chocolate. I certainly didn't mean to taste your croissant. It was only one bite, though. I'm sure it will be fine." He turned to the glass counter. "I'll get some sausage rolls for you. They're delicious."

Kate led him two doors down to an ironwork gate. "Hard to believe this is a hostel." She fumbled with the lock.

"May I?" Brad held out his hand for the key.

They walked into a courtyard filled with greenery. Kate surveyed the three large buildings surrounding the courtyard.

"Isn't it great? The clerk told me Abbey Court rents two apartments here and we got the only vacant one."

"Be glad it isn't a six-bed dorm. Which building?"

"Left, the clerk said." Kate used the second key. "Voila."

The apartment had a bedroom, living room and kitchen. Kate opened the bathroom door. "Our own bathroom. No sharing. And it's only sixty dollars a night, each."

Brad peered into the bedroom at the queen size bed. "Are we going to share that?"

"In your dreams, buddy. The clerk told me there's a roll-away bed in the closet. Why don't you be a gentleman and offer to take it? Or we could take turns?"

Brad yawned. "I'm too tired to care. I'll take the rollaway. How about a nap before we explore?"

"Aren't you hungry?"

Brad looked a little queasy. "No. I ate at the bakery. The sausage rolls, are for you."

Kate took the paper bag from him and sniffed. "Cold sausage in pastry doesn't do it for me."

He waved the second bag under her nose. "But you should definitely sample the croissant. It's out of this world."

Kate broke off a piece. There was an odd honey taste behind the rich chocolate. "I'll pass."

Brad's face fell. "I thought it was excellent."

"I'll save it for you then."

The kitchen had a full-sized fridge. There were dishes in the cupboard, a stove, and . . . "There's even a microwave. Score! This place is twice the size of my New York apartment."

Brad trundled the rollaway into the living room. He opened it up and sat down to test the mattress. "Not bad." He kicked off his shoes and pulled up the covers. "Night."

Kate looked out the window into the alley below. A boy trudged by, shoving a cart full of odd-sized boxes in front of him. He stopped in an overhung doorway and lit a cigarette. A gentle rain started. "Irish mist." Kate hugged herself. She'd made it. Despite cranky editors and a scarily low bank account, she was really here.

And by the time it was over, she'd have all the research for the book. Simmering in her subconscious was the article she had read in the Times about the matchmaking festival in Cluhalaugh.

Kate's eyes threatened to close. It was still the middle of the night in New York. She turned to Brad. "I'll shower; then take a nap. Wake me if I sleep past two hours."

Her only answer was a snore.

* * * *

Kate's eyes snapped open. What was that noise?

The toilet flushed. Brad walked into the hall and braced himself with both hands on the doorframe of her room. The light from the hall made his skin look green. "I think I ate too much chocolate."

Kate sat up. "I'm sorry. Are you sure it wasn't the sausage rolls?"

Brad clapped his hands over his mouth and sprinted for the bathroom.

Kate winced at the unpleasant noises echoing through the apartment. The best thing to do was leave him to his misery. She dressed and tapped on the bathroom door. "I'm going out. Can I get you anything?"

"Urgh!"

"Well better out than in. That's what my grandmother used to say."

"Go away."

"Going. Phone if you need me."

This was right. She wanted her first exploration of Ireland to be on her own. Kate zipped up her new North Face parka. There was a bit of dampness in the air. It wasn't rain so much as a memory of rain. Breathing in the smell of wet cobblestones made her soul tingle. It felt like a trip back in time. She almost expected to hear the rumbling of wooden cart wheels and the jingle of harnesses.

She crossed to the other side of the street and walked the river path, craning her neck, trying to take in everything at once. A couple passed her carrying on a conversation in a language she couldn't identify. The next bridge was a graceful white iron arch.

Halfway across, Kate stopped to look down at the river. She closed her eyes and whispered a wish. "I still need a hero." An image of Michael's smile flashed on her mental screen. She should have taken notes.

She opened her eyes to see a young girl smiling at her as if they shared a secret. Kate smiled back. "Quit wishing on stuff, Kate." she scolded under her breath. "You're thirty-two. Get a grip."

Kate looked for street signs, but didn't see any. Well, in lieu of a map she'd use her phone. Pressing repeatedly on the start button did nothing. *Drat.* She'd forgotten to charge it. Looking through the gray stone entryway arching over a branching cobblestone street, she saw a policeman chatting with a man in a green baize apron. What were police called over here? Garda. A nice soft name. Sounded more like milk and cookies than guns and nightsticks. She was thinking food references. A sure sign she was hungry.

Kate made her way to the Garda. "Excuse me. I'm new to Dublin and I can't find a street sign. Could you tell me where I am?"

The Garda smiled nicely. "It's a bit of a confusion for tourists. The streets are signed in the British style with all signs being placed on buildings adjacent to street junctions." He pointed to the side of the building in front of them.

Kate looked at the white lettered blue sign. Below the words Airse Na gCeanna was the English translation - Merchants Arch followed by the numeral 2. "What's the 2 for?"

"It's the Dublin Postal district number."

That seemed odd. But she didn't want to ask any more questions. "Thanks. I'll be sure to remember that."

"You're in the Temple Bar district. Where are you staying?"

"Abbey Court," Kate said.

"Ah, nice place that. Well, if you get lost, ask for directions to Ha'penny Bridge. That's the white one. You can see your hostel from there."

Ha-Penny Bridge. What a magical name. "Thank you. Next time I'll remember to charge my phone before I come out."

"You need a special charger for Ireland. Did you buy one before you left home?"

Kate remembered Carrie telling her about chargers. But it was part of a stream of advice her best friend gave her, and she'd forgotten to put it on her list. If it wasn't on her list, nothing got done. "I didn't. Can you tell me where I can buy one?" Please don't let it be expensive.

"Your hostel probably sells them. Otherwise, you can pick one up at a Boots."

"Thanks. I'll do that." Sounded like a shoe store. Odd place to get electronics.

The Garda smiled at her. "Have a care to yourself, and enjoy your stay."

Kate wandered Merchants Alley over to Dame Street and turned on to Grafton.

Mistake. Grafton Street was lined with too many familiar shops. She hadn't come to Dublin to visit Urban Outfitters or Apple. Kate turned back to find a more local area and hit a barrier of tall male.

"Sorry." Kate looked up into a surprised face. Michael's. He gave off a heady aroma of spice and rain. She pushed away from him. Wild thoughts of espionage entered her head. She wished she had a pair of sunglasses. "Are you following me?"

Michael laughed. "Hardly. Did you find your hostel?"

"Yes. We're across the river. Where's your grandmother?"

"She's not my grandmother. She's my friend. I haven't done away with her if that's what you're thinking. Are you always this suspicious?"

"Well, it seems odd to be meeting you again." *Lame, Kate.* He'll think you're a complete idiot.

"Not that odd. Dublin's city center is a relatively small area. I'm staying at the Cormorant. It's a couple of blocks from here." Michael matched his step to hers. "Where are you staying? Where's your friend?"

Kate shrugged. "Brad's a victim of some local cuisine."

"Ah, well, better out than in," Michael said.

"That's what my grandmother used to say."

"Mine too. When he can take something, give him some Pulsatilla. You can get it at a Boots."

"Right." Boots must be the local name for a pharmacy. "What's Pulsatilla?"

"It's a homeopathic remedy for food poisoning. I find homeopathy does as well as traditional medicine for some ailments." Michael smiled down at her. "How do you like Dublin?"

"It's wonderful. I feel like I'm living in a book. Look at that sign, Bride Street. Sráid Bhríde Nua." She stumbled over the pronunciation. "I wish I knew how to say it properly. It sounds like a very musical language."

Michael pointed down the street to a green sign lettered in gold. "I haven't been to a pub yet. You can't visit Ireland and not try the Guinness. Come on. I'll treat you."

Kate shook her head. "I haven't got time for a pub. I want to keep taking in the local atmosphere."

"You can't get better local atmosphere than a pub. They're the center of life here in Ireland."

"How do you know that?"

"Essie told me." He took her arm and guided her inside.

The scent of beer, and fish and chips mingled with other delightful food aromas Kate couldn't identify. The dark wood paneled walls were lined with frames, some filled with what looked to be antique theatre posters. Others were announcements of sporting events. The gleaming mahogany bar was backed by mirrored shelves filled with bottles. Three large globed lights hung from the ceiling over the bar, giving a muted shine to the black-tiled floor.

A flat screen TV to one side of the bar flashed a sports game of some kind. The neon-lit jukebox ground out Johnny Cash.

Kate wrinkled her nose. "Never thought of *I Walk the Line* as an Irish ballad."

Michael seated her at one of the tall polished tables. "Me neither. I expected something more traditional at a place called *Failte*. Perhaps we're too close to Grafton Street. This is probably for the tourists." He studied the menu. "Hungry? They have a beef and Guinness stew. Or fish and chips?"

Kate scanned the prices on the menu. Not too bad and she was starving. "The beef stew with Guinness sounds properly traditional. I'll try that."

Michael ordered a Guinness and some soda bread.

"Aren't you hungry?"

"No. I took Essie to stay with her brother. His wife feasted us on Irish bacon and the best bread I ever tasted. Actually, I'd never tasted soda bread before. It's replaced biscuits in my heart."

Kate tried to decipher one of the theatre posters. "This place looks really old."

"It probably is. This may be one of the pubs where James Joyce and Sean O'Casey hung out. Maybe Brendan Behan."

Kate erased the flat screen in her mind; changed Johnny Cash to Celtic fiddles; added clouds of pipe smoke, and literary giants leaning against the bar, imbibing Irish whiskey. "That's what I love about being here. It's saturated with history. I have a list of things to see."

"A list sounds more like a duty trip than a pleasure excursion."

"It's both." Michael's crooked tooth kept his smile from being movie star perfect. Was there any way to discreetly snap a photo of him for reference? "I'm here to research my next book. I'm a writer."

He actually looked interested. "What kind of things do you write?"

"I write romances." She waited for the inevitable male leer. It didn't come.

"My mom reads romances. So does Essie. She'll be very excited to know she met a writer. What name should she look for?"

Wonder of wonders, he sounded respectful. "Carnahan. Katherine Carnahan. My first book came out last year. *Miss Minerva takes a Dare.*"

Michael pulled a small notebook from his jacket pocket. "I'll buy it for her when we get home. I don't imagine book-stores here carry many American titles."

He carried a notebook? "Are you a writer too?"

"No. I'm really good at forgetting things unless I write them down."

The sound of his voice was . . . "Me too." Kate palmed her own notebook. *Lord Rotherham's voice. Whiskey smooth with a hint of smoke in it?*

"Food's up," called the barkeep.

Michael retrieved their meal from the bar. He set down the plates and went back for their Guinnesses.

"Now this is history. I'm having my first Guinness at a real

Irish pub." Kate held her glass up to the light, admiring the brew's amber color and the crown of foam.

"I'm pleased to be present at your first." Michael held up his glass to hers. "Slainte."

"Slainte," Kate let the word roll off her tongue, loving the sound of it. She sipped cautiously. The cool dark taste tickled her palate. "A bit bitter, but I like it." The stew was a blissful combination of beef, potatoes, and vegetables with a tangy flavor which must be the Guinness. She pushed her bowl toward Michael. "This is sinfully delicious. You have to taste it."

He had the oddest expression on his face. Did he think she was too forward? She pulled it back. "Sorry."

"No. I'd like to try it." He broke off a piece of soda bread and dipped it into the stew. "Wonderful." He broke off another piece, buttered it and put it between her lips.

Kate chewed it slowly and smiled. "I'm in love." His eyes drew her in. A touch of darkness behind their smile. The eyes of a dreamer who'd maybe seen too much. What kind of stories did he have? She lowered her gaze and sipped her Guinness. This was crazy. She wanted him to reach over and . . . She felt a feather light dab at the corner of her mouth.

"Sorry." Michael withdrew the napkin. "You had a crumb caught in the corner of your lip." He turned away and stared fixedly at the television. "Cricket. I haven't seen that in a while."

Kate pushed away her bowl. She wasn't hungry anymore for stew. Why did a touch from a napkin feel like erotic foreplay? She fought off a vision of Michael's lips pressed to hers. What was in the Guinness? "Excuse me. I'm going to find the bathroom."

He swung round. "Are you feeling ill, too?"

He was staring again. Kate's face flamed. "No I . . . uh. . ."

"The signs say second floor."

Kate walked up the stairs, trying for nonchalance. There were two signs *Mna* and *Fir*. Fortunately there was a tiny picture, or else she would have assumed women were firs. She went into the Mna and sank down on the shabby sofa. Her traitorous body wanted to race downstairs into Michael's arms.

"You don't even know him." Her body had clearly run mad. "You will stop this right now," she ordered her body. Using him as a hero in her book didn't mean she needed to get close to him. "I am the captain of my fate. I refuse to be attracted to some stranger because he has a story behind his eyes and an amazing smile. Look what happened last time?"

Kate shivered at the memory of her ex-fiancé. Two years of her life following the wizard of wonderful. Pathetically grateful he found her worth loving. *You complete me, babe. We're going to build a beautiful life together.* Right. His life. Using all her spare time to entertain his clients. Allowing him to redecorate her apartment to his taste. Letting her own friends go in favor of his. Making sure every aspect of his life ran smoothly. And the final wrenching scene where Eric explained kindly they'd grown apart and she'd be better off without him. *The most important thing, Kate, is to follow one's heart.* Right. The heart he'd been following was below his belt.

She moved to the sink and splashed water on her heated face, wishing she could splash some where it counted. "You have no judgment when it comes to men, Kate. Remember that."

She'd go downstairs, pay for her share of the meal, smile and say she had to get back to Brad. She'd find the nearest Boots and buy a charger and some Pulsa-something and go back to the hotel. "You have a plan to follow. A book to write."

Michael saw her descending the stairs and pulled out her chair.

Kate shook her head politely and laid fifteen Euros on the table. "I'm sorry. I think I'd better get back to the hotel and see how Brad's doing. Thanks for the company. I hope you have a great vacation."

Michael's smiling eyes frosted over. He looked down at her as if she were a fly he wanted to brush off. "No problem. You didn't finish your drink. Mind if I finish it for you?"

Kate shrugged. "Whatever. Keep the money, though. I like to pay my own way." She attempted a breezy smile and walked out of the pub.

9

Michael reached for Kate's discarded Guinness and drained it. They weren't just companions, then. They were involved. Why the hell hadn't she said that? He winced at the memory of her eyes looking into his, bright with interest and something else. The air between them felt like the space before a summer storm. Alive with electricity. When she'd offered him a taste of her stew, he'd wanted to pull her to her feet and kiss her senseless. He'd felt attraction before, but never like that. He could have sworn she felt it too.

"Which proves once again, you know nothing about women." Michael picked up Kate's spoon and finished the stew. No point wasting it.

A crack of the bat and cheers from the bar's patrons fixed his attention on the running figures on the flat screen. His head felt buzzed from the second drink. Guinness was stronger than California beers. Better walk it off, he decided.

The bartender grinned at him. "Not interested in the end of the match? Ireland's one up on Somalia."

Michael handed him his credit card. "I didn't realize you played cricket here in Ireland."

"It's not our national sport, but it comes in the top three."

"What's your national sport? Rugby?"

"No. Hurling."

Michael smiled inwardly at the mental picture he got. Wonder how Brad was doing?

"It's played with nets on sticks. A very fast paced game. You should try to catch a match." The barkeep rested his elbow on the bar. He had the look of someone settling in for a long conversation. "The lady left in a hurry. Had she forgotten something?"

"You could put it that way." Michael signed the slip. He glanced at the money Kate left on the table. "She left you a tip. She said to tell you she thought you were cute."

The fine mist had started again. No one seemed bothered by it. He zipped up his jacket and pulled down the brim of his Dodgers cap. No use trying to make up his run after a couple of pints and a meal. He'd settle for a brisk walk.

Michael let his feet lead him. His eyes took in his surroundings while his thoughts wandered off on their own. Essie looked ten years younger. He enjoyed visiting Declan and Shauna until their daughter came home. When Essie announced Michael was a doctor and unmarried, Brenna's eyes lit up like she'd won a carnival prize. He felt like a pop star. Hell's Bells, why couldn't women leave a body alone? Everyone didn't have to go through life two by two. His steps took him across Ha'penny Bridge.

"Braedon!" A mother's scream turned him around. A young boy had his arm stuck between the bridge rails. His mother tried to jerk him free. The boy howled.

"Stop!" Michael raced to the boy. "Don't try to jerk it. Here, let me." He put his arm round the boy. "I'm going to turn your arm very slowly and you're going to pretend you are a Ninja trying to sneak out of the robbers' den."

The boy stopped mid-howl.

People crossing the bridge began to gather round them. Michael let their murmurs of sympathy and advice fade into the background. All his attention was on the tear-stained eyes looking into his.

"Now the only way to sneak out is to relax your arm completely and slide out." Michael turned the arm and put his hand through the bar on top of the boy's arm. "Follow my hand and we'll sneak out together. Slowly now."

The boy followed Michael's hand and pulled free of the bridge. His breath hitched.

"Braedon, you scared ten years off me." His mother wrapped her arms around him.

Braedon screamed.

The mother dropped her arms. "I think he's broken something." She looked ready to pass out.

A woman wearing a sari stepped from the crowd to support her. "There's a Garda right over the bridge. Jamal, go fetch him." Her accent was as Irish as Johnny's mother's.

Braedon settled into a series of hiccupping wails.

He couldn't stand there and do nothing. "I'm a doctor. Do you mind if I take a look?" At the mother's nod, he unzipped the boy's jacket and examined the arm. "Braedon, you put your elbow out. I want to put it back in for you."

"Will it hurt?"

"Yes. But only for a second." Michael looked at the mother's terrified face. "Don't worry. I've put elbows back in before."

The mother attempted a smile. "Do what the man says, Braedon."

Michael felt Braedon's arm till he found the place. "Hold your breath and count backward from ten."

Braedon puffed out his cheeks. "Ten nine . . . Ow!"

Michael felt the bone pop back into place. "All over." He zipped up Braedon's jacket. "Doesn't that feel better?"

Braedon nodded.

The crowd applauded.

Michael smiled at the mom. "He had a good scare. It may prevent him from doing it again."

"I hope to God it does." She hugged her son. "But this one's a limb of Satan. He'll find something else to try. He always does."

Michael knelt down next to the boy. "Braedon, you scared your mother very badly. I think you need to take her to get a cup of hot chocolate."

Braedon beamed.

"And next time, think about what a Ninja would do. Ninjas are very careful people because if they get hurt, their usefulness is over."

The crowd drifted away, leaving Michael free to see a familiar green-eyed figure leaning on the bridge rail watching him.

"You're good with kids," Kate said. "How did you learn to put an elbow back in like that?"

"In med school." Michael tipped his cap to her and walked back the way he'd come. He forced himself not to turn around. His nurse, Lynne, said if you met a person three times accidentally, it was fate. Well, he had no intention of letting fate play games with his head. Straight back to the hotel. He'd check out the bar there. Scare up some conversation and perhaps a pretty face. But nothing serious. He wanted history and stories. He was going to finish this trip the way he started it. Heart-whole and single.

10

THAT WAS THE THIRD TIME SHE'D RUN INTO MICHAEL. SURELY Dublin wasn't that small?

No. Fate, the thing that always popped up in her books, was toying with them. From the way Michael tipped his cap and walked away, he didn't want to play with destiny any more than she did.

The mist turned into a fine steady rain. Kate quickened her steps.

He was a doctor? With the ball cap and the sexy beard shadow, she would have cast him as a baseball player. Or maybe a movie star in disguise. But doctor suited who he seemed to be inside. He had such kindness in him. She'd seen it when he spoke to Essie and again with the boy.

Kate shifted her Boots' purchases to her other hand and unlocked the door. Brad was cocooned on the cot, snoring lightly. She felt his forehead. Cold and clammy. She got an extra blanket out of the closet and added to the two he already had. He turned over and snuggled in.

Kate stifled a laugh at the contrast between his little-boy-sleep look and his street-tough face.

She wrestled the charger out of its plastic packaging and read the directions. Simple enough. Kate plugged her phone into the apparatus and attached it to the wall. The charging light blinked.

"Kate?"

She turned around. One bloodshot eye peeked out from the covers. "How are you feeling?"

"Like a cold empty balloon. I may survive. Not sure yet."

Kate twisted the top off the tiny tube she'd bought at Boots. "The pharmacist said to take three of these under your tongue."

Brad looked at the tiny white pellets and swallowed hard. He shook his head weakly.

"Try."

"I don't think ..."

She popped them in his mouth.

He started to spit them out. "They are sweet." He rolled them under his tongue and closed his eyes. "Not bad," he mumbled.

"I brought you some ginger tea too." Kate hauled his blankets down.

"Hey," Brad protested.

"Go sleep in the bedroom. You'll be more comfortable in there. When you wake up, I'll make tea."

"Thanks." Brad wrapped himself in the blankets and wavered to the bedroom.

Kate sat cross-legged on the sofa and fired up her laptop. Time to work. She opened the last draft of *Chasing Cressida*.

Bold move, Kate. You're actually facing your manuscript. Now write something. Her brain felt like stale pudding

She entered the Wi-Fi code they'd given her at the desk. Five minutes. *Check my email and off.*

An email from her agent emitted a siren call. *Congratulations, you made the top twenty bestsellers on Amazon. I don't know how you got her to do it, but she gave you a great review.*

Who? Kate clicked on the link Rhoda embedded and froze looking at her favorite author's well-read Facebook page. Andrea Saint Claire had posted a link to *Miss Minerva takes a Dare* and told her readers to check it out.

Kate stared at the thumbnail of the Miss Minerva cover—a glimpse of red curls and a wisp of dress and a hand holding out a string of pearls. Andrea Saint Claire liked her book. Someone whose work she adored liked her novel.

Kate floated to the fridge and got out the Coke she'd bought. Flipping the top, she raised the can in the air. "Here's to me. I can do this."

She took a swig. The bubbles poured down her throat in a cool sweet stream. One matchless moment and then Ethel, her inner critic, took over. *One book isn't being a writer. You'd better fix this one, or everybody will know you're a flash in the pan.*

Back to Lord Rotherham and Cressida. "No Googling. Turn off the computer," she ordered herself. "Use the legal pad."

Lord Rotherham mesmerized Cressida. His eyes promised adventure of a sort she'd never known before. And his mouth? She felt a sense of something in the pit of her stomach . . . Danger? Excitement? Was this the mysterious thing her governess warned her against? She wanted to reach up and put her arms around his neck and draw him close and feel the tender scraping of his rough whiskers against ~~my~~ ~~lips~~.

"Aargh." *her lips*

Rough whiskers? In Regency novels, heroes shaved. Kate scratched out the whole last sentence. Her pen dried up. She sucked and stabbed the page several times. She stared at the holes on the page; absentmindedly tracing blue ink hearts around them.

"Stop it"

Ethel, the Critic chimed in. *You can't even concentrate for two minutes. How do you plan to finish a book?*

Kate turned a fresh page and started over.

Drawn as she was by Lord Rotherham's desire-filled eyes, Cressida knew she must not succumb. Once he knew her secret, he would despise her. Better to walk away before her heart was involved. "Lord Rotherham, I find I cannot like you." *She wasn't accustomed to telling ~~fibs~~ bouncers.* "I must ask you to leave."

Lord Rotherham brought Cressida's hand to his lips. "Cressida, do not fear me," *he said in a voice like rough velvet.*

Kate sucked the end of her pen. Rough velvet? Really?

His hooded eyes held a gentleness she never thought to see there. "I would give my life to protect you. I know something frightens you. Won't you please take me into your confidence?"

Kate's eyes closed. She snapped them open.

Ethel sneered. *You're tired because you don't want to write.*

Ethel had to go. "No. I'm tired because I've slept three hours in the last twenty-four."

You need to write your ten pages.

"Shut up, Ethel. We're going to sleep." Kate tiptoed into the bedroom and grabbed her flannel Pjs. By the time she'd brushed her teeth she could barely keep her eyes open. She went back to the living room and realized Brad had taken the blankets. Back to the closet, but there weren't any more extra. Drat.

Brad lay on his side bundled in the extra blankets. He hadn't gotten under the bedspread. She slipped in beside Brad and eased under the covers.

Well, Kate, you want to write about this? Fate was an odd duck. Her first night in Ireland and there was a man in her bed. But not the one she wanted. Her eyes weighted closed.

11

"WAKE UP, SUNSHINE."

Brad's disgustingly cheerful voice penetrated her nightmare. Kate fought her way to consciousness past slow motion scenes of her editor chasing her with a red pen the size of an axe screaming, "Where is it?" Images of Michael swirled past her. Michael's smiling eyes. His mouth murmuring "Trust me. I'm a doctor." His arms were around her and it was . . . smothering. Kate tried to move her arms, but they were pinned to her side. She forced her eyes open.

Brad stood over her, holding a cup of tea. His color was good and his eyes bright with amusement. "Want some help unwrapping yourself? You look like a sausage roll."

All Kate could muster was an umph. How had she managed to roll herself up like this?

Brad set down the teacup; took one edge of the blanket and pulled.

She unwrapped like a dancing girl in a rug, ending up against the wall. "That was weird." Ugh. Her tongue felt like a woolen mitten.

Brad handed her the tea. It could have used some sugar, but she was grateful for the wetness.

"It looked like you might be having a bad dream. I thought you'd be pleased to be woken."

"I am." She took another sip. The lingering miasma slipped back. "My editor was chasing me and I couldn't remember what I'd done with the book and Michael . . ." She shuddered.

"Michael? The man who gave us a ride from the airport? Wow. If you are dreaming about him, he must have made quite an impression on you."

Kate handed Brad the tea and stretched. "How did I end up with all the blankets?"

"I have no idea. Why were you sleeping with me, by the way? Couldn't bear to leave my side?"

"You hogged all the blankets when you went to sleep it off. I guess the pills worked."

"Yeah. I felt good when I woke up around three and better when I took another dose. Woke again at six and took a third. Then I tried the ginger tea. Where did you learn about Pulsatilla?"

"Michael. I bumped into him on Grafton Street." Kate yawned. Images from the dream still hovered at the edge of her consciousness.

Brad's face lost its cheery look. "Then what?"

"I told him you had food poisoning and he told me about the pills." Kate's stomach rumbled. She remembered the meal she hadn't eaten. "I'm starving."

"Me too. Get dressed and we'll go find breakfast."

Kate crawled to the end of the bed and grabbed clothes at random from her suitcase.

"Honestly, Kate, you have the fashion sense of a six-year-old boy." He took the sweatshirt from her hand and substituted a dark green blouse. "At least, someone helped you pack a few nice things."

"Gah." She would have to travel with someone who looked like he shopped at GQ. Kate stalked into the bathroom.

"Comb your hair," he called after her.

Kate improvised a shower cap out of one of the hostel's thin white towels. No way she wanted to take the time to dry her hair. She washed and dried quickly. Her stupid curls made her look like a sultry ad for L'Oréal. She yanked a brush through her hair and plaited it into submission, securing the braid with a twist tie. One of these days she'd remember to buy new scrunchies. "I'm ready."

Brad stared at the twist tie. "Sad. Very sad."

Kate grabbed a wool cap out of her suitcase and stuffed the braid inside. "Take it or leave it. I'm not fooling with it anymore." She grabbed her cell phone, purse, and jacket.

"You look more a college dropout than an up and coming author."

"The book! You got Andrea Saint Claire to read my book." She wrapped her arms around him. He wasn't as short as she'd thought. Maybe two inches shorter than she

Brad returned her hug. His arms felt hard and strong against her back.

"Do you have any idea how it feels to have someone whose work you love praise your book? It's completely awesome."

Brad pulled away and took her hands. "Did you happen to note where you are on the Amazon list?"

"Yes and I can't believe it. You're a magician. How did you do it?"

"Trade secret. You owe me a meal. That's my fee."

"I owe you more than a meal."

"How 'bout you buy some better hair doodads? Then you can take me somewhere for dinner. I'll check the Michelin Guide."

"You'll have to wait till we get back to New York. I may be up in the top twenty, but that doesn't translate to money till the quarterly statement. Last quarter I made about three hundred dollars."

"Oh, I think you can count on more next quarter. How do you feel about appearing on Oprah?"

Kate's heart stuttered. "You're kidding."

Brad grinned. "Yeah. I am. *Miss Minerva Takes a Dare* isn't Oprah's kind of book."

Kate curled her hands into strangling position.

Brad stepped back. "But you do have an interview coming up with Happily Ever After, USA Today when we get back."

Kate consulted her watch. Almost eight-thirty. Still time. "About breakfast. We have a free one over at the hostel dining room. We might as well take advantage of it."

"You're joking. I want a full Irish breakfast. You owe me."

"And you had food poisoning yesterday. Let's start with something simple."

"This is about Oprah, isn't it? You're trying to kill me." Brad mumbled things Kate was glad she couldn't hear all the way to the main hostel.

The small hostel kitchen had two attached dining rooms. Each had several long tables covered with blue plastic oilcloth. A smiling girl, her brown curls covered with a gauze cap, put a tray of white toast on the kitchen's hutch.

Brad took a couple of slices. He bypassed the granola in favor of a cup of tea.

"At least, take an apple." Kate filled a Styrofoam cup with coffee.

Brad grabbed several pats of butter for the toast.

They moved into the adjoining room, and found seats at an almost full table. At the front of the room, a well-worn sofa and a couple of chairs were grouped around a television tuned to a morning news show. On the opposite side of the room stood a fridge.

Kate nudged Brad and pointed to the large sign on the

fridge door. *Mark and date your food or it will be thrown out.* "See. If we hadn't gotten a kitchen, we could cook our food right here. It's good to know for the next hostel. This is the way to travel."

Kate sliced a banana over her granola.

Brad buttered his cold toast and grunted.

Almost all their fellow diners were in their early twenties. Several had taken advantage of the wall plugs and were on their computers. Others tapped busily on their phones. Different conversations in different languages surrounded them.

This was exactly how she imagined her trip. Journeyers. Wayfarers coming together. They were all here to explore and seek adventure. She caught a flash from the computer screen on the other side of Brad and averted her eyes. Should the man be watching that in public? Maybe things were different in Europe.

The pots of jam decorating the table looked home-made. She spread some on her toast. "Mmm. Blackberry. Have some. It's wonderful."

Brad dabbed some jam on top of the cold butter icing his slice of toast. "It does improve the flavor. We're not eating here again. Promise."

The bearded guy watching the porn snapped his computer shut and walked to the outside door.

"Pity," Brad commented. "Things were getting interesting."

The opened door let in a wave of smells. Tobacco and . . . marijuana?

"Is pot legal here?" Kate whispered.

Brad shrugged. "I'm betting they don't care whether it's legal or not. Kids think they are invulnerable." He picked up his tray and followed the signs to the disposal area.

Kate stuffed the last of her toast in her mouth. "I thought we'd start by taking a bus tour of the city and get our bearings."

"No buses. Remember?"

"Oh." Kate pouted. "I thought it would be over by now. This is really inconvenient."

"Yeah. A lot of Ireland's revenue comes from tourism. I'm sure they're going to try and settle it quickly. But in the meantime, we'd better see about renting a car. Let's ask at the front desk."

The front desk had a line of people waiting to check out.

"Let's not wait," Kate said. "I picked up a map; Trinity College and Dublin Castle are within walking distance. Come on."

"Let me see the map." He walked along, seemingly oblivious to the pedestrians, but somehow managing to avoid collisions. "The Guinness factory is close too. That's where I want to go."

"College first," Kate stated. "We have to see the Book of Kells. That's one of the most famous things to do in Dublin."

"Not more famous than the Guinness factory," Brad grumbled.

"But much more educational."

"Fine. But I get to choose where we eat lunch." He tapped something into his phone. A rich British voice rolled out. "Head northeast on Bachelors Walk toward O'Connell Street."

Kate's mouth dropped. "Your phone sounds like Dumbledore in the Harry Potter films."

"Turn right on "O'Connell Bridge."

"Put the phone away," Kate hissed. "We look like tourists."

"Kate, we are tourists." Brad stuck the phone in his pocket. "It's going to look even weirder having a voice issue from my pants."

She snatched the phone out of his pocket and turned it off. "We'll use the map. Discreetly. If we get lost, we can always ask a Garda."

"Ooh, sounds like fun. If there's one thing I love, it's a uniform."

Kate stared at him suspiciously. Was he gay or not? The way he'd returned her hug this morning was . . . she tripped on the thought. And he'd seemed to enjoy the man's porn at the breakfast table.

Brad took her hand. His palm felt warm against hers. "Come on, Kate." He hummed under his breath. "Over the river and through the woods, turn left on College Green."

Kate giggled. "I love you."

His hand convulsed on hers. "But in a platonic way, of course," he said, his voice flat.

"Of course." She wished she hadn't used the L word. Brad's grasp on her hand didn't feel platonic. Exactly how gay was he?

12

THE PHONE DRAGGED MICHAEL OUT OF A DREAM OF RUNNING through endless streets chasing a green-eyed mermaid. He sat up, squinting at the sliver of daylight coming through the curtain and fumbled for the phone. "Hello?"

"Michael. Declan, and Shauna are going to drive to Galway, and they have plenty of room for me," Essie chirped.

Michael suppressed a groan. How could Essie sound wide awake at, he squinted at his watch. *Nine?* He couldn't remember when he'd last slept this late. "That's good." Michael yawned. "How are you feeling?"

"I'm wonderful. We talked till . . . oh, I don't know what time. My body and my head are saying different things about that. Declan and Shauna both took time off work so we could travel together. And Brenna took time off too. She wants to visit with her cousins and," Essie lowered her voice, "she's that excited to have time to know you better. Would you be wanting to let go of your car and travel with us? There's plenty of room."

"Thanks. No. I want to see more of Dublin before moving on. Why don't I meet you in Clu . . . ah?" His brain fumbled for the name of her hometown.

"No. I want to be with you when you catch your first sight of Cluhalaugh. Hold for a minute. Shauna wants to tell me something."

Michael rubbed his hand over his chin. He really needed a shave. Nah. This was his vacation and he was going to do what he wanted.

"Michael, we've another plan. We'll stop by and visit with my cousin Iona's husband, Padraic in Athlone. Shauna says he could use a bit of company. That will give you some time to explore on your own. We'll meet up with you in Galway in three days. My sister Maire is expecting us then." A voice rumbled in the background. "Declan says you'll want to stop and see the Burren."

Declan's voice echoed over the wire. "We'll take good care of Essie. Can you give me your cell phone number?"

Michael heard a female voice in the background. "Brenna says she wants to take you to see the Burren. It's a great draw for the tourists. It's got some Neolithic sites, and a bear cave."

"Bear cave, huh? I have to see that." Preferably without company.

"Why don't you come by for breakfast and see us off then?" Declan asked.

"I'd be delighted." Time on his own sounded great. Wonder if Declan knew any good fishing spots?

Brenna's face lit up when she opened the door for him. "Mum's been making a full Irish for you. She says you need fattening up." Her tongue flicked out, moistening her upper lip. "I don't know. You look pretty good to me."

Essie bustled in from the kitchen with a steaming plate in her hand. "I hope you brought a good appetite. Shauna wanted you to experience the full breakfast."

"That's fine." Michael took the plate from Essie. "You look ready to climb the cliffs of Moher. Traveling agrees with you. You should do more of it."

"It's the pleasure of family, and well you know it," Shauna bustled in with the teapot and a plate of steaming biscuits. "Sit yourself down."

"Shauna's scones are even better than her soda bread," Essie said.

Brenna set a thermos shaped pot in front of him. "Aunty says you prefer coffee so I made you some special."

"Thank you." Michael looked at the piled-high plate. Eggs, potatoes, sausage, bacon, tomatoes, mushrooms, and a square black object he couldn't identify. "What's this?"

"That's blood sausage," Essie said proudly. "It's a traditional part of the breakfast."

"Ah." Michael slid his fork past it and stabbed a sausage. It cracked and bubbled scenting the room with sage.

Shauna passed the plate of scones. They didn't look anything like the hard objects found in a Starbucks display case. He bit into one. "Amazing. Are you sure I can't persuade you to dump your husband and marry me instead?"

"Go on wid ya?" Shauna patted his arm. "It wouldna be a good bargain for you, but I'd fine fair like to see America. If Declan doesn't stop turning off my programs to watch a sports match, I'd consider it."

"Woman, we've gone on forty-three years the way we are," Declan said. "I'm thinking we'd better stick to our bargain. And don't forget who matched us."

"You went to a matchmaker?" Michael's inner vision flashed to Barry Fitzgerald driving John Wayne and Maureen O'Hara through the Irish countryside in a wagon instructing them in the rules of courtship. *The Quiet Man* was on his watch-once-a-year list.

"Aye and we did. The best matchmaker Cluhalaugh ever had. When she moved to America, the whole town wept."

Michael looked at Essie. "You?"

"And who do you think matched half the couples in Parsonville?" Essie asked. "I haven't found the right woman for you yet, but I have high hopes for . . ."

"Me?" Brenna fluttered her lashes at Michael. "I think we'd do fine together."

Maybe he'd better seek out the bear cave and stay there. Essie had a determined look in her eyes. "Matchmaker . . . How do you choose who to match?"

"I'm a seer and my talent is for matching lives and hearts." Essie folded her hands in her lap. "It's a talent come down in the family. There were two of us in my generation. Me and my cousin, Iona." Essie's eyes filled. "After Iona passed, I knew I was meant to come back. But I didn't know how to manage it until Br . . ." Essie clamped her lips shut.

How had she managed it? Michael knew Essie had barely enough to get by. Where had she gotten the money for the airfare?

"I would say it's perfect timing," Declan said. "Here's Brenna broken it off with her teacher friend. I knew they weren't right for each other. And Sean and Catriona's Danny courting Enid Motheroe, and no one to say if it's good or not. Too many divorces these days. No one's got any respect for the sanctity of the marriage vow."

Shauna nodded in agreement. "These days it's like the Telly. Changing your partner is as easy as changing the channel."

Michael winced at the memory of his Mom and Dad telling him and his brother they were getting a divorce. "And having a matchmaker makes it all right?"

Essie lifted her chin. "In all my days only one couple I matched ever broke their marriage vows, my own brother, Fiercra. He left his wife and ran off to Australia. Never came back. His wife emigrated to Canada. I hear she got a divorce and married a banker. Nelly was always one for the money, so I suppose she did well for herself. Fiercra was the wildest of my brothers."

"That's a very impressive record." Michael tried not to sound skeptical. He looked down at his plate and discovered he'd eaten everything but the blood sausage. "How far is it to Athlone?"

"About two and a half hours depending on the traffic," Declan said. "We don't want to be taking the M6. You miss too many fine sights on the way."

"You'll want to get on the road then. I'll say goodbye to you now." Michael smiled at Essie. "How long will you be staying with your cousin?"

"Long enough to persuade him to come to Cluhalaugh with us." Essie had a militant look in her eye. "Iona's been gone five years now and it's time Padraic found a new partner."

Michael spared of a pang of sympathy for the unwary cousin. "Perhaps he's content the way he is. Some people like to live singly."

Essie shook her head. "Man was meant to live two by two. Some people simply haven't found the right person. Now, Michael, I have Maire's address all written out for you." She handed him a slip of paper covered with her elegant cursive penmanship. "I know you want to see the Guinness factory, but go see the Book of Kells first. It's a piece of history I think you'll be appreciating."

Essie's innocent look told him she was up to something, but he couldn't imagine what. "Book of Kells it is."

"The grand thing about Dublin is everything's close by." Shauna handed him a foil package of scones. "You can take these back to your hotel room. It's a scandal what they charge for snackies at hotels. Trinity College Library is no more than an a few minutes by foot from The Cormorant. And the Guinness Factory is just the other side of Temple Bar. Not far from Dublin Castle."

They saw him to the door with a chorus of additional sights to be sure and see.

The weather had shifted. Lamb's wool clouds chased each other through the blue sky. Good thing he walked to Declan's for he surely needed to walk off breakfast. Michael slung his jacket over his shoulder and strode out briskly toward Dolphin Road. Three days of freedom before he had to meet whatever Essie planned for him in Galway and he was going to make the most of it.

13

Kate took a photo of the blue shield over the arched stone gateway in front of Trinity College. Its golden images—a lion and a harp above a clasped book and a castle—spoke to her imagination. "Trinity College looks like a medieval monastery. I would love to have gone to school here." She noticed people going around, rather than through the gateway. "Why's everybody avoiding the arch?

"It's a superstition," Brad said. "If you go through it, you might have good luck, but you'll never graduate from Trinity."

Kate snapped rapid pictures of the cobblestone quadrangle. The excitement of standing in a place chock full of history fizzed through her body. "Do you have any idea of who went here? Samuel Beckett, Bram Stoker and Jonathan Swift, among others."

"You're forgetting Oliver Goldsmith. His is the statue up front." He consulted his phone's guidebook. "Goldsmith was best known for his plays. But he was also a doctor and wrote the nursery rhyme, *Hickory Dickory Dock*."

"It does not say that." Kate reached for his phone.

Brad held it away from her. "But it's true. My high school

drama teacher told us about *Hickory Dickory Dock* when we did Goldsmith's *She Stoops to Conquer.* I played Tony Hardcastle, the wild and crazy son."

"How apt," Kate snarked.

"The eminent Oscar Fingal O'Flahertie Wills also wore the green cap and gown."

"Who?"

"Oscar Wilde, my personal hero. Who could ever forget a man who wrote 'To lose one parent may be regarded as a misfortune; to lose both looks like carelessness.'"

Kate turned away and surveyed the huge quadrangle, storing up details in her mind. The ordered beauty of the gray stone pillared buildings, the swathes of emerald green grass dwarfed by huge expanses of cobblestone. She looked at the bike racks lining the buildings. "I don't think I'd want to ride a bike on cobblestone."

"Well, plenty do." Brad nodded at the stream of people headed to the right. "If we follow the crowd we'll probably find your book."

"It's not my book. The Book of Kells is a manuscript dating from about 800 AD. Show some proper respect."

"It's your book in the sense that *you* want to see it," Brad pointed out. "*I* suggested the Guinness factory."

Kate frowned. "My trip. Remember?"

Brad sighed. "Fine. Age before Guinness. I understand."

They paid their admission and joined the line of tourists wending their way through the exhibit. Kate stopped to examine the display of the book's original binding. She lifted her phone for a picture.

A guard stepped forward. "No pictures, Miss."

"I'm sorry." Kate put the phone away. She'd have to content herself with postcards.

Brad stopped in front of the first of a series of huge poster boards lining the stone room. "They used more than a hundred and eighty-five calf skins to make this book. That's a lot of calves. The book better be worth it."

Kate sniffed. "It is. Because it preserved words and pictures and created art."

They moved through three more rooms to get to the book itself. Four glass-topped cases displayed pages of the original book.

"Those poster boards of the book are easier to see," Brad said.

"You don't get it." Kate studied the illustrations, colors faded from age, envisioning what the pages would have looked like when they were written.

Dark abbey lit by torches. A young monk hunched over a piece of calfskin painstakingly copying the words of his faith and then worshipping the words with his own gift. Each drawing created with black ink, and carefully filled with color. A bell tolled the hour. He rubbed his cold hands and warmed them inside his robe.

How many years had it taken to create this book? She looked down at the darkened pages and felt a sense of kinship with the monk. "Rest well," she whispered. "The beauty is still here and what you have created still exists. Thank you."

"What are you mumbling?" Brad asked.

"Nothing." She pushed away from the wood-framed glass case and tripped over a large foot.

Warm hands caught her arms and steadied her. "Amazing piece of work, isn't it?"

She turned around. Michael. "This can't be happening," she said. "Why are you here?"

"Michael." Brad clapped him on the back. "Good to see you. Thanks for telling Kate about the pills."

"I see you are none the worse for wear. Glad you're on your feet again."

"Why are you here?" Kate repeated.

"Essie told me I had to be sure and see the Book of Kells." Michael's eyes crinkled. He looked amused by some private joke.

The crowd flowed them up the stairs and into a new hall.

Kate stopped fuming and let the beauty of the place wash over her. Rows and rows of arches stretching into infinity. Each arched niche was two stories tall, with a balcony separating the stories. Ladders ran to the tops of the floor-to-ceiling book-shelves. Each arch was lit by two huge rectangular windows, one on top of another.

Down the center aisle were glass cases showcasing open books. White marble busts lined the arches. Thick carpet muffled the sound of footsteps. Hushed whispers rose and floated away.

Kate pulled out her phone to snap a picture; then remembered and started to put it away

Michael stopped her, "It's all right in here. I read it's only in the Kells exhibit you can't take photos. Here let me." He took the phone from her.

Kate stood haloed in a shaft of light, books rising dark around her.

Michael's indrawn breath was audible.

"Let me take it." Brad took the phone from him. "Go stand beside her. You two make a pretty picture. Beauty and the Scruffy."

Michael rubbed his hand across his two-day old beard. "It's vacation. I don't plan to shave till it's over." He retrieved the phone from Brad. "You go stand beside her. I'll snap you both."

Kate took her phone back. "Thanks," she said brusquely. "I'd rather take pictures of the room. Did you ever see anything like it?"

"It's called the Long Room." Brad tapped his brochure. "It's the longest library room in the world. And it's making me thirsty. Shall we get on with it? I want to get over to the Guinness Brewery."

Michael nodded. "I'm with you."

Kate frowned. "Seriously?"

"Dublin's a small town and the tourists all want to hit the same places," Michael said. "I bet if you looked it up, you'd find the Book of Kells and the Guinness factory are two of the top destinations."

Kate sighed. "I would have put a bus tour at number one, but it's off the list."

Brad clapped a hand on Michael's shoulder. "Join us. The more the merrier."

Kate followed them out of the library and back to the courtyard. Brad stopped to take a picture of the 'giant gold ball within a ball' statue.

"Where's your friend?" Kate asked.

"Essie's with her brother and his wife. I'm supposed to meet them in Galway in three days."

Michael's smile made her want to do stupid things. Like, kiss a man she'd seen four times in twenty-four hours. Kate stomped ahead muttering to herself, "Get a grip, Kate. It's just coincidence." She stepped on a cobblestone the wrong way and fell to her knees.

"Are you all right?" Michael helped her to her feet.

"I'm fine. It's just a twist." Her breath quickened.

He knelt beside her. "Let me check. The last thing you want to do is limp around Dublin all day."

Kate resisted the urge to run her fingers through his tumble of brown hair. Every time he got near her, she lost all sense.

He ran expert fingers around her ankle. "I can't feel anything. Are your knees okay?"

"Yeah. I caught myself on my hands." She winced at their sting.

Michael turned her palms over. "These need to be washed up."

His touch sent feelings swirling through her stomach. Kate pulled away. "It's nothing."

"Don't be stupid, Kate." Brad took her arm. "There's a ladies room over by the gift shop." He steered her toward it. "We'll wait for you out here."

"Fine." Kate stomped away, cursing her thoughts and her clumsiness.

She found the M'na, washed her palms carefully, and dried them with the thin paper towels. She stared at her flushed cheeks in the mirror. She could not be having sexual thoughts about a complete stranger. It was wrong and embarrassing.

She caught up with Brad and Michael in the gift shop.

Brad looked smug. "I talked to Michael and since we're going the same way he is, he offered us a ride."

Michael looked like he wasn't sure what hit him. She had the same feeling around Brad sometimes. She opened her mouth to refuse.

"Come on, Kate. It's a piece of luck us running into him again. I've got us accommodations at a Castle. If we took a train, it would be standing room only, with the buses on strike. And we couldn't stop at the Burren. I wanted you to see that."

Kate bowed to the inevitable. "Do you really think you should offer a ride to two complete strangers?"

"Not complete," Michael said wryly. "There seems a certain inevitability about our meetings. I'm beginning to suspect Leprechauns."

It was hard to resist his crooked smile. "Thank you, Michael. It's very nice of you." Leprechauns were as good an explanation as any.

The men bonded further over glasses of Guinness at the Warehouse. Kate dreamed out the window of the bar at the top of the building. She didn't care about the ale, although seeing the process of brewing was fascinating. What drew her was what the Guinness family had done for the people of Dublin. When the Great Lockout occurred in the early twentieth century, Guinness kept their people working. They founded schools, hospitals, all manner of things. She'd been awed by the sight of the ninety-thousand-year lease the Guinness family signed for their brewery. That showed an extravagant belief in the future. She wished she had that kind of belief about her own work. How did they manage to keep believing what they were doing was worthwhile?

MICHAEL RESISTED the temptation to ask Kate what she was dreaming about. He was becoming far too fond of studying her expression. Time to part ways. "The Abbey Theatre is doing a revival of *Noises Off* tonight," he found himself saying. "Would you both like to join me?"

Kate blinked. "You like theatre?"

"I do," Michael said. "My godmother has an old friend in this production. And she threatened my Christmas gift if I didn't see it while I was here. She gives very good Christmas gifts. I wouldn't want to risk it."

"I love plays." Kate looked like he'd just given her a box of chocolates. "When I have the money, I haunt the TKTS tickets booth in Times Square."

Brad turned to Kate. "You've done Guinness for me. I'll do theatre for you. Michael, where can we meet you?"

"I'm staying at the Cormorant in Temple Bar. I'll ask them to recommend a restaurant. Shall we meet at my hotel around six?"

"I didn't bring anything to wear to the theatre," Kate objected.

"Not a problem," Brad said. "We'll go shopping. We've both

got souvenirs to buy and you could use a wardrobe refresh. Perhaps you could donate the contents of your suitcase to Goodwill."

Kate glared at Brad. "Brad doesn't approve of my taste."

Michael wanted her to stay the way she was. Bundled in a too large jacket with her silky mass of auburn hair covered by a cap. "I don't think people dress for the theatre anymore. What you're wearing will be fine."

"Pity." Brad sighed. "But you still have to buy an Irish sweater and some lace stuff. That's what people bring home from Ireland. Would you like to go to a lace making factory?"

"No thanks." Kate yawned. "I don't think my inner time's caught up with my outer time. I'm going to head back to the hostel for a nap."

"Fine," Michael said. "See you tonight then?"

"Tonight." Brad put his arm round Kate's shoulders. "Come on, sleeping beauty. Let's get you home."

Michael watched them leave. His brain and his tongue were obviously no longer communicating. Why on earth had he asked them to the theatre? And why had he offered them a lift. He contemplated his half-finished Guinness. "So much for fishing."

14

BRAD STOPPED OUTSIDE THE THREE-STORY BUILDING ON THE corner of Jervis and Abbey Street. The crest saying *National Leprechaun Museum* blended into the surrounding tan brick. Even with their museum, leprechauns weren't all that keen on being noticed.

He tried the handle on the door. Locked of course. Humans couldn't visit the museum without an appointment. He pressed the bell repeatedly.

The grumpy face of his cousin Eamon peered through the mirrored glass. He unlocked the door. "It's about time you came home. Had enough of this New York nonsense, have you? The McPhee will be overjoyed."

"No. I haven't had enough of it and when are you going to get off your arse and come visit me?"

He and his cousin were much of a height. There the resemblance ended. Eamon was the handsomer of the two of them. In Brad's opinion, Eamon would be better looking if he'd shaved off his cherished beard. While Brad embraced his human heritage, Eamon hated it. He'd taken the gold their grandfather left them and started a museum dedicated to preserving leprechaun legends. The beard and his old-fashioned green shirt were all part of the image.

Eamon led him through a room with rainbow painted walls, past a forest of giant mushrooms. "You'll no catch me visiting that devil's place. It's claimed too many Irishmen already."

Brad craned his neck to look up at the twelve-foot-high table flanked by two ten-foot chairs. "This is new."

"I want visitors to feel what it's like to be tiny in a human world." Eamon motioned to the souvenir shop. "Those statues you sent me are selling well. And I can't keep the *Find the Leprechaun* books in stock. I wrote you to send me another fifty. I don't know where you found the artist, but he's a marvel."

"He's one of my clients. I suggested the books to him. If you come to New York, I'll introduce you."

Eamon motioned him into the tiny office and offered him a seat in from of a carved desk pile high with papers. "What are you doing home then?"

"McPhee gave me a wish client, knowing damn well she was coming to Ireland and that I'd have to accompany her. I think he's counting on me not being able to grant the wish. He put a geas on me not to use magic."

Eamon scowled. "That's harsh. He used magic to stop you from using magic? Knowing you, I'm betting you tried. How sick did you get?"

Brad grimaced at the memory. "Sick enough. Kate, my wish client, gave me some medicine which took it away."

Eamon looked surprised. "Does she have healing magic? A hedgewitch, perhaps?"

"No. She's a human with a fine sympathy for her fellow man." And a grand companion who laughed at his jokes. And a beautiful woman who insisted on disguising it. And a temptation he'd do well to avoid.

"Does she know you're part of the fair folk?"

"No, and she's not going to find out. I think I'm close to granting her wish."

Eamon lit the long meerschaum pipe he always carried. "And what does your client want?"

"A hero."

Eamon inhaled sharply and choked on a cloud of smoke. Brad leaned over the desk, and pounded him on the back.

Eamon wheezed. "Bradley Flynn, you're not thinking of offering yourself, are you?"

"Of course not. I've found someone else."

"Without using magic? How did you manage that one?"

"I called in a favor from an old friend. Aisling O'Callaghan. She found me someone." Michael seemed like a good match for Kate. Certainly he was perfect hero material for her book.

Eamon raised a bushy eyebrow. "The Lady of Cluhalaugh? I thought she'd be dead by now."

"She's in her seventies and very much alive." Humans aged much faster than the fair folk. Another reason thinking about Kate was a bad idea.

"Where is your wish client? Why don't you bring her to the museum? I'd be happy to give her a tour."

Brad shook his head. "Ah, no. You'd give me away for sure just for the fun of it."

Eamon grinned. "That I would. It would be a grand joke to see you try to wiggle out of it."

Brad looked away. Shifted a few of the papers on the desk. "You really need a secretary, Eamon. What happened to Piri?"

Eamon's face darkened. "I let her go. I don't need anyone to be sticking their nose in my business. I am happy enough alone."

But he wasn't. He was a fellow halfling who never quite made his peace with either world. "Too bad. I thought you and she made a fine pair, both of you loving the legends like you do."

"Hah! Finn, save me from half-fairies. The only legends she was interested in were her own." Eamon dropped his voice to a whisper. "She called me a damn shoemaker."

Brad stifled the grin that wanted to pop out. Oh, to have been a fly on the wall for that strammash. Piri and Eamon were tinder and flame. The two of them would have a grand making up, if only they would come to their senses. "I need a favor. I want you to meet me in Cluhalaugh in three days' time."

"Ah, don't want to face the family on your own do you?"

"True enough. The thought scares me silly. They want me in Ireland, tied to one of their own producing wee little grandchildren for them to spoil. They want an end to the bargain."

"And you don't."

"No. I've been more human than fae most of my life. I love their world and I've made a fine place for myself in it."

"Why don't you just marry a human then? You'll never have to dance to McPhee's tune again."

"Because I'm not ready to give up half of what I am. I'm escorting Kate to Cluhalaugh"

Eamon looked at him incredulously. "You're taking a human to visit the family?"

"Of course not. It's the Equinox, Eamon, and the Lady is back. Kate will find her hero at the choosing ceremony. I need you to stand with me in the line."

His cousin blew a cloud of smoke at him. "I know what it is you want. You want some of my magic to make sure she doesn't choose you."

No. He needed his cousin to stop avoiding his own fate. "That's the way of it," Brad said aloud, tweaking his power of persuasion up a notch. If his cousin had forgotten leprechaun magic didn't work at the time of choosing, who was he to remind him? Eamon was past his hundredth birthday. And humans weren't the only attendees at the ceremony.

Eamon sighed heavily. "I'll come. I'd fair hate to see you dangling from a human wench's hook. But you'll owe me."

"That I will. Shake hands on it then?" Brad pulsed a little magic through his palm. McPhee's geas only forbid him to use love magic on Kate.

Eamon grasped his hand firmly. "Three days' time. Someone has to save you from yourself. Shall we drink on it then?"

"If I start drinking with you, I might not stop till morning." Brad consulted his Bulgari watch. "I left Kate napping, but by this time she's probably up and choosing something terrible to wear to the play tonight. From the way she doesn't want to be noticed, you'd almost think she was one of us. I'll meet you in Cluhalaugh."

15

THE RESTAURANT LOOKED LIKE IT STEPPED OUT OF THE PAST. OIL portraits of Victorian ladies and gentleman hung on the cream paneled walls. Kate drank in the details. Rose shaded candles, White damask tablecloths. The spicy scent of carnations vying with the incredible aromas of food wafting toward them. The quiet swish of obsequious waiters.

Kate blessed Carrie's additions to her suitcase. The lace-trimmed chiffon blouse and the St Laurent blueberry wool jacket Brad unearthed from the bottom of her bag blended nicely with the Victorian ambiance and made her feel rather like one of her own characters. The elegant Maître de gave Kate a Gallic nod of approval and ushered them to a central table. With a flourish, he presented menus and sent the wine steward.

Brad's spate of French with the steward resulted in the presentation of Champagne in an iced-filled silver bucket. Brad examined the bottle and nodded. "Good year."

Kate kicked him under the table. "I cannot afford Champagne."

"Relax. Michael provided the theatre tickets and dinner is on me."

The steward filled their glasses and discreetly vanished.

Kate sipped her Champagne, enjoying the cool tickle of bubbles. "This is what I imagine the Victorian era looked like. I should be wearing a dress with leg of mutton sleeves."

Michael cleared his throat. "You look . . . nice. Is that St Laurent?"

"Yes. My friend Carrie haunts vintage stores whenever she has a chance. She snuck it into my suitcase." He recognized the designer? "How did you know it was St. Laurent?"

"My mom runs a vintage shop and I worked for her in the summers during high school. She was a stickler for us knowing designer names and period styles."

"Us?" Kate had a quick flash of a teen-aged Michael and a hot girlfriend necking in the stock room.

"My brother John worked there too, till he managed to get a job at The Golden Apple."

"Beauty Parlor?" Brad asked.

"No. Comic book store. John's personal Nirvana."

"I'd have loved a job like that," Kate said wistfully. "I never had enough comics."

"Yet another thing you two have in common. If I'd known you liked comics, I would have invited you to my lair to see my first edition Spider-Man," Brad said.

"Really?" Kate and Michael said simultaneously.

"No. But it was fun watching your heads whip round." Brad laid down the menu. "I'm having the goose."

Kate studied the gold cursive entrees on the maroon leather menu, looking for prices. There were none. This was so far beyond her means, it was ridiculous.

Brad's hand covered hers. "Relax, Kate. I can afford it. Why don't you enjoy the moment? No strings attached."

Michael looked up from the menu. "The duck looks good."

"Excellent choice." Brad took the menu from Kate. "She'll have the Oysters Au Poivre.

"No, I won't. No poor little oyster is going to be murdered for my sake. I'll have the . . ." She'd taken a stand against oyster murder. It would be inconsistent to order the duck."

Brad sighed. "She'll have the duck."

Michael took a roll and a curl of butter from a cut crystal dish. "Brad, what's your line of work?"

"I grant wishes."

Kate rolled her eyes. "He owns a public relations firm in New York. He promotes things."

"I prefer to think of it as wish granting," Brad said. "People come to me with an idea of how they want to be perceived. I make it happen."

"And how do you do that?" Michael asked.

Brad shrugged. "Various ways. I used to program video games before deciding there were more social ways to make a living. The two jobs are rather similar. You know what you want the end-result to be, and all you have to do is figure out how to make the players get there."

The waiter wheeled up a cloth-covered cart and lifted the silver dome. "Your duck with brandied cherries."

The plates were beautifully presented with slices of glazed duck garnished with swirls of sauce which trailed over the large plate toward the miniature vegetables and the tablespoon-size portion of artistically whipped potatoes.

"It looks wonderful." Kate said. She got more food in a Weight Watchers entrée. Her eyes caught Michael's. He looked like he had similar thoughts.

Michael looked at the waiter. "Could you please bring some more rolls?"

Brad's plate was better filled. "Cheer up, kiddies. It smells fabulous and maybe the desserts are big. If not, we'll order extra."

Brad guessed right. The duck was the best thing she'd ever tasted. And the portions of chocolate walnut torte were huge.

Kate set down her fork. "I can't finish it. If I take another bite, you'll have to roll me to the theatre."

Michael looked at her unfinished slice. "If you're sure you don't want it? . . ."

"Be my guest."

"Thanks. I had a very large breakfast and a very small lunch to make up for it. This will fill in the cracks."

Brad pushed his plate toward Michael. "As tall as you are, you've got a lot of cracks to fill. Finish mine too."

Kate watched Michael finish both slices with devout enjoyment. Whatever carnal thoughts he'd been thinking about her were now devoted to chocolate. Just as well. Helped her remember all men were fickle. The caramel colored sweater he wore over his button-down shirt brought out the brandy color in his eyes and the dark green striped tie . . . she peered at the tiny print figures. "What's on your tie?"

"Yoda. My brother gave it to me in memory of the nights we spent in line to see Episode One. We were both class-A geeks. I outgrew it, of course."

"Yes. I can see that from your tie."

His smile warmed her all the way down to her . . . Kate looked away. The heat in his eyes was contagious. She felt color stain her cheeks. "I've never heard of *Noises Off*. Is it Irish?"

"I've no idea."

Brad beckoned to the waiter for the check. "In thirty minutes, you'll find out."

THE ABBEY THEATRE'S square-pillared front facade spilled light from the double-storied plate glass windows. Kate stifled a twinge of disappointment. "This can't be the original theatre."

"The old one burnt down," Brad said. "This massive brick monster is a mistaken tribute to modernism. I looked in the guidebook, but no one wants to own up to having designed it. You'd have thought they'd do better for the National Theatre of Ireland."

Noises Off was a fast-paced farce. The lines were punctuated by rolling gales of laughter from the packed house. Kate had to grip the padded armrest to keep from falling out of her seat.

"Want to go backstage?" Michael asked afterward. "I have to say hello to John to prove I've been here."

Kate nodded. "If I can still walk. I ache from laughing."

JOHN LUTERMAN SHOOK hands with Michael, but his eyes were on Kate. "Hello, gorgeous. Why don't you ditch these two and come out for a drink with me?"

John had to be in his seventies, but he was still a fox. Kate knew the zing of attraction she felt wasn't real. His portrayal of Lloyd, the director of the 'play within the play' was brilliantly funny, and the glamor of theatre bathed him in a golden light. But what fun to have a drink with an actor? She smiled back at him. "I'd love to."

Brad clamped his hand around her arm. "Kate, time to go home and take your meds." He looked at John, apologetically. "No telling what she'll do once they wear off."

Kate felt the heat once again flooding her cheeks. Torn between rage and laughter, she pried his hand off her arm. "Brad's just . . ."

Michael stepped up to flank her.

John's eyes twinkled. "You should see your faces. You're right, gentlemen. Never trust a beautiful lady to an amorous lecher. We'll all go." He offered Kate a courtly arm. "Your guardians can follow at twelve paces. There's a pub right around the corner."

CORMAC'S WAS DECORATED with theatrical posters and packed with people. Kate recognized some of the other actors from the play. The barkeep waved John to a corner table with a reserved sign.

"Thanks, Rory." John pulled out a chair for Kate and sat down next to her. "What would you like, lovely?"

Kate ignored the glowering duo in front of her. "I'd love a red wine. Merlot, if they have it."

"If they don't, I'll go out and stomp the grapes myself."

The barkeep came over with a Guinness and a shot glass of whiskey for John.

"Thank you, Rory. This exquisite creature beside me will have a glass of your best Merlot and her companions can state their own needs."

"I'll have a Guinness," Michael said shortly.

Brad motioned to the shot glass in front of John. "Bring me three of those."

John flirted with Kate till Rory served them. "Here's to beautiful women, God love em. May he keep making more." He clinked glasses with Kate's and turned to Michael. "Lorena told me you're involved with Tracy Jay. How's that working out?"

Kate was glad she'd set her wine glass down. Tracy Jay? The actress the critics were comparing to a young Marilyn Monroe?

Brad put down his empty shot glass. "I *have* seen you before. Star Magazine a couple of weeks ago. That was you on the cover with Tracy Jay?"

Michael nodded, his face expressionless.

John lifted an eyebrow. "Tabloid picture, eh. That's rarely a good sign. What happened?"

"We broke up."

John nodded wisely. "Good thing. We actors aren't a steady bunch."

16

MICHAEL TOSSED HIS JACKET ON A CHAIR AND SAT DOWN ON THE bed. The evening had gone downhill after John's announcement that he was involved with Tracy. He saw Kate raise her eyebrows. Noticed her slight withdrawal. He didn't blame her.

The dratted tabloid had been on the rack in front of every checkout counter in the US. The cover shot of him staring down at Tracy like she'd fallen off the Christmas tree, just for him. Tracy looking up at him like he was Superman come to save her. He winced at the memory.

When he first met Tracy the combination of her sultry beauty and little-girl-lost attitude had knocked him for a loop. They'd become lovers after their first date.

Tracy had wanted to keep their relationship a secret. She said the world needed to see her as available. She'd laughed off the tabloid stories of her lovers and wild parties. "All publicity is good publicity. It keeps the fans happy. Price of fame, darling. But I don't want them to do that to you."

They'd made a game of avoiding the paparazzi. For months, they'd snuck around in their own world of two. Secret rendezvous. A private picnic at the beach after she'd come home from a premiere. It wasn't enough for him.

Michael had wanted to claim Tracy publicly. He wanted to have the right to shield her from every ill wind that blew. He wanted to climb mountains for her, and leap tall buildings with a single bound. He'd bought her a ring. When he'd shown up to surprise her, she'd been in bed. With someone else.

He'd listened to Tracy's first tearful message explaining Chad was business. They were playing lovers and they had to know each other on an intimate level. "I need you, Michael. You're the only one I've ever felt safe with."

The problem was he recognized the line. Laura, her character in *Just the Girls*, said it to her boyfriend, Steve. After that, he deleted Tracy's voicemails unheard.

Until Tracy broke the story to the tabloids.

Michael checked his phone. No new messages. He changed his cell number after the press onslaught. Lynne insisted on addressing him as Doctor Heartbreaker while she dealt with the paparazzi and the stampede of curious patients and found a doctor to sub into the practice. She was worth her weight in gold.

His phone buzzed. Jen wanting FaceTime.

"How's my favorite aunt?" Jen didn't look like anyone's aunt. More like a much younger Maggie Smith ready for mischief. They'd been friends since his pre-med days when she rescued him from a dragon customer when he'd been in charge of his mom's shop. A few years later her brother Jeremy married his mom.

"Languishing in London waiting to hear from you. Why didn't you tell me you were going to Ireland?"

Because he didn't want any more sympathy. He knew he'd been a damn fool. "How did you know I was in Ireland?"

"John called me."

"John? My brother?"

"No. John Luterman. He's my friend as well as Lorena's. I knew him first. We acted together for years. He still loves keeping me up on the latest gossip. How did you like the play?"

"I loved it."

"John was marvelous I suppose?"

"Yes, he was. Kate . . ." He caught himself. Not going there.

"Yes. Kate. That's why I called. John said you and the other chappie looked like two dogs guarding a bone. Does this mean you're over Tracy? I wanted to kill that bitch."

"Yes, I'm over her." Jen seemed to be waiting for more. The nicest thing about Jen was the way she listened. "The worst part was feeling such an idiot. "I believed her completely, convinced only I knew the real Tracy. How could I have missed the signs?"

"She's an actress, darling. It's her business to make you miss them. Tell me more about Kate."

Michael fought to keep his expression relaxed. He wished Jen hadn't made this a FaceTime call. She could read him too easily. "There's nothing to tell. She and her friend Brad were stranded by the bus strike. I offered them a lift."

"John was quite taken with Kate. Said she had wonderful eyes. Windows to her soul as it were. What do you think of her?"

"I don't know much about her beyond the fact she's a writer and this is her first trip to Ireland." And I feel this crazy magnetic pull every time I get near her. "Don't match-make, Jen. She's already got a boyfriend."

"Pity. I want to see you settled. Making nephews and nieces for me and Lance to spoil."

"Not going to happen. I don't see any point in getting married. I'm heart-whole, and planning to stay that way."

"I'd worry if I didn't know you'll change your mind when the right person comes along."

Michael yawned. "Sorry. My body hasn't caught up with the time change."

"I'll let you go then. Send us a picture of Kate. I like to know whom I'm worrying about."

"I'll send you a picture of Kate and her boyfriend."

"Make it a selfie. I'd like to see all three of you. Bye, darling. Take care."

Michael yawned again. Twelve-thirty. He was supposed to meet Kate and Brad at nine. If he didn't know better, he'd think Brad had hypnotized him into giving them a ride to Galway. He'd never met a man so persuasive. His mind turned back to Kate. Tonight she'd looked more elegant lady than mermaid. Until the play started and then she was helpless with laughter. What the hell had she found so mesmerizing about John?

"You can tell its men and women by the wearing of the green," Brad's tenor was true and surprisingly un-slurred by the whiskeys he'd consumed. His gait was another matter. Kate propped him up against the wall while she opened their apartment door.

"Ah, Kate, sweet Kate. John's not the man for you. He's far too old, for one thing. I didn't bring you all the way to Ireland to give you to an actor."

Kate slipped his arm around her shoulder; guided him to the rollaway bed. "You didn't bring me. I brought you."

"That's the outside truth. The inside truth is more important." Brad sat heavily. "That last whiskey may have been a mistake. Some Irish don't hold their whiskey well. Especially those with Leprechaun blood." He smiled up at her sweetly. "Want to hear a joke? An Irishman walks out of a bar."

Kate tossed him a blanket. "I'm not going to undress you. You can sleep it off on the rollaway."

"All right. G'night, sweet Kate. Don't worry. The matchmaker will sort it out."

Kate scrubbed her face and frowned in the mirror. Leprechaun blood? Brad definitely shouldn't have insisted on stopping for a nightcap at the corner pub.

Flirting with John was fun and safe. They both knew it wasn't going anywhere. Michael was another matter. When he looked at her, she felt like she was balancing on the edge of a cliff. So easy to fall over the edge.

Kate pulled back the covers, trying to ignore the computer on the bedside table. No use. Writers write. She'd never be able to sleep unless . . .

She booted up her computer.

"I came to warn you that if you trifle with Thea's affections, I will see you punished." Cressida lifted her chin, wishing she had a square uncompromising jaw instead of a silly dimple.

Lord Rotherham stepped closer.

Parsley's tiny body stiffened. Stepping between them, he barked his outrage at Lord Rotherham.

Lord Rotherham snapped a negligent finger. "Down, Sirrah. Your mistress is safe enough with me. For now."

Cressida quailed before the hint of danger in his eyes.

Parsley's barking shut off like a spigot. He lay down; eyes fixed on Lord Rotherham, tail wriggling with excitement.

Lord Rotherham bent down and stroked him.

The room was suddenly too hot. What would it be like to have those long tapering fingers stroke a path down her body?

Lord Rotherham's glance caressed her. How dare he look at her like that when he was all but engaged to her dear friend, Theodosia? Surely he couldn't tell what she was thinking? ~~Thank the Lord he didn't have any Leprechaun blood."~~

Kate stared at the screen. Hopeless. Where was her mind?

The funny thing was, even though she knew a lot of what Brad said was nonsense, the Leprechaun blood felt like a niggle of truth to her. Which was ridiculous because . . .

Kate Googled *Leprechauns*. Not a lot of information there. A small race of people who lived in Ancient Ireland. The Fairy's shoemakers. A news snippet about a woman who swore she and her dog had seen a little green man. A part of Ireland in County Louth sacred to the preservation of all living Leprechauns. The words blurred. How did Leprechauns produce other Leprechauns? Her eyes closed. She jerked them open.

She Googled *Tracy Jay*. The cover of Star Magazine popped up. *No Wedding Bells for Tracy*. There was Michael smiling down at her, obviously in love. The article read like a true confession. Tracy disclosed she'd fallen in love with Michael when her dear friend, Lorena Anderson introduced them. According to Tracy, Lorena had whispered in her ear, "This is a good one. Don't let him get away."

Tracy made Michael sound like a self-important ass. A small-town doctor, jealous of her career. Refusing to be seen with her in public. Tracy said she went along with it because she loved Michael. Then Michael gave her an ultimatum: It was him or her acting career.

What a load of twaddle. Anyone could see Michael wasn't the sort of . . . "There you go again, Kate, assuming you know what a man is really like. When are you going to learn your judgment's not worth a tinker's damn? Back to your book. That's how to find your happy-ever-after. Write it."

17

The Abbey Court dining room was almost full. Kate slid into a seat at the long table next to a man holding up a copy of *The Irish Independent*. She snuck a look at the lead story. *Irish Rail Joins Bus Eireann strike.* Another plan down the drain.

"I thought we'd agreed not to eat here again." Brad loomed over her, eyes bloodshot.

"You sound cranky. Have some coffee."

"I am cranky. I wake up and you're gone. Not even a note. I thought you'd run away."

"If I'd run away, I *would* have left you a note. As it turns out, I'm stuck with you and Michael." Kate pointed to the headline in her neighbor's paper.

"That's a relief. I wouldn't want to lose you at this stage. Come on. Let me buy you a better breakfast."

"I'm fine where I am, thanks. You go ahead."

"Of all the stubborn . . ." Brad stomped off muttering under his breath.

The jam pot was empty. Kate crunched her dry toast, washing it down with coffee. At least it was free.

Brad returned with two Styrofoam cups of coffee and a plate of toast. "Jam pot's empty."

"I know."

He snagged a pot of jam from the adjoining table and sat next to her. He chugged the first cup of coffee. Picked up the second. "What are you studying so intently?"

"The plan for what was supposed to have been my bus trip."

"You crossed out Blarney Castle."

"I had to. Michael said he was giving us a ride to Galway. Blarney Castle's in the south of Ireland. I thought I could get a train and meet you in Galway. The train map said it was possible. Except there's no train." Kate put her notebook back in her purse. "I'll go check us out."

"You have to go to Blarney Castle. You're a writer. It's your duty to kiss the Blarney stone. I'll handle Michael."

"Do you really think you can convince—"

"I do. It's a lovely drive from Dublin to Blarney. We'll take the coastal route and spend the night in Cork."

* * *

Kate marveled at the ease with which Brad persuaded Michael to take the detour. Once Brad pointed out that Blarney Castle was only three and a half hours from Dublin and that among other things, it was famous for its poison garden, Michael agreed instantly. Very natural. What doctor wouldn't want to visit a poison garden?

"The Blarney Stone is well known to endow those who kiss it with the power of eloquence." Kate looked up from her guidebook. "I wish the guidebook didn't have such clear pictures. When I decided I had to include kissing the Blarney Stone on my itinerary, I didn't realize it was on top of a castle."

"Essie told me the Blarney Stone was brought to Ireland by the prophet Jeremiah," Michael said.

"There are many stories about the provenance of the Blarney Stone," Brad said. "The truth of it is that Cormac Laidir McCarthy, builder of the castle, prayed to the goddess Cliodhna to help him keep the castle which had become the prize in a lawsuit. She told him to kiss the first stone he found on his way to court. He did so and won his case. Cormac was convinced the power of the stone helped him win it so he gave the stone a place of honor in the outer wall of the castle."

"I wish he'd put it in a more accessible place," Kate grumbled.

"Ah, well then, it wouldn't be such an accomplishment to kiss it then, would it? You have to dare fortune for a great prize."

The car turned into the winding road leading to Blarney Castle. Kate took in the magnificent stone edifice set in rolling acres of green. "It has to be six stories high. What is the round tower next to it?"

"It's a watchtower," Brad said. "It was part of the curtain wall of the original castle. There's also a bit of a dungeon for you to explore and a Victorian septic tank house, if you so desire."

"No, thanks," Kate and Michael chorused.

Kate looked into the rearview mirror and saw Michael smiling at her. She could feel her cheeks turning red. She lowered her gaze to her guidebook. "I'd rather explore the gardens. I'd like to see the wishing steps."

The winding path from the car-park led them under a wooden pergola twined with pink and white roses.

A cheery wisp of a woman took their money and they joined the line of pilgrims waiting to kiss the stone.

"You two go on up," Brad said.

"Aren't you coming?"

"Ah, no. I kissed the Blarney Stone a long time ago."

Of course he had. He'd talked her into letting him accompany her, hadn't he? Drat the man and his stupid cherubic smile. She turned to Michael. "You don't have to come along."

"Actually, I like climbing. And I like castles."

One out of two things in common. She climbed only when she had to.

"Enjoy," Brad called out cheerily. "There are one hundred and twenty steps to the top."

Kate winced. That was five times the distance she climbed to her apartment.

The narrow triangular stairs spiraled upward. There was no bannister. A thick rope hanging down from the parapet, fastened to the wall at intervals with iron braces was the only handhold.

If she kept her eyes on the steps it wasn't so bad. The sounds of footsteps, heavy breathing, and muttered remarks enveloped her. She and Michael were surrounded fore and aft by a line of tourists. She turned to Michael, whispering, "I hadn't realized we'd have so much company."

Michael nodded agreement.

Halfway up, she stepped into a room labeled as a former bedroom and looked out one of the open stone windows. Green lawns and trees flaming with autumn made a patchwork of color below.

Michael stood sentinel behind her. "The climb's worth it for the view alone."

He didn't even sound out of breath. Disgusting. Her heart was sending *slow-down* signals to her mind.

Up on the ramparts, the wind blew away conversation. Kate clutched her cap with both hands. They followed the line of people waiting to kiss the stone. The attendant had a portable music player which blared out a tinny version of *Staying Alive*.

"Perhaps not the best song to reassure prospective kissers," Michael remarked.

The stone keeper's voice was a monotonous litany. "Lay down. Arch backward. Put your head down."

Kate looked down at the distance to the ground and shuddered. She watched the person in front of her get into position. The stone keeper kept his hands around the man's waist. The upper half of his body hung over the side in an almost full backbend as he reached to clutch the supporting iron bars on the curtain wall. One quick kiss and he was out.

It was her turn. She could see the iron bars below which would prevent her from falling to her death. Nevertheless, that was a lot of trust to place in three spindly bars of iron.

"Lay down. Arch backward. Put your head down," the stone keeper droned

Kate stepped back. Michael urged her forward. "I'll hold you. I promise I won't let go."

Better Michael than a stranger with a poor taste in music. Kate took a deep breath. It didn't matter how scary the journey, she had to take it. Lord Rotherham and her next book required Blarney Stone intervention.

She lay backward over the padding on the stone wall and reached for the bars set in the outer wall. They were too far away.

"Kate, I'm going to move you a little closer to the edge."

She felt Michael's hands encircle her waist. He was leaning with her. Her whole upper body was now hanging over the parapet. She grabbed for the bars in the outer wall and clenched the cold iron for all she was worth, her eyes scanning for the stone.

"That's the spot," the stone keeper said. "Now kiss it."

She saw a spot, darker than the rest of the wall, no doubt from generations of wet lips imprinting it. She closed her eyes and kissed it.

Michael eased her back onto solid ground.

"Come again. Enjoy your trip to Ireland," the stone keeper said. "Next."

Kate buried her face in Michael's chest. "I'm never coming again. If it didn't work this time, then I'll go back to full time bookkeeping."

Michael's arms circled her. "I'm sure it worked. It did for Winston Churchill and Mick Jagger, among others. And they've both written brilliantly. An added bonus is that you've probably been inoculated against a million different people's germs."

Kate rubbed her hand over her lips. "Ew. I didn't think about that part."

"I don't imagine many do. If they did, there would be far fewer kissers."

"I don't feel more articulate." Being held in Michael's arms felt very right. "Maybe it seeps in slowly."

They found Brad at the Stable Yard café sitting at a table with a pot of tea and a plate containing a lone scone.

"How was it, Kate? Do you feel properly eloquent?"

Lady Cressida's lips twisted into an expression quite improper for a Lady of Quality. "You left me alone with Lord Rotherham and now I find you've had tea without me. No doubt you think your unctuous smile is attractive. Don't you dare eat that last scone. I shall inform my mother that you are unfit as chaperone. Had it not been for Parsley I could have been tarnished.

"Earth to Kate. Did you kiss the stone?"

Kate snatched the last scone of Brad's plate. "Yes. And you're mean not to have ordered us tea too."

"I didn't want it to get cold," Brad said. "I'll order it now."

"Don't bother." Kate flounced over to the counter and ordered a pot of tea and a sandwich.

Michael joined them with his own order. "Does anyone else want to see the Poison Garden?"

"I do," Kate said. "Writers need to know how to do away with characters that don't cooperate."

Michael grinned at her. "I read a book of Mark Twain's where he threw all the characters he didn't like down a well. He said eventually the well got choked and he had to think of a new way to get rid of them."

Kate smiled back. *"Pudd'nhead Wilson."* He read Mark Twain. Wonder what other books they had in common.

The Poison Garden was a small railed-in plot behind the battlements. The sign at the entrance warned against touching any of the plants. Inside many of the plants were caged in iron tubing. The very informative skull and crossbones decorated signs gave the plant's history and usage in both ancient and modern times.

Kate stopped at a caged shrub sporting mauve bell-shaped flowers and black berries. *"Atropa Belladona,* Deadly nightshade," she read aloud. "I know this one. Historically women used belladonna drops to enlarge their pupils to obtain a fashionable wide-eyed look."

"It's used in a great many medicinal compounds. Very carefully. One of its side effects is hallucinations." Michael pointed at a leaf full of worm holes. "Somewhere in this garden are some very tripped-out worms."

"It's also an ingredient in witch-made love potions," Brad said.

Kate snorted. "Love potions are a stupid device. I would never use one in a story."

Brad stepped back. "You're right. Making love happen magically is never a good idea. Too many ways for it to backfire."

"Shades of Harry Potter. Here's mandrake." Kate crouched to take a snapshot of the caged plant. "It looks like a salad green."

"A salad green which can cause madness and death." Michael pushed her hand away from a leaf poking through the bars. "They put the bars there for a reason."

"I wasn't going to touch it." Kate jumped up and stalked

down the path. "Idiot," she muttered under her breath. "I don't need a big, stupid, unreasonably attractive man to look after me."

18

BRAD CAUGHT UP WITH KATE IN FRONT OF THE WISHING STEPS, where moss-furred boulders overhung a tunnel excavated out of solid rock. An iron rail fastened to the left side of the rock wall served as a bannister for the irregular stone slab stairway leading down to the glade.

"If you want a wish, Kate, you have to close your eyes and walk down the steps backward. Then up again. All the while thinking only of your wish."

"If I closed my eyes and walked down backward, the only thing I'd be thinking about would be not breaking my neck. I do want to see where that water sound is coming from though." Kate grasped the rail and started down.

"Ah, the lure of splashing water. Mind your steps, now." Brad followed her down, knowing quite well what she would see. A series of different steams shaped like bony Banshee fingers, flowing from a rocky overhang into a pond below, creating a water symphony. The pond was surrounded by rocks and greens ferns and all manner of mosses. He'd never bothered to learn their names.

Kate held out her hand letting the water flow over it. "The

sound is perfectly magical. In this setting it's easy to believe in the possibility of fairies."

Brad caught a glimpse of a figure across the pond disappearing into the shadows. It might be coincidence. But he had to check. "You stay here and admire the waterfall. I'll see if there's another way out."

He skirted the pond to a place out of Kate's view. A familiar whiskered face peered out from the shadow of a rock fissure. His uncle Collum. McPhee's chief lieutenant.

"He's having you follow me? Why?"

Collum sidled out from the fissure. "It's good to see you home, lad. You've been away far too long."

Brad hunkered down next to his uncle. The crimson witch alder effectively screened them both from Kate's view. "Uncle Collum, you're avoiding the question."

Collum pulled out a pipe, twin to the one Eamon always carried, and struck a match on the rock. "I was having a wee craic with Eamon and he mentioned you were courting a human girl. He was that worried about you."

"And you passed on his worry to the McPhee?"

"Brad," Kate called. "Where are you?"

Uncle Collum nodded in the direction of Kate's voice. "McPhee doesn't know. But I wanted to have a look at her. Make my own estimate of the situation."

"There is no situation." Brad was aware his voice had risen a notch or two. He lowered it. "Kate is my wish client and there's nothing between us but friendship."

"Good to hear. I've naught against humans. My Deidre and your Mam were both human, and two more glorious creatures never lived."

Collum laid his gnarled hand on Brad's knee. "But loving a human carries a terrible price. Their lifespan is a fraction of ours. And you Flynn's love once. Your Da never recovered from losing your Mam. It wasn't the Abhartach that killed him. It was sorrow."

"I know." He barely remembered his mother. She was a picture in a frame to him. But the gray ghost image of his father was as clear as day. He'd died battling a marauding Abhartach when Brad was nine. Collum and Deirdre had taken him in. When Deirdre died, they'd all sorrowed. But Collum hadn't withered like his Da had. Collum remembered he had a son.

"Eamon says he's going to meet you in Cluhalaugh." Collum looked away. Fiddled with his pipe. "I was wondering .. . Have you heard from Pirikit lately?"

Ah, that's why Collum followed him. "No, I haven't. She cut me off when she quarreled with Eamon."

"She cut me off, too. Me, who was like a second father to her." Cullum puffed on his pipe emitting smoky exclamation points.

"More like a first father since that string of misery who fathered her hared off before she was born."

"It was his loss. There never was a more delightful child than our Pirikit, even if she did have a wee bit of a temper." Collum sighed heavily. "I always thought Eamon and Piri would make a match of it. Then she ups and moves to Connemara."

"You want me to meddle, don't you?"

"She's taken a job with Regan MacCatháin in Maigh Cuilin. Do you suppose you could pay her a wee visit? Lovely crystal work they do there. Your American friend might enjoy seeing how Irish crystal is made."

"I'm sure Kate will find it fascinating. And it's time Piri and I mended fences."

"And perhaps you could mention to Piri that you and Eamon will be in Cluhalaugh at the time of choosing?"

"Perhaps I could." This was one case where he'd be happy to meddle.

Collum smiled. He tamped out the smoldering tobacco with his forefinger. "You're a good lad."

Brad rose. "I'm off to my wish client. Tell the McPhee I don't need a nursemaid."

"I won't say a word to McPhee. This is between you and me. Good luck to you."

"I may need it," he muttered under his breath. He circled back to the waterfall. The only people in the glade were two tourists posing for a selfie in front of the steps.

He caught up with Kate and Michael near the Seven Sisters. Shafts of sunlight slanting through the trees highlighted the granite monoliths turning the grey stone to gold.

Kate looked up from the sign she'd been studying. "Did you know there was a Druid's Circle here?"

"I did." The sunlight gilded her delicate features. But it was her eyes that drew him in. The eyes of a dreamer. A story teller. Eyes that could easily reel in his soul if he wasn't careful.

He turned to Michael. "Did you learn anything new at the Poison Garden?"

"Yes." Michael glanced at Kate. "To mind my own business. Are you about ready to drive on?"

"Where did you disappear to at the Wishing Steps?" Kate asked Brad. "I looked around and you were gone."

"I heard you calling me, but I was on the phone," Brad lied. "Checking availability for rooms for tonight."

He *had* checked availability. While Kate and Michael were climbing to the Blarney Stone. He was not trusting Kate to find accommodations. "The Clayton has rooms."

"No." Kate pulled a brochure from her purse. "I asked at Abbey Court before we left and they recommended Sheila's. They said it's clean and has a very good breakfast."

"I'm not staying at another hostel. Come on, Kate. I'll treat."

Kate's fist tightened on her brochure. "And I'm not letting

you treat me. I can afford Sheila's and that's where I'm staying. You can do what you like."

Might as well argue with a stone as a stubborn woman. It wouldn't hurt her to be on her own for a night. He turned to Michael. "I think you'll like Cork. It was once an island. The streets are surrounded with water on both sides. Rather like Venice. The Clayton's right in the heart of Cork City, very close to all the nightlife."

"Sound's good. I'd like to look around the city. Maybe hit a pub or two." Michael looked at Kate. "Do you want to join us for dinner?"

"No, thank you, I've got some writing to do."

SHEILA'S HAD no private rooms available. "There's a vacancy in our six-bed dormitory," the receptionist said. "We've a large party checking in later. I'm sorry, but this is the best we can do."

"I'll take it."

Kate climbed the two flights of stairs to a large room with three sets of red-enamel bunk beds—all currently empty. Each bed had two pull-out drawers under the bottom bunk. The slip the receptionist gave her said she was in bed 1L. Surely that stood for lower.

The narrow mattress looked adequate and if it wasn't the equal of Abbey Court, well, you can't win them all.

A door next to the one she'd come in led to a bathroom. She peeked in. Two toilets stalls, two sinks, and one shower.

Between two of the bunk beds was a narrow shelf with an electrical outlet and a stool underneath. One narrow shelf for six people. It paid to be first in.

Time to test whether the Blarney Stone had improved her plotting skills. Kate removed the laptop from her carry on, re-

134 | *Irish Magic*

zipped the bag, and stowed it in one of the pullout drawers under her bunk.

She attached her transformer to the outlet and plugged in the laptop. Resisting the urge to email Brad and ask how his room was, she opened a new document and transferred the bit of scene she'd thought of at Blarney Castle onto the page. The mere act of putting words on paper flowed into a scene that promised to be a turning point in her Lord Rotherham dilemma. The words and plot points flowed gloriously until . . .

"Oh look, we've got company." A teenage girl with purple spiked hair dressed in unrelieved black walked in, followed by three more teenagers all wearing emerald green jackets.

A petite brunette chirped, "Hi, we're the Jennys. It's our drinking team name. We're doing a backpack-slash-pub crawl. We've come over from Brittany on the ferry. Don't do it. God, I was so sick." She peeked into the bathroom. "Hopefully that's all over."

The four girls chose beds, chattering nonstop.

"You have madly great hair."

"Why've you got it all twisted up like that?"

"Who are you writing to? A boyfriend?"

Kate clicked save. "No. I'm working on a novel."

"Are you a published writer?"

"What's your name?"

"Do you make lots of money?"

Kate gave up trying to sort out who asked what.

"My name is Kate Carnahan. I have one published novel and no, I don't make lots of money. Who are you?"

Out of the babble of Dari and Cherise and Trina one voice was piercingly clear. "Aren't you a bit old to be dorming it? I thought your sort took private rooms."

"Stuff it, Angel. That's rude."

The Goth girl's name was Angel? Maybe her appearance was a protest against her name.

"There were no private rooms available. Where are you headed?"

"Dublin," they chorused.

"Are you traveling alone?"

"Want to join us for dinner?"

"Drinks? Cork has some extra savage pubs."

That brought up a lovely mental picture. Hordes of drinkers assaulting each other with bottles. "No. But thanks for the invitation. I've really got to write."

Angel shrugged. "Your loss. Come on, Jennys. We're wasting drinking time.'

The door slammed on their chatter leaving a lovely silence.

Kate re-read what she'd written. She needed another complication. What if Cressida wandered into a bar?

The Leaky Pig stunk of strong spirits and unwashed bodies. Cressida clutched the crumpled note in her fist, looking around for a person wearing a blue striped waistcoat.

An ill-favored seaman rose from his seat and cracked a bottle over his companion's head. "Curse you, you tap hackled dunghill."

His companion fell backward giving Cressida a clear view of his blue striped waistcoat. The onlookers roared their approval. Cressida stifled a scream.

Strong hands grabbed Cressida and pulled her out of the tavern. They spun her around and she found herself looking into Lord Rotherham's fulminating gaze.

"Of all the foolish things I've seen you do, this is the worst. If Theodosia hadn't thought to send me word of your direction, you could be dead."

Cressida wanted to sink into the comfort of his arms, but that wouldn't help Parsley. She lifted her chin. "Parsley's been stolen. The ransom note told me to come here with twenty guineas and tell no one. It's my duty to rescue him."

Lord Rotherham's face softened. "A woman who braves physical danger to rescue a companion is a rare find, indeed."

Kate unwrapped the sandwich she'd bought downstairs at the hostel's coffee spot. Lord Rotherham was improving nicely. She finished her sandwich, rescued Parsley, brushed her teeth and crawled into bed.

Music, the sound of cars, and passing voices echoed through the open window. Kate got up and tried to close it. No use. It was frozen open. She winced at the lights slanting up through the blinds. Cork City appeared to have an active night life.

She crawled back into her bunk and pulled the pillow over her head. What were Brad and Michael doing tonight? Closing down the pubs, maybe? She could see Brad doing that, but Michael didn't feel like that kind of man. She shouldn't have reacted so strongly to him brushing her hand away from the Mandrake. He was only trying to save her. The memory of his arms around her on the parapet of the castle heated her body far better than the thin blanket. What would it be like to kiss him?

Thoughts of the day and her new chapters drifted, cocooned, and spun her into a dream punctuated with noisy taverns, waterfalls, and whiskey brown eyes.

19

Kate waited outside for Michael and Brad on one of the hostel's blue painted park benches. Better outside than in the dining room with her unreasonably bright-eyed dorm mates. They hadn't rolled into bed until after three. And they were up and at it five hours later with no visible ill effects. Angel had the right of it. Women over thirty didn't belong in dormitories.

She warmed her hands on her second cup of hot tea, reveling in the absence of human voices. From where she sat she could see down the hill, past rows of houses, all the way to the river and the hills beyond. The air was crisp and tangy with the scents of damp earth, smoke, and fallen leaves.

Michael's rental car pulled up in front of her. Brad opened the passenger door and rose gingerly. His eyes were bloodshot. "Good morning. Did you sleep well?"

"Better than you, apparently. Did you close down the bars? I've got some aspirin, if you want one."

Brad ignored her offer. "If the team of your host city wins, there's a certain amount of obligatory drinking. And a grand game it was."

Kate looked at Michael. He appeared to have suffered no ill effects.

"Cork won their match twenty five to ten. I left after the first celebratory round," Michael said.

"That's because you're not Irish. You don't understand the way of these things. Kate, do you want to sit up front?"

"No, thanks." Kate slung her suitcase into the back seat and slid in after it. The last thing she wanted this morning was more conversation.

The drive to County Clare was marked by sheep, cows, and more sheep, all posing picturesquely in crayon green pastures marked off with hand-set stone walls. White farm houses and cottages were surrounded by pretty beds of flowers. The clouds in the autumn-blue sky looked like cousins to the sheep.

Brad twisted around carefully as though he were afraid his head might come loose. "Kate, every time we pass a field, I hear your phone clicking. Don't you think you have enough livestock pictures?"

"No." Animals were predictable. You knew where you were with a sheep. The only thing she wanted from a sheep was a picture and maybe a sweater or two. A one-way kind of love with no complications.

"I like the cows best," Michael said. "They loll about those huge fields doing yoga poses. The epitome of happiness. No wonder people like Irish butter."

Kate caught Michael's eyes in the rearview mirror. He smiled at her as though they shared a private joke.

Kate's heart skipped. He really had the most beautiful eyes. She resisted the urge to take a picture of them. *No. Back to the sheep.*

Brad turned to Michael. "Turn right at the next stop sign. Follow the signs for Connemara."

Michael glanced at his GPS. "According to Lola, we should proceed straight for the next ten miles."

"That instrument of yours is most efficient. But not very imaginative. There are more interesting ways to get to The Burren.

"Why not?" Michael turned off his GPS. "I'm in no real hurry."

Kate pulled out the guidebook she'd brought. Connemara wasn't one of the places she'd planned to stop on her now-mythical bus tour. "Connemara's nowhere near The Burren."

"It's a bit of a detour." Brad held out his hand to Kate for the aspirin she'd offered him earlier. "But well worth your while. I'd like to show you a bit of the real Ireland."

Kate handed him the bottle. "What do you mean, the real Ireland?"

"Wait and see."

The new road wound up a hill and settled down beside a river. Trees interspersed with metal rail guards where the water ran too close to the road. Stone and wire cut fences bordered the far side.

The road curved inland again, past trees and the occasional stone ruin. The motion of the car was soothing. Last nights interrupted sleep was catching up to her. Kate's eyelids began to droop.

She startled awake to the sound of Brad's voice. "There it is." Brad pointed at a green road sign *Maigh Cuilin*. Beyond it was another sign.

"*Failte Go Conamara*" Brad read aloud. "It means Welcome to Connemara. We're officially in the Gaeltacht."

The words sounded lovely rolling off Brad's tongue.

"What does that mean?" Michael asked.

"Irish speaking." You are in one of the few places left in Ireland where Irish is the major language."

A place where they still spoke Irish? The magic of it tingled Kate's mind. "It's a bit like stepping into a past where Ireland was truly a foreign country."

The road curved into a main street fronted with two-story white plaster buildings. Many had flower boxes in the upper windows. The shop doors and windows below were painted blue, red, pink. All of the signs were in Irish.

"But they do speak English too, right?" Kate asked.

"Of course." Brad pointed to the forest of antennas above the buildings. "How else could they enjoy the telly?"

He directed Michael to a shop called Claddagh Crystal. The two-story brick building sat squarely in the center of a large parking lot. Lots of room for tour buses.

Kate felt a twinge of disappointment. "It's not exactly quaint."

"It was built in the 1970s on the site of the old rail station, which was part of the now defunct Clifden line," Brad said. "That makes the building a spring chicken by Irish standards. But they've a fine shop and one of the few factories where all the crystal cutting is done by hand."

They followed Brad into the shop. Kate drew in a deep breath. The wall-to-wall deep wooden cases were arched at the top. Built-in lights illuminated clear glass shelves filled with the most beautiful crystal Kate had ever seen. Vases, fanciful jars, crystal stemware with matching decanters, intricate baskets. Some of the pieces were colored; ruby, emerald, and sapphire shimmering with deep crystal carvings. Her eyes fixed on a sapphire blue box incised with Celtic runes. If she could afford a souvenir, this would be the one she coveted.

Michael's voice broke the silence. "I think I just solved Christmas. My female relatives are going to love me."

A tall elderly woman, wearing a beige suit stepped out from behind the counter.

Brad took the woman's hands and kissed them. "Regan MacCatháin, how is it you look younger every time I see you? I've brought you some visitors. They want to see how you make the glass."

The door to the back of the shop flew open. A small woman darted out. Hugged Brad. Her hair was a rich dark brown with streaks of red and orange that looked like tongues of flame when they caught the light. She had an arresting face with long-lashed slanting eyes, a pointed chin and brown-gold skin that reminded Kate of autumn leaves. "Bradley Flynn, what are you doing in Ireland? I thought you were settled in New York."

Brad returned her hug. "Well, I had to see what my favorite cousin was up to didn't I?"

The woman's slanting brown eyes narrowed. "I'm not your favorite cousin. You and that fool Eamon are closer than twine. What are you up to? *An bhfuil tú ag rá as neamhchiontach astray. Tú fear olc?*"

"Hold now. My friends only speak English."

"Well, they're not my friends, are they now? Why should I care?"

Brad turned to Kate and Michael. "This is my old friend Piri MacKenna. She wanted to know what I was doing here, and she thinks you two make a lovely couple."

Piri folded her arms and glared at Brad. "The name's Pirikit Mac Cionaoith and that's not what I said at all. I said Bradley was a wicked man who was up to no good." She looked Michael up and down. "Oh, this one's lovely. I'd like a little of that."

Michael's face reddened.

Kate felt a sudden urge to protect him from Pirikit's predatory glance. Which was ridiculous.

Regan sighed. "I knew well enough this one would be trouble. But she has a magic touch when it comes to infusing the glass with color." She smiled at Kate and Michael. "Let's leave them to sort themselves out and I'll show you through the factory. Arbin is finishing up a trophy for the All County Hurling competition. We are one of the few places left that cut the traditional designs."

She opened the door to the back. The sharp bright buzz of glass against rotating-diamond-saw filled the air.

"Yes, you two follow Regan," Brad said. "It's a fascinating business. Get her to tell you how they mix the lead into the glass to make it soft for cutting." He waited till the door closed behind them. "Explain yourself, Pirikit. What possessed you to leave Dublin and come back here? I thought you hated Maigh Cuilin."

Piri picked up the dusting cloth and reached for a fine crystal basket. "I thought I could make a difference in Dublin. But that thick-headed Eamon cannot see beyond the end of his nose."

"He said you call him a shoemaker."

"Well, he deserved it. He acts as if he were the only halfling in Ireland."

Brad leaned against the counter. He enjoyed watching Piri in tempest mode, as long as it wasn't aimed at him. "Eamon has as much love for being a halfling as you do. That's why he's determined to preserve the leprechaun heritage."

"There's nothing wrong with that. It's the way he goes about it. Does he explain how leprechauns mate? No. There are damn few true facts in that museum of his. Does he admit the existence of fairies? Of course not." The fire in her eyes could have melted glass. "The fact that fairies have been in Ireland longer that leprechauns means nothing to him. All I wanted was to make facts about *all* the Fae available to his museum patrons. And he wants to keep the legend pure. Stupid."

"*All* the facts? Including the fact that halflings exist? Come on Piri, do you seriously want the world to know you are part Fae?"

Piri dropped her gaze. "I wouldn't care. It's not as if many would believe it."

"Perhaps all Eamon wanted was to protect you."

"I don't need protecting." A ruby glass vase flew off the shelf.

"Stop it, Pirikit." Brad caught it before it fell to the floor and shattered. "I think it's time you thought about being matched."

A pair of crystal goblets flew off the shelf. "There *is* no match for me."

Brad barely caught them in time. "Ah, but what if you're wrong? The Lady of Cluhalaugh is back."

The fire died out of Piri's eyes. "I thought she was dead."

"No, she's been in America the past forty-five years. She came back to help me grant a wish."

"Aisling O'Callaghan." Piri smiled. "I well remember that Samhain you brought her into the hill. It appears your good deed has a reward at the end."

Brad's temper flared. "That wasn't why I rescued her and you damn well know it."

"I do. You've a kind heart, Bradley Flynn, and a weakness for humans."

"Which you'd do well to share, Pirikit. Not all humans are like your father."

"I've yet to see that," she snapped.

They'd had this conversation many times. He was beating his head against a will of steel. He took her hand, pulsing a bit of persuasion through his palm. "You are both, Pirikit. Your father gave you half of what you are. It's a bad thing to deny what made you."

Piri pulled her hand away. "And what of you? And what of Eamon? Have you made peace with your beginnings?"

Brad looked up at the rows of sparkling crystal. "Eamon hasn't. I have. But the McPhee wants me to choose. And I'm not ready to do that yet. What about you? If you had to choose, what would you do?"

"I'd choose the Fae, of course. But none of my mother's kind would have me. I stink of human."

"Now you're being dramatic. You and Eamon and I were welcomed by both races as children. We didn't feel left out."

"Speak for yourself. Do you think I liked being used as a football because of my size?"

"Eamon put a stop to that, Piri. He shadowed you. He watched every move you made, and he came between those who wanted to tease you. He's loved you his whole life."

"Well, he has a poor way of showing it. Talking to me as if I had no sense at all. It wasn't as if I was going to tell humans how to find us."

Piri could match The McPhee for stubborn. "I can't stay. I'm going home in three days' time. It's the Equinox and I must stand in the choosing line."

Piri's look was decidedly skeptical. "I thought you weren't ready to choose."

"I'm not, but I've a wish to see fulfilled. I've asked Eamon to support me."

"Ah, who would match with him?"

"That's for the Lady to say. Are you sure you don't want to come to Cluhalaugh and find out?" A blue crystal box flew up and careened across the room, shattering against the workroom door.

The door to the workroom cracked open. "Is it safe to come out?" Regan asked.

"All's well," Brad said. "Piri and I have negotiated a ceasefire. Mind the glass now."

Michael and Kate slid out through the partially blocked door.

"Oh, what a shame." Kate knelt to pick up the broken crystal.

Michael pulled her to her feet. "No. You don't want glass embedded in your knees."

"Michael's right," Brad said. "Regan, where's the dustpan?"

Piri lifted her chin. "twas my fault and I'll clean it up, and

I'll pay for the damage." She fluttered her eyelashes at Michael. "Perhaps I will come join you after all, Brad. As you say, they aren't all bad."

Brad noticed the bright flash of color in Kate's cheeks. She wasn't as indifferent to Michael as she liked to pretend.

Michael bought every piece Piri showed him. Kate bought nothing. That damn budget of hers, probably. Brad had Regan wrap the two ruby stemmed goblets etched with the harp and shamrock. He'd give them to her at the end of their journey. "Hungry work, shopping," he said cheerily. "It's time for lunch."

THE VINES OVERHANGING the arched doorway of the teashop reached up to join the spill of purple and pink petunias from the flower boxes on the second story. Kate snapped a picture.

Inside, most of the tables were occupied. Kate was glad Piri refused her cousin's invitation to join them. Something about that pointy faced little witch rubbed her the wrong way. "You were right, Brad. Watching the glass artist at work was an experience not to be missed. I got a video of the process. I wish I could have seen the blowing of the glass, but Regan says they only do that once a week."

"It's a beautiful process," Brad agreed. "As long as you're not the one doing it. It didn't suit me at all."

Kate sampled a cream bun from the three-tiered tray of goodies Brad ordered for them. "Yum. So, what is the Burren exactly?"

"It's an odd magic area steeped in legends," Brad answered. "The ghost of Marie Rua haunts the area near the hollow tree where the people of Burren imprisoned her after she murdered the last of her twenty-five husbands

"I think you should write a novel," Kate said.

"You don't believe me? I'm wounded." Brad reached across

her and snagged the last scone. "Go on the internet and look it up."

Michael picked up the empty scone plate. "Think I'll get us a refill."

Brad waited till Michael was out of earshot. "Did I detect a flash of jealousy when Piri made a play for Michael?"

"No," Kate lied. "The man was engaged to Tracy Jay. Piri is more his type than I am."

"You're missing a bet there. He's perfect hero material," Brad commented.

That much was true. Lord Rotherham had improved enormously. Her editor was going to be delighted.

AN HOUR'S drive brought them to the Burren National Park. Michael pulled up in the nearly empty car park.

Kate took in the ocean of rock in front of them. She heard no sound but the soft sighing of wind. "Are there any birds or animals here?"

"Well, there's supposed to be a bear cave," Michael said. "Essie told me that."

"I never knew there were bears in Ireland," Kate said. "Somehow I never think of them having big wildlife. Just deer and rabbits."

"And snakes." Brad added. "Surely you've heard of Irish snakes?"

They followed the signs to the walking trail.

"Essie told me Saint Patrick drove the snakes out," Michael said.

"What about spiders?" Kate asked. "Did he get rid of those?" She loathed spiders.

"I don't know, but I hope so." Michael grimaced. "I'd kiss a snake before I'd touch a spider. Spiders give me the creeps."

"So if a spider should happen to sit down beside her, you wouldn't be the one Kate should run to."

"Nope. I'd probably jump into her arms and scream."

Kate stifled a giggle.

The bear cave was a disappointment. Brightly lit and floored with limestone. "I'm having trouble imagining bears here," Kate said.

"Yogi Bear, maybe," Michael said. "On a trip from Jellystone Park."

Brad agreed. "Not at all like it used to be. It's a bloody souvenir shop. Let's go on to the Castle Drumlogie. That's been kept up properly."

They took another route back to the car park picking their way carefully through the giant slabs of limestone and occasional pockets of green. Straw colored thistle heads and wildflowers poked their way through the cracks in the rock.

"There's an important lesson in here. Flowers break rocks." Kate bent to snap a picture of a patch of tiny lavender flowers. "I'm not sure what the lesson is, but I know it's important."

"It means," Brad said, "that the seeming fragile things of life are often tougher than the big heavy things. Like, love. Love is stronger than all the crappy stuff we've done to each other. There's still hope for this world."

Michael and Kate looked at Brad in silence.

"That was very profound," Kate said. "I didn't know you could be profound."

"There're a lot of things you don't know about me." Brad strode ahead.

Michael turned to Kate. "He's a very clever man. You've chosen well."

"How kind of you to say so," Kate said sweetly. Stupid man and his stupid assumptions. "And you chose Tracy Jay. Too bad it didn't work out. What happened?"

Michael's look could have frozen a popsicle. "We had different ideas on what constituted a relationship."

"Ah." Kate tried for a bright smile to cover her embarrassment at having asked him for details. What had she been thinking? That he'd pour out his feelings and lay them at her feet? "Better luck next time."

20

"THERE'S THE ENTRANCE." BRAD POINTED TO A HUGE STONE structure straddling the road in front of them. Its crenellated roof was partially obscured by overhanging trees. The ancient two- story stone building had beautiful diamond-paned windows, but looked a bit small for guests.

"Is that the castle?" Kate asked, stifling a twinge of disappointment.

"No. It's the gate house. Drive through."

Michael drove under the arch and continued up the winding road. The long expanse of green on either side was broken by hand-set stone fences.

Perched on a rise was a massive square building flanked by four towers. Weathered stone. Three stories. Crenellated roof between the towers.

Now that was a proper castle. Kate's heart dropped. Accommodations here probably cost the earth and there was no way she was letting Brad pay for it. "Brad, it's beautiful, but I can't afford a hotel like this."

"I didn't say it was a hotel, Kate. Drumlogie belongs to a friend of mine. There'll be a room for you too, Michael."

Michael parked the car in the cobblestone forecourt next to a lorry and a four wheel drive. On one side of the forecourt couple of inquisitive horses inspected them from beyond a high-barred fence. The silence was broken only by the whistle of the wind and some distant barking.

A jovial man in a snap-brimmed cap came round the side of the building carrying a basket of vegetables. "Ah, you'll be the guests himself is expecting. Come away in."

His brogue was so thick Kate could barely understand it.

The great wood doors must have been two stories high, but they opened easily. Their footsteps echoed on the stone paving. Kate looked up at the narrow windows raying the floor with dusty slabs of sunlight. "I feel like I've gone back in time."

The man led them to a large library. Two walls were lined floor to ceiling with books. The wall facing the entrance had a huge window with maroon curtains drawn back. An oval desk faced the window, an enormous computer screen covering most of its surface. A high-backed leather chair hid whoever was tapping at the keyboard.

"Hugh, we've made it," Brad shouted. "Come away from the machine and give us a proper greeting."

The chair swiveled around. The middle-aged man sitting in it looked up at them. His light blue eyes and befuddled expression called to Kate's mind the White Rabbit. She almost expected to hear *Oh, my paws and whiskers*. But instead a beautiful tenor voice with a tinge of an Irish brogue said, "Brad, good to see you old boy. I was just . . . er—"

"I can see perfectly well what you were doing. Betting on the ponies. I thought you'd given that sort of thing up."

"Er, not the ponies exactly. I've gotten into bigger things." Hugh came around the desk to greet them. "Good to see you again, Boggle." He thumped Brad on the back. "That's what we called him at school. Boggle. He was always being surprised at things."

"Hugh, these are my friends, Kate, and Michael. We're traveling together."

"School?" Kate questioned. Hugh's thinning sandy hair made him look a lot older than Brad.

"Boarding school. I was a prefect when Boggle enrolled. He took years from my life." Hugh shook hands with Michael. "Welcome. I've told Sheila to put you and your wife in the Queen's bedroom."

Kate and Michael took a step back from each other.

"We're not married," Kate said. "We've just met."

Hugh blinked. "Sorry, I got it all wrong. Boggle, I thought you said . . ."

"That's the trouble with cell phones," Brad interrupted. "Sometimes the message gets garbled. I didn't say anything of the sort. I'm sure you have enough room for all of us in this great barn of a place."

"It's the devil to manage," Hugh admitted. "But fortunately, I've gotten rather good at picking stocks."

A woman with flyaway wispy hair and a dreamy smile entered the room. "Oh, there you are. Peter told me you'd arrived. I asked the cook to put tea in the sitting room. I'm Sheila, and the children are upstairs. We thought we'd spare you as long as possible."

The sitting room was much smaller than the entry hall. No elegance here. This was a room for families. A faded oriental carpet covered the flagstone floor. A square coffee table the size of a small pond occupied the center of the room. Legos and magazines and the beginnings of a jigsaw puzzle vied for space. A fire crackled in the huge stone carved fireplace.

Sheila gestured at the sofa and chairs clustered around it. "Have a seat, but mind the Legos. They can be anywhere."

Kate sank into a delightfully squishy wingback chair close to the fire.

A chorus of shrieks erupted from the second floor. Footsteps pounded down the stairs. "Give it back or I'll stuff your Barbie in the Loo."

"Family life," remarked Hugh. "It's hard to say too much about it."

A girl of about eight with Sheila's wispy brown hair erupted into the room holding a toy bow and arrow. "Mum, Connor and Pat stole my Barbies. Make them stop."

Two red-faced boys with identical mops of ginger curls skidded into the room. "We weren't doing anything. We were just going to —"

"I know exactly what you were going to do." Sheila retrieved the bow and arrow from her daughter and held out her hand to the boys. "Give them over."

The boys surrendered the naked Barbies they'd had behind their backs.

Kate tried to keep a straight face.

A plump woman with gray curls twisted into a knot, high on her head wheeled in a tea cart. "What do you mean screaming like a pack of hooligans when your mam and dad have guests?"

"Treysa, you made ginger cakes." All three children made a break for the tea cart.

Treysa caught the boys by the seats of their pants. "They aren't for you, me boyos." She fixed the girl with a stern glare. "Kayla, Connor, Patrick. All of you go wash your hands and report to the kitchen, and if I see one pinch or one look, it's bread and butter for you. Apologize at once."

Kayla dropped a curtsey to Kate and Michael and Brad. She'd gone from Virago to Angel in one look. "Sorry. Welcome to Castle Drumlogie. If you like, we can do the clan dance for you after tea." She flew from the room as quickly as she entered it. The boys followed.

"Have your tea in peace, then." Treysa turned back. "Mind Sheila gives you the tour."

Sheila handed Kate a cup of tea. "I've put you both in the Queen's room. Pay no attention to any odd noises you hear. It's almost assuredly going to be the children. I think the legend of the ghost is highly overstated. I've never seen her."

"Of course there's a ghost. My own mother swore it." Hugh cleared his throat. "The thing is, Bunny, I'm afraid I got hold of the wrong end of the stick. They aren't married."

"That's all right. It's the twenty-first century, Hugh. Not everyone likes to do the deed."

Michael accepted a cup of tea from Sheila. "I just met Kate two days ago. We're strangers.

"My goodness and you are living together already?"

"No," Michael and Kate chorused.

Kate shot Brad a death at the earliest opportunity look.

Brad grinned. "Seems I've made a right muddle of it. Kate and I encountered Michael at the Dublin airport, and since he was planning to meet up with friends in Galway, he graciously offered us a lift."

Sheila's head swung from one to another. "None of you are sleeping together? How disappointing. I suppose I'd better see about getting another room made up." She turned to Hugh. "Be a dear and give Poppy a shout."

Hugh picked up his cell phone and tapped out a number. "Poppy, can you make up the blue room as well? Nobody will be sleeping together."

How gorgeously incongruous. "You use a cell phone to call your housekeeper?" Kate asked. "I expected you would have speaking tubes that went from room to room."

"Too much trouble. Everybody's got a cell phone these days. Ireland's got more cell phones per capita than any country in Europe. Glad I invested in them. Try the ginger cakes. They're extraordinary."

Conversation became general. Kate bit into a ginger cake. The soft gingery molasses taste perfectly suited her mood. She was in a real castle and they had a ghost. Maybe more than one. She could slip a ghost scene into *Chasing Cressida*. "Who is your ghost? Does she have a name?"

"The Queen's lady. That's all we know," Hugh said. "Queen Anne visited here in 1706. Think it was the only time she toured out of England. She had a fondness for the lady of the castle, Iona of Skye. She also had a fondness for the drink, as did her ladies. The legend is one of her ladies went to meet a lover, and fell down the round stair and broke her neck. Not sure who the lover might have been. There are two male ghosts I know of. Could have been one of them."

Better and better. Hugh sounded as though ghosts were a normal occurrence. "Do the male ghosts have names?"

"Hugh, stop it," Sheila said.

Hugh sent his wife a wounded look. "It's all true, Bunny. I think you must be ghost proof." He turned to Kate. "Donal MacBride met his end in a duel said to have taken place in the North Tower. Or perhaps it was foul play. He favors the North Tower, but he's fond of books. I've seen him pass through the library on occasion. Don't know the other one's name. Seems a quiet chap."

"Yes, Hugh. On the occasion of your third brandy." Sheila shook her head and turned to Kate. "Hugh's a terrible romantic. How long will you be in County Clare? What have you seen?"

MICHAEL SIPPED his tea and listened to the talk around him, hopefully nodding in the right places.

He stole a surreptitious glance at Kate. If he had any sense, he'd manufacture an emergency with Essie and skedaddle. With her bright spill of hair catching the light, and her face alive with interest, she made him ache. He had no intention of falling into that particular trap. Not again. Not after Tracy. Love cost too bloody damn much.

21

KATE CLOSED HER NOVEL. A GHOST STORY WAS A POOR CHOICE OF reading in a haunted castle. She shivered, grateful for the fire still flickering on her bedroom hearth. Over the mantelpiece, a portrait of a woman, Queen Anne, possibly, stared down on her reprovingly. The top of the room was lost in shadow. The chill smell of the stone wall seeped through the wood paneling covering it. The unknown Poppy or someone had put a vase of asters on the dresser.

Kate snuggled into the feather duvet and gazed up at the royal blue bed hangings. Her mind pictured the Queen's lady and her lover. The lady tiptoeing out of the room, shielded candle in hand. Her dark haired lover, dressed in knee britches and flowing shirt, taking her in his arms, his brown eyes intent on his beloved. Yawning, she turned off the light. *Wonder what her name was?*

Elise came to her on a drift of air.

Kate sat up, heart pounding. She heard a breathy whisper. "*Elise.*" The air shivered with it.

The space at the foot of the bed shimmered. Kate's scream

froze in her throat. A small figure took form. A woman with hair in gold ringlets, wearing a tight waisted gown with a voluminous skirt took form. Lace fell from the elbow length sleeves to her delicate wrists.

Kate couldn't move. She felt encased in ice.

The girl held up her hands, beseeching. "Find him for me. Please. I beg you."

Helplessly Kate felt the ghost's sorrow and longing become her own. "I will try," She whispered. "Where is he?"

The apparition floated to the wall. "Michael. My Michael. Find him."

The light winked out. The room grew warmer.

Kate's frozen posture dissolved. She snapped on the light. Looked round wildly. No sign of anything and there was no way she was staying in this room

She grabbed the duvet as a shawl and ran for the door. Halfway down the corridor, she bumped into a warm solid form.

Michael caught her against his chest. "We've got to stop meeting like this."

Kate clutched him as if her life depended on it.

He put his arms around her. "What's wrong? Had a bad dream?"

She burrowed into him, her breath coming in small shallow gasps.

"It's all right," he said, his voice soothing. He picked her up and started back toward her room.

Kate fought him. "No," she rasped. "Not there. Please."

"All right. Stop kicking me." He carried her into his room, using his elbow to switch on the overhead light. "Better?"

Kate looked around and relaxed a fraction, but she couldn't make her fingers let go.

Michael sat down in the upholstered reading chair with her in his lap. "You're freezing." He unfisted her hands from his T-shirt, covering them with his own, massaging his warmth into them. "I don't know what scared you, but it did a damn fine job." He reached for the decanter on the side table and poured amber liquid into a small cut crystal glass. "Drink this."

Her teeth chattered on the rim of the glass.

"It's brandy. Good for shock. Drink."

The brandy burned in her throat and blazed a trail of warmth down to her stomach.

"Better?"

Kate nodded mutely.

"Care to tell me what happened?"

She took another sip. The nightmare feeling receded.

Kate looked into Michael's face. His whiskey-brown, caring eyes mesmerized her. Could she drown in them? She ran the pads of her fingers over his stubbled cheek. Her fingers tingled.

She heard Michael's swift intake of breath.

Kate, what are you doing? She closed her ears to the voice of reason. She set down the brandy. "Would you mind kissing me, please?"

Michael's eyes disengaged from hers and moved to her mouth. "This is a bad idea," he whispered. His hand cupped the back of her neck.

"I know." Her breath caught in her throat. "Please?"

Michael bent to take her mouth.

Kate wound her arms around his neck, needing to bring him closer, to become a part of him. His tongue tasted of brandy. Or was it hers? They tasted, touched, sought.

He slipped a hand into her pajama top, blazing a fiery trail down her breast. "More," he rasped. He opened another button, baring her to his heated gaze.

Kate gasped and arched backward reveling in the feel of his tongue against her nipple. The warmth in the pit of her stomach flowed down, igniting her core. The evidence of his desire was hard against her legs. She reached for it

"No." He stopped her hand. "I won't make it if you do that." He picked her up, carried her to the bed and set her down as lightly as a feather.

The brush of his tongue prickled her skin to attention as he kissed his way down her abdomen. Her breath quickened. The need to have him inside her consumed any shred of sanity. "Now. Please."

"Not yet," he murmured and slipped a finger inside her.

Kate arched up, and shattered.

As she slowly floated back to earth, he nudged her legs wider and entered her, driving through the trembling of her aftershocks, taking them both higher. Nothing existed but their bodies and the friction between them. He muffled her scream with his mouth as they reached glory. Together.

His body collapsed on her.

Exhausted; replete, she listened to their heartbeats intermingling.

Michael lifted dazed eyes to her face. "That was . . . You are . . . We were . . ."

Kate pulled his face down to hers. "Yes." She took his lips in a questing kiss. He dived deeper and their tongues danced. She felt him rise again inside her. This couldn't be happening. She'd never wanted to make love twice in a row but . . .

On the air, she heard a ghostly echo. *Michaelllllll.*

Her body froze. What had she done? Who had just made love? Was it her and Michael, or some ghost doing it through them? She pushed him away.

A voice wailed. "No. *Michaelllll . . .*"

Michael tensed and eased out of her. "Did you hear that?"

Kate nodded, her eyes wide with terror.

Michael shivered. "It just got colder in here." He pulled up the covers around them. "Shall I get you a—"

"No. Don't leave." Kate clutched his hand.

"What's wrong?"

"I saw the ghost."

"You did? Was that what sent you flying into me?"

"Before I went to sleep I was wondering about the ghost and whether she'd died before or after meeting her lover. Then I woke up and she was there. At the foot of my bed."

"Maybe she was part of your dream," he suggested gently. "Dreams can feel very real."

Kate shook her head. "I didn't only see her. I felt her. Her name is Elise. She was beautiful, about twenty and in her face, such misery. She was looking for something. Someone. She was weeping and she said 'find him. Find him for me.' And then she disappeared."

Michael clearly thought she had a screw loose. "You know they say what appears to be a ghost is simply a random disturbance of energy . . ."

"In the force?" Kate interrupted. "Come on, Michael, you can do better than that. Didn't you hear that sound?"

"I heard something. Probably the wind through a crack in the fireplace."

The fireplace embers swirled and sparked to life. "*Michaelllllll.*"

Michael stiffened. "I heard that. It sounded oddly like my name."

"That's who she was looking for." Kate felt adrenaline blast through her veins. "Michael. Her Michael."

"But I'm not her Michael."

Michaelllllll. The window curtains fluttered in a wild dance.

Kate pulled him out of bed and dragged him toward the door.

"Wait." Michael tossed her pajamas to her.

She'd been about to rush into the hall naked. The shocks from the aftermath of loving combined with the terror of the ghost left no room for thought. She hurried into her pajamas and grabbed the duvet she'd brought with her.

Michael pulled on the sweatpants he'd been sleeping in. "Want to go back to your room?"

"No. Downstairs. Living room. Outside." Kate felt for the stair handle rail. In the dim light, she didn't want to end up as the ghost had done.

THE BANKED EMBERS in the living room fireplace emitted a dim red glow. Michael stumbled into the low table and caught himself with his hands. His leg felt on fire. "Mind the table," he muttered through gritted teeth. He inched his way to the wall and found the light switch. The wrought iron wall sconces cast a warm golden light. "It's safe now. Except for the Legos. Come in and sit."

Kate still stood in the doorway, eyes blank. She shivered. "Michael, I don't know if we made love or the ghosts did."

He didn't share her ghost theory. But her terrified bewilderment was real. He had to fix that. "Let's go raid the kitchen. There's something very non-ghostly about apple tart."

Kate followed him, wrapping the duvet closer.

Michael poked about in the stainless steel double-door fridge and brought out the lamb roast from dinner, a dish of apple tart and a bottle of milk.

"I heard a crash." Brad stood in the kitchen doorway, sleepy-eyed. "What are you two doing down here at this hour?" He looked from Kate to Michael to the food on the table. His eyebrows lifted. "Midnight snack? Lovely thought. I'll make the cocoa."

Michael felt like he'd been doused with cold water. Kate was involved with Brad. What kind of heel was he to have forgotten that? And what kind of woman was she to have initiated it? He'd fallen for another Tracy.

He pushed away from the table. "I bumped into Kate in the

hall and she was terrified. A nightmare or something. I'll just leave you two."

Kate reached for his hand. "Michael, stay. Please?"

"No. You're boyfriend's here. Let him take care of it." Michael edged past Brad and slipped out of the room.

22

Kate slumped against the table. "Oh hell. He thinks you're my boyfriend which makes me a total slut in his eyes."

Brad opened the tin of Cadbury's cocoa above the stove and measured it into the saucepan of milk. "Well, it's rather obvious you two just had sex. I thought you didn't like him."

"I don't. I didn't. I . . ."

"I think you changed your mind. What happened?"

She filled Brad in on the ghost. "When I bumped into Michael I couldn't let go. Then Michael took me into his room and gave me a brandy and then . . ."

Brad looked at her dryly. "I deduced the 'and then' part."

"I don't know what came over me. I looked at him and suddenly I needed him more than I needed air." Kate clasped her hands together to still their shaking. "I don't know if it was me feeling that, or the ghost."

Brad rescued the chocolate before it bubbled over. "This is an occasion that calls for marshmallows. But I don't think they do marshmallows in Ireland. Pity."

"What am I going to do?"

"I don't know." Brad wrapped her hands around a cup of cocoa. "What do you want to do?"

She wanted to go back upstairs and make love to Michael.

Brad read her face. "Ah. Well, it seems you found what you were looking for."

"No, Brad, I was not looking for this. This wasn't supposed to happen." Kate sipped the cocoa letting its warm sweetness steady her.

Brad's face got serious. "By any chance did you remember to use protection?"

"Well, of course, we . . ." But they hadn't. Neither of them thought to stop. "It's okay. I'm on the pill."

Brad looked skeptical. "Because of your promiscuous lifestyle?"

"No," Kate snapped. "Because they regulate my period. Not that it's any of your business."

Brad finished building a huge lamb sandwich and took a bite. He chewed thoughtfully and swallowed. "Let me get this straight. You felt a sudden intense attraction to Michael which the two of you took to its logical conclusion, and now you think that you might have been possessed by a ghost?"

"What else could it have been? I have never felt that intense about anyone before."

Brad patted the crumbs from the corner of his mouth. "I make a terrific sandwich. Would you like a bite?"

"No."

"Are you ready to go back to bed?"

"No! I can't go back in that room."

"Fine. But you can't stay down here all night."

"Yes, I can. I'll get a book from the library and read until morning. Then we can leave."

Brad put the tart and the sandwich makings away and left the cocoa pan to soak.

Kate sat there sipping her chocolate. Why had she ever

thought she wanted to see a ghost? She felt exhausted and ashamed and miserable. How could she ever explain this to Michael?

"I've got an idea, poppet. Come upstairs with me to my room."

"Great. Then Michael will know for sure I'm a total sleazebag."

"I don't think you were possessed. And I'm going to prove it to you. I'm betting if you come with me to my room, nothing at all will happen."

"Why's that?"

"If you see a ghost, I don't think you'll suddenly feel a need to jump my bones. I'm your friend. Not your lover. It's possible the ghost intensified your feelings, sort of an echo effect, but she didn't create what you feel for Michael. That was already there."

She looked at Brad and felt a sprig of hope. It sounded logical, but . . . "No. I'm staying down here."

"All alone? There's another ghost you know. I hate to leave you prey to him."

Kate felt like a trapped field mouse. "Fine, but you'd better be right. I don't want to see another ghost as long as I live." She followed Brad up the stairs and into his room, tensing for the first sliver of movement or unnatural coldness.

"Nothing will happen. Here I'll prove it to you." Brad bent and touched his lips to her.

The warm touch of his lips was nice. Sweet, but she felt no stirring of desire. No curtains blew. She just felt . . . safe. She yawned. "Suddenly very sleepy."

"Take the bed. I'll take your room. No dreams now."

Kate stumbled to the bed and sank into sleep.

≈

KATE WOKE TO WAR WHOOPS. She cautiously peeked out from under the covers. Connor and Patrick, wearing Indian head-dresses and carrying tomahawks war-danced in front of the bed.

When they saw her they froze. "You're not Brad," one of the twins, said.

Kate sat up and stretched. "No. Were you going to scalp him?"

"No," the other twin said, "We were going to tie him to a tree."

Kayla burst in. "Mam says no matches. We'll have to pretend the fire. Oh." She stopped short. "You're not Brad."

"No." Kate stared in fascination at Kayla's lipsticked war paint. "You were going to tie him to a tree and burn him?"

"Only for pretend," Kayla said. "He gave us the war bonnets and said he'd play with us today. Where is he?"

"Um, we swapped rooms last night. He's in the Queens room."

"Brilliant," Kayla crowed. "We can use the secret passage."

A secret passage? Kate swung her legs over the edge of the bed and caught hold of the bedpost to keep from falling. The ground was much further away than she'd thought. She opened the door to the hall and peeked out. Nothing. But she could still hear the war whoops. Where were they coming from?

Michael's door opened. His hair was still damp from the shower. He wore a brown long sleeved shirt the exact color of his eyes and carried his bag and a jacket. He smelled like a breath of forest.

Kate reached up to smooth her hair and felt the tangles around her face. She looked down at her shabby pajamas. Way to go Kate. Look of the month for dates-you-never-want-to-wake-up-with. "Michael, I —"

"I see you're none the worse for wear." His cool glance

swept over her and landed on the room she'd just left. "Is your boyfriend still asleep?"

"That's what I wanted to explain to you."

Brad erupted from the queen's room. "Banshees," he yelled. "Do you hear them?"

The muffled war whoops did sound a lot like wails. "It's not the ghost, Brad." Kate aimed a pointed glance at Michael. "Brad swapped rooms with me after you left."

The whooping grew louder.

Michael looked startled. "That doesn't sound like last night's ghost."

"It isn't." Kate marched Brad into the Queen's room and yelled. "Come out, you Indians. I've got your prisoner."

A portion of the wall slid open and Connor, Patrick, and Kayla flew into the room brandishing their hatchets.

"What's all the commotion?" Hugh appeared in the doorway, natty in a plaid shirt and tan suede jacket. He frowned at his tomahawk-waving brood. "Ah, Brad, I warned you about giving them weapons. The headdresses would have been enough." He eyed the children. "How many times have you been told never to wake a sleeping adult?"

"But Brad said we could wake him," The twins chorused.

Hugh looked at Brad.

Brad shrugged and nodded. "I told them we'd have a game before breakfast."

Hugh shook his head at the children. "But you know perfectly well Brad sleeps in the yellow room when he visits."

One of the twins pointed at Kate. "He wasn't there. She was."

"Oh dear." Hugh turned to Kate. "Did the ghost bother you? She's been rather quiet of late. I rather thought she'd moved on."

Kate wrapped her arms around her thin pajama top. She wished they'd all move away so she could grab her clothes and get dressed. She frowned at Hugh. "Yes, the ghost appeared and then she disappeared right there." She pointed to the open secret passage. "If you put someone in a room with a secret passage, I think you ought to tell them it exists."

"Well then, it wouldn't be a secret anymore, would it?" Hugh said reasonably. "Children, go wash the war paint off before your mother finds out you've used her lipstick."

The boys scampered down the hall. Kayla sidled up to Kate and stroked her pajamas. "You've got Tinkerbell on your pajamas. I have a Tinkerbell nightgown. Do you want to play fairies?"

Kate looked at her hopeful face and surrendered. "First you'd better wash. You can't play fairies in war paint."

Kayla beamed. "I'll go get my magic wand."

"Do you mind if I have a look at the secret passage?" Michael asked Hugh. "My brother and I always wished we had one."

"I'll come with you," Hugh said. "Show you around. Of course, it's much shorter now. My father blocked off the round stair after we discovered it. He didn't want us tumbling down them like the Queen's Lady did."

Kate watched Hugh and Michael disappear into the entry; then turned on Brad. "You've been here before. Did you know about the secret passage?"

"I'm sure I knew, but I'd forgotten about it. Sorry, it never entered my mind. How did you sleep?"

"Fine, till the war party woke me."

"Any dreams?"

"No. You kissed me and then I got sleepy."

"Lovely to know I have such a soothing effect."

Brad's eyes widened. Kate turned around to see Michael and Hugh walking back into the room. From his icy expression, Michael overheard her say Brad kissed her. She opened her mouth to explain. Then closed it. What was the use? "I'd better go wash up."

Hugh beamed. "I was telling Michael that Degan, the hawker was coming this morning. I thought you might all enjoy seeing the mews."

Kate didn't want to be anywhere Michael was. "I've a date with your daughter to play Fairies." She grabbed clothes at random.

"Serves you right for wearing Tinkerbell pajamas." Brad took her favorite NYU sweatshirt out of her hand. Rummaging in her suitcase, he came up with a periwinkle blue sweater. "Wear this instead."

Kate fingered the soft luxurious wool; looked at the label. Cashmere. "This isn't mine. I've never seen it before."

"It was in your suitcase. Perhaps it's a gift from the faerie folk."

"The faerie folk have really good taste." Kate fixed Brad with a hard stare. "Almost as good as yours."

Brad could have given lessons in innocence to the twins. "You must have forgotten you packed it. Perhaps Carrie put it in as a gift."

"I checked all Carrie's additions before I packed up at Abbey Court."

Michael edged past them with a murmured, "Excuse me."

"Hurry down, you two. Before the breakfast is all gone." Hugh left whistling a tune Kate almost recognized.

"I can't take gifts from you, Brad. It's not right."

Brad sighed. "Kate, you don't need to hide all the time. Give the rest of us some credit. You're smart. You're funny and you have a beautiful heart. I think you should dress to match it."

"Yeah, well if I am ever going to find Mr. Right, he's going to have to see past my looks." Kate pulled the NYU sweatshirt out of Brad's hands. "I'm going to go shower."

"Ok, Cinderella, but someday you're going to have to come

out of the ashes. Michael saw you at your worst and he didn't seem to have any problem being attracted to you."

She turned around. "Sure. And he's convinced I am a slut. Cause that's what beautiful people do. They sleep around. They take your heart and leave it bleeding."

"I'm beginning to get a picture here. What did your last boyfriend look like?"

"Go away." Kate slammed the door into the bathroom. She turned on the water and threw her pajamas on the floor. Stepping into the shower, she let the tears mingle with the spray.

Last night has been one of the most wonderful and terrible nights of her life. No one had ever affected her the way Michael did, and it was all wrong. Why on earth had she thrown herself at him like that? Well, no more.

Kate dried off. She would play with Kayla and stay out of his sight for the rest of the day. She yanked the brush through her hair hard enough to make her eyes smart. "He can go to hell," she muttered, twisting the wet strands into a bun. How dare he think she was the kind of person who would sleep with one man while attached to another? She slipped the sweatshirt over her head and pulled on her oldest jeans.

Brad tapped on the door. "Finished yet?

"Yes."

Brad looked her over and shook his head. "I don't think fairies wear teacher buns."

"This fairy does," Kate snapped.

"You forgot your Tinkerbells."

She snatched up her pajamas and padded back to her room; found socks, and pulled on her fleece lined Uggs.

Kayla was lurking by the scones. "I brought an extra wand," she mumbled through a mouthful of scone and jam. "Can we go trap some other fairies? Then we could have a tea party."

Kate could hear rumbling voices coming from the direction of the library. Good. Hugh and Michael had already finished.

The smell of bacon mingled with the aroma of fresh baked scones. Suddenly she was starving. She lifted the lid off a covered dish and helped herself to eggs and bacon and broiled tomatoes. She buttered a still-warm scone. "Where are your brothers?"

"Throwing up."

Kate pushed her plate away. "Why? What happened?"

"I gave them medicine. I told them it was Indian whiskey and they drank some."

"Why would you do that?"

"They used my Barbie's dresses to wipe their war paint off." Kayla's smile was angelic. "I knew the medicine would make them throw up. Mam gave me some when I was little because I ate some of her pills."

Sheila's voice thundered down the hall. "Kayla Drumlogie you march yourself in here right now."

Kayla's smile disappeared. "I'll wait in the stables. We can play there." She grabbed the wands and fled.

Michael and Hugh poked their heads into the dining room. "What's the problem?"

Sheila appeared with two limp wan-faced boys. "Hugh, take them outside. I think they are empty. I am going upstairs to lie down. After that, I shall write a letter to Mumsie asking her how it is she let me and my brothers live to grow up. I'm not sure I'm that forbearing."

"What happened?" Michael asked.

"Ipecac happened. Hugh, if you find your daughter, discipline her in some terrible manner."

"Hair of the dog?" Hugh asked.

"Only if you are willing to clean it up. Go. Now. Take them away. Good morning, Kate. If you are thinking of having children, think again."

Hugh looked after Sheila. "She loves them really. Well, so do I. Don't know where we'd be without them."

Connor made a suspicious noise. Michael and Hugh each grabbed a child.

"But sometimes I'd like to find out." Hugh hurried them through the French doors.

Brad entered the dining room. "Where are they off to? Going to see the hawking?"

"In a manner of speaking. I wouldn't follow them if I were you."

"Not going anywhere till I'm fed." Brad piled a plate with eggs, sausage and potatoes.

Treysa came in carrying a steaming pot of coffee. Brad got down on one knee. "Treysa, oh love of my life. How soon can we be married?"

Treysa chuckled. "Men. You're always slaves of your stomach. I'll wager Queen Cleopatra had a good biscuit recipe."

Kate took her cup of tea and joined Kayla in the stable.

"Good. You've come." Kayla handed Kate a wand. "Is Mam still mad?"

"I think so."

"Never mind. We'll trap her a fairy and then she'll be happy with me again." Kayla led the way out of the barn, using her wand like a dowsing stick. "Mum loves magic things. She writes stories you know."

"Does she? So do I." Kate eyed the brambles Kayla seemed to be heading for. "I don't think fairies hide in thorn bushes. We're more apt to find them under a flower or by an ancient oak. Do you have any of those?"

"We've got flowers, but they are the boring kind. Let's go to the forest. It's okay if I am with you."

Kate mistrusted Kayla's innocent face. "I'd have to ask your mother or father first."

"They won't mind. Honest." Kayla climbed over the bars of the fence and headed for the woods on the other side of the pasture. "What kind of books do you write? Do they have ghosts and pirates? Can I read them?"

Kate looked around. No parental figures or livestock in sight. Should she follow her or scream for help? She couldn't let the child go off alone. "I don't think you'd like my stories. They are about grownups who fall in love."

"Oh."

Kate could see she'd lost face in Kayla's eyes. "Grownups like them," she said defensively.

"I think love is stupid. I always run out of the theatre when they kiss. I don't like the happy ever after stuff. It means no more adventure."

"I don't like it either," Kate said. "But I'm good at writing it."

"Is there any adventure in your books?"

Kate flushed at the thought of a child reading one of her love scenes. "Not the kind you would like."

"You should put ghosts in your books. We have ghosts. Would you like to meet them?"

Kate's foot found a gopher hole. She put out her hands to catch herself. Behind her, she heard a loud snort. She turned and locked eyes with a very large bull.

Kayla's face turned the color of skimmed milk. "I thought Caesar was in the other pasture. Run for it."

Kate picked herself up ignoring the pain in her hands and ankle and hobbled after Kayla. Snorts turned to a thudding of hooves pounding the ground.

Kayla made it over the fence and turned to look for Kate. Her eyes widened. "Kate. Hurry."

Kate ran for her life. Her heartbeat sounded as loud in her ears as the hooves behind her. She reached the fence and threw herself over.

Caesar hit the fence with a bang. It sounded like an explosion, Kayla stuck out her tongue at Caesar. "Missed again."

176 | *Irish Magic*

Kate sat up and tried to brush the leaves out of her hair. Her teacher bun was a thing of the past. "Let's go back to the house."

"But we haven't found a fairy yet."

"You knew the bull was in the pasture."

"No, I didn't. I looked first. Honest. Oh. You're bleeding." Kayla tried to help Kate to her feet. "I'm sorry. I didn't mean for you to get hurt."

"I think you lied to me, Kayla. I don't like being lied to."

Kayla hung her head. "I really thought Caesar was in the other pasture. Connor and Patrick and I like to make him chase us and we are not supposed to do it. But I wouldn't have made *you* play that game. I just wanted to take the fastest way to the woods."

How could she fault Kayla when she'd looked herself, and not seen anything either. Her ankle still throbbed. "Why don't we sit here a moment and you can tell me about your mother's stories. She writes about fairies?"

Kayla made herself comfortable leaning against Kate's side. "Mam likes to write about real people meeting fairies. And I want to meet one. Just like the Girl of Ennisinch in her story. It's funny because she believes in magic creatures, but she doesn't believe in ghosts. I've seen the ghosts. I've never seen a fairy. I think she's making them up."

"You've seen the ghosts?"

"Oh yes. Elise plays with me sometimes when she's not moaning over her boyfriend. Why do grownups do that? I've told her Michael is in the north tower, but she keeps losing him."

"What does she look like?"

"She's shorter than Mom and has gold curls and big lace on her sleeves. Mostly her dress is blue, but sometimes she gets misty. You know what? I wish there was a ghost who was the same age as me. And maybe a dog and cat ghost too?"

"That would be lovely," Kate said absent-mindedly. Elise's sad voice still echoed in her heart. Her mind sorted through possibilities. Kayla had seen Elise's Michael. She knew where he was. Maybe . . . "Kayla, has Elise ever been to the North Tower?"

"I've never seen her there. Maybe she's trapped in the Queen's room and the secret stair. Why don't ghosts change clothes? I tried to give her Mam's nightgown, but she wouldn't take it."

Kate's ankle felt marginally better. She'd love to make it back to the house and clean up before anyone saw her. The warm trickle on her forehead felt like blood. "Have you ever tried telling Michael where to find Elise?" Some part of her mind knew this was a ridiculous conversation. She was sitting in a wood, bramble-scratched, discussing ghost relations with an eight-year-old. Never mind. It was better than thinking about last night.

Kayla circled the patch of green they sat on, touching her wand to each toadstool. "Come out, fairies. I've got honey for you."

Honey? Kate noticed a bee flying lazy circles around Kayla. Five more followed. "Kayla, put the honey down. The bees want it."

Kayla looked up and screamed. She scrambled over the fence.

"No, Kayla. The bull."

The bees followed Kayla. Kayla's scream sounded like a fire siren. Her head swung from the bees to the snorting behemoth in the pasture. She scrambled back over the fence, running straight for Kate. "Hide me."

Kate pulled off her NYU sweatshirt, bundling the child in its folds. The bees circled landing on the material. Kate heard Kayla's muffled sobbing. She held her breath, willing the bees to leave.

The bees made a final circle and flew toward a patch of clover.

"It's all right. You can come out now." Kate tried to pull the sweatshirt away

Kayla clung to it with desperate fingers. "No. I hate bees."

Great. She was sitting in the woods in her bra. Why hadn't she put on a T-shirt? Fat drops of rain fell on her naked shoulders. Or remembered her rain jacket? "Get up, Kayla. It's starting to rain."

Kayla stood up, a small figure tented in blue. "I'm not coming out. You'll have to carry me."

Kate drew a deep breath. "Right." She blinked raindrops out of her eyes. How hard could it be?

By the time she's skirted half the distance of the fence she was ready to give up. The trickle of rain settled into a steady downpour. Kayla felt like a fifty-pound sack of potatoes. "Kayla, bees don't come out in the rain. Pop your head out and look."

Kayla's head poked out of the sweatshirt like a small wet turtle. She hiccupped back a sob. "They've gone. Hurry before they come back." She rolled out of Kate's arms and streaked for the house.

"Give me back my sweatshirt." Kate hobbled after her.

Head down, Kayla crashed into her father. "What's all this then?" Hugh picked her up. "Where did you get the . . .? Aah."

Kill me now. Kate wrapped her arms around her bra, trying to keep her teeth from chattering. "We ran into some bees."

Hugh put down the weeping Kayla. He took off his jacket, handing it to Kate. "Thank you. Kayla's got a thing about bees. It's the only thing that terrifies her."

Kate wrapped herself in the coat gratefully.

Strong arms swung her around. "What happened?"

She looked up into Michael's concerned eyes.

"Bees." This was beyond embarrassing,

"No bee did that to you. He lifted her wet hair away from her forehead. "You're bleeding."

"It's just a scratch." She turned away. Her ankle buckled.

Michael lifted her into his arms. "What else have you done to yourself?"

She fought the urge to lean into his warmth. "Nothing. I'm fine."

Michael looked at her scratched palms. "What were the two of you doing? *Digging* for fairies?"

Hugh had the look of a man about to mete serious retribution. "Kayla. You had your last warning. Did you go through the pasture?"

Kate looked at Kayla's woeful face. She couldn't betray her. "It's my fault. I hopped over the fence before Kayla could stop me. She saw the bull coming and screamed to warn me."

Michael's arms tightened around her. "A bull chased you?"

"I've never run so fast. I got scratched climbing over the fence. Kayla saved my life."

Hugh patted his daughter's head. "Well done. I suppose that gets you off for this morning's crimes.

Michael looked from Kayla to Kate. "Let's get you cleaned up. Hugh, where's your first aid kit?"

"There's one in every bathroom. Given our children's suicidal tendencies, we find it best to be prepared." Hugh swatted his daughter lightly on her bottom. "Kayla, change your clothes before you catch a chill."

Michael strode toward the back door.

Kate knew she ought to struggle more. But it was too much trouble. "Put me down. I'm fine." It would have sounded better if she could stop her teeth from chattering.

The downstairs bathroom had a tub. Michael turned on the taps. "I'll bring you down some clothes after I see to your forehead." He poured something from the first aid kit onto a pad, using it to blot away the blood on her forehead.

It stung. She pressed her lips together.

"You don't need a stitch. That's good. A butterfly bandage will do it." He moved onto her hands. "You seem to have a talent for tripping."

"I do not. Normally I'm very graceful."

"You lied, didn't you?"

She looked down at her scraped hands. "It's not a lie. It's an affirmation. I want to be graceful."

"I'm betting Kayla led you into mischief."

"Oh. That." The steam rising from the tub eased her shivers. "Well, I couldn't throw her to the wolves, could I? She was in enough trouble for the ipecac incident."

Michael bent over her ankle. She tried not to breathe in the scent of his hair. Clean. Fresh. Some kind of herbal scent. She wanted to bury her face in it. *Think of something else.* She cleared her throat. "Kayla's talked to the ghosts. She says Elise's Michael lives it the North Tower. I thought I might ask her to take me to see him."

Michael's head came up so fast it almost bumped her chin. "I think she's gotten you in enough trouble. No telling what she could do with a winding staircase."

Don't say it, Kate. "You could always come with us. Don't you want to meet your namesake?"

Michael stood up abruptly. "Get in the bath. I'll send Brad down with some clothes for you. After you're done, I'll tape the ankle."

Blockhead! After he left, Kate peeled off the rest of her clothes. He hadn't even asked if she was involved with Brad.

Let it go, Kate. He was worried because you were hurt. It's a doctor thing. It doesn't mean he wants anything more to do with you. He still thinks you are a two timing slut.

The steaming water stung her hands, but the rest of her body welcomed it. Kate concentrated on shampooing the leaf debris out of her hair, willing away the memory of Michael carrying her.

She'd gotten what she needed from him. The perfect hero. The sex was simply an aberration. The memory of Michael's body covering hers flashed through her mind. Her senses screamed *liar*.

"Stop thinking!" Kate sank beneath the surface holding her breath.

A knock interrupted her yoga moment. "Michael said you needed clothes. Shall I come in?"

"No. Leave them outside."

Brad popped his head around the door. "What happened to you?"

"Go away."

"Fine. I didn't see anything. I wasn't peeking. Just demonstrating friendly concern." Brad nudged the clothes inside the door. "Aside from the bandage on your forehead, you look fine."

"Out."

"Going." The door clicked shut.

BRAD LEANED against the door and smiled. "Beautiful in fact," he said aloud. Now she'd have to wear the blue sweater. Unless she wanted to walk through the hall in a lacy bra. The woman clearly had a weakness for Victoria's Secret.

The Wearing of The Green tinkled on his cell phone. Brad blanched.

"What part of no magic didn't you understand?" Finn McPhee's voice sounded like nails coated in Irish whiskey.

"I haven't. I'm not." How was it The McPhee could always make him sound like a schoolboy brought before the headmaster? "Perhaps I made a mistake with the potion, but she didn't eat it. And I've already been punished."

"Then how do you explain last night?"

Brad willed his voice back to the rich creamy tenor he used to soothe nervous clients. "I had nothing to do with last night. It was all the fault of the ghosts."

Finn snorted. "Ghosts, is it? A fine tale to tell the council."

"It's the truth." The trouble with Leprechauns is they had a hard time believing in things they couldn't see.

Finn's voice softened into benevolent uncle. "Two days till the Autumn Equinox. Your family's looking forward to a wee visit."

And if Finn had his way, the visit might be for forever. "You struck the bargain. I've a right to be in the human world as long as I keep it."

"You're not thinking of marrying her yourself are you?" Finn bit off the words like a clink of gold coins. "Because you know what that means."

He *had* thought of it. Kate pulled at him the way no other human had. Was he ready to choose? "No. I'll stick to the bargain."

"You haven't much time." The phone clicked off.

23

Kate peeked out the bathroom door. Coast clear. She'd put a towel over the beautiful blue sweater. She'd get Brad later for forcing her to wear his gift.

"You left your hair down."

Michael's tone revealed nothing. He might have been asking about the weather. But his eyes were another matter. Their hot possessive gaze made her want to run. Preferably straight into his arms. His fingers tightened on the elastic bandage he'd been tossing like a tennis ball.

"It dries faster that way."

"I want to tape your ankle. It's a slight strain, but with all the stairs in this place you need the support."

He was right. Kate followed him to the living room. The fire's crackling warmth felt like a blessing. She sat down, careful to put some distance between them, lifting her foot onto the sofa.

The feel of his hands winding the bandage around her ankle felt like some kind of erotic foreplay. But then everything about Michael made her feel like that. She cleared the lust from her throat. "When did you know you wanted to be a doctor?"

"Since I discovered the hard way I wasn't Superman, I had to find another way to save people."

"The hard way?"

"My brother dared me to fly from the porch roof. My cape failed to save me."

"Aah." She wanted to smooth away the crinkle his eyes made when he smiled.

"The doctor who cast my leg became my next hero. Hospital emergency rooms can be very exciting. I was hooked."

Kate focused on those clever fingers winding the bandage around her foot and ankle as if it were a yardarm. "I never got to be Superman. It always went to my boy cousins. But I could beat any of them playing Nintendo."

Michael looked like a dog who'd just heard the word 'squirrel'.

She stifled a giggle.

"Zelda? Super Mario Brothers? Star Fox?"

"Any of them. I was an only child. Being the divorce kid meant I got a lot of guilt gifts. The housekeeper didn't care what I did, so I had a lot of time to practice."

Michael grinned. "My brother and I got guilt gifts. John was the oldest, so he always told me what to ask for. Of course, we had to share the Nintendo. Which means I didn't get much time as I wanted to practice. Too bad they don't make Nintendo anymore. I'd like to take you on."

Heat shot to her core. Get a grip, Kate. He's talking about a video game. She took a yoga breath. "Michael, about last night. Brad—"

"We've got an Xbox." A voice piped up from behind the sofa. "Would you like to play? We could make teams."

Kate jumped.

"It's a twin, Kate. No ghosts involved." Michael twisted to peer behind the sofa. "What are you doing back there?"

"Playing hide and seek. Only Connor forgot to find me. I fell asleep." Patrick tumbled over the back of the sofa barely avoiding kicking Kate in the face. "We've got lots of good games. We could be teams."

Kate and Michael exchanged glances.

"You ought to rest your ankle. It's as good a way as any."

Kate nodded. "Fine. Go get your brother."

Patrick screamed, "Connor!" His voice could have sunk ships.

Kate covered her ears.

Michael nudged Patrick off the sofa. "She meant go look for him."

Patrick raced out of the room.

Kate put her hands down. "My ears may never be the same. They have three children all of the time. I'd go mad."

"I hear it's different when they're your own."

"I don't plan to find out."

"Me neither."

Their eyes locked.

Connor and Kayla beat Patrick into the living room.

"Patrick says you play Xbox," Connor said as if he didn't believe it.

"Do you play Mario Kart?" Kayla asked.

Kate and Michael both nodded.

"Good. You can be on my team." Kayla marched over to Kate.

Connor sat down next to Michael. "I'm way better than Kayla. I'll help you win."

"Care to make a bet?" Brad strolled into the room.

"He's on my team," Patrick said, clutching Brad's hand.

Kayla scowled at Brad. "No cheating. No magi—" Her mouth snapped shut. "Mmmph. Mmmph."

Brad smiled at her. "I wouldn't dream of it, dear girl. Fair game to the finish. Winner gets to take all the desserts."

Patrick pushed open the antique carved wardrobe revealing a flat-screen TV and shelves which held a media player and an Xbox.

Michael leaned over to Kate. "Xbox isn't the same as Nintendo. You might be a tad rusty."

Perhaps this wasn't the time to mention her father had given her an Xbox for Christmas last year. There were advantages to having a father who still saw her as twelve. It kept him thinking he was young, and it gave her something to do when she got stuck on a scene. "I'm game if you are."

The boys were good. Connor made it to level five before he fumbled. He handed the controller to Kayla with a smirk. "Bet you can't beat that."

She couldn't. She fumbled on level three.

Brad was up next. He brought himself and Patrick to level six. "I used to be better than that. Been slacking off lately. Too much work at the office."

Michael flexed his fingers. "This is my game. We're going to beat them, Connor."

Kate watched him dance past mushrooms and steer flying carpets with a skill a jet pilot might have envied. "You're really good."

Michael glanced at her. His fingers lost their rhythm. Mario gave a moan and died. "You broke my concentration."

"Sorry." Kate took the controller. She'd played the Mario Kart so often it had become sense memory. She reached level ten without a hitch. Music soared. Princess Peach kissed Mario.

She smiled at the stunned faces surrounding her. "I'll get fat eating all the desserts. Maybe I'll share."

"I'm overwhelmed. Kate, will you marry me?" Brad kissed her in a very unbrotherly way.

"Stop it." She could feel Michael mentally pinning the letter A on her chest.

"Why don't we give Kate and Brad some privacy?" Michael said. "Your dad told me you have a nice fishing stream. Care to show me?"

Kate pushed Brad away. She turned to see the boys leading Michael out the French doors. Kayla looked at her reproachfully. "You were kissing. That's a bad thing to do. You should never kiss a Le . . ."

Brad snapped his fingers at Kayla. She clapped her hands over her mouth.

"Do you remember the story of the girl who broke a promise to one of the wee folk? It's a sad one, that."

Kayla hung her head.

Brad snapped his fingers again. "Of course, you aren't the sort of person who would break a promise. So it will never happen to you."

Kayla lifted her head. "I'm sorry. I meant you should never kiss a man because terrible things will happen."

"I didn't kiss Brad. He kissed me. And terrible things may happen." Kate thought of several creative ways to murder him. "Why did you do that? What were you thinking?"

Brad actually looked embarrassed. That was a first. "I'm sorry. I was overcome by your skill and the way you finely tricked us. Consider the proposal unsaid."

Kayla seized Kate's hand. "Would you like to go to the North Tower? I'll show you my hiding place."

Sheila drifted into the room. "Kayla. I've been looking for you. Your punishment for this morning's debacle is to clean up the playroom by yourself. Hop to it."

Kayla left the room with the dragging step of a serf sentenced to a week in the dungeon.

Sheila turned to Brad and Kate. "Do either of you know the proper name for King Arthur's Chalice? I'm sending my

Gwyneth on a quest to find it and I can't remember what it's called."

"Do you mean the Holy Grail?" Kate asked.

"Holy Grail? How disappointing. I'll have to think of another object. Holy Grail sounds improper for a fairy tale."

Brad shrugged. "Call it the Fairy Grail then. The holy relic of the first of the Omaeara."

Sheila's eyes brightened. "That's perfect. Excuse me. I have to finish my chapter."

Kate looked at Brad with respect. "The holy relic of the first of the Omaeara? That's brilliant. I wish you could help me out like that. What could Cressida do to make Lord Rotherham fall in love with her?"

"She could tell her the truth about herself. But that's not likely to happen. Truth's a dangerous weapon and one doesn't offer it to one's adversaries."

"If there is going to be a happy ever after, they have to stop being adversaries."

"True," Brad said. "But it has to happen in the proper time and place."

Kate slumped back on the sofa. "I haven't a clue when the time might be. My writer's mind seems closed for repair."

"You'll figure it out Kate. I have faith in you."

24

THE QUEEN'S ROOM WASN'T SPOOKY BY DAYLIGHT. KATE snuggled in the window seat on the down-filled blue velvet cushions. The narrow window looked across pastures made magic by a veiling of mist. The silver shimmer of the stream was barely visible.

Her laptop purred. She stroked it absentmindedly.

"*Stop dreaming ,*" Ethel, the critic, shrilled. "*Cressida needs to tell Lord Rotherham the truth.*"

Like that was going to happen. Let him go first. Kate's fingers circled the touchpad. Lord Rotherham's dread secret. Fix it.

The backstory where he'd disowned his wife, sending her out into a snowstorm with only the clothes on her back hadn't endeared him to her editor.

The new Lord Rotherham. The one with warm, wary brown eyes and a deep velvet voice needed a new secret. Why was his heart locked away?

"*I had a wife once. Annabel was everything I ever dreamed of in a spouse. Wellborn, dutiful.*"

"*Was she beautiful?*"

Lord Rotherham looked down at Cressida, a wry smile curving his well-shaped lips. "That goes without saying. When I initiated her into the art of lovemaking, she liked it so well, she wanted to practice at every opportunity. I was enthralled to have a courtesan in my bedroom and a perfect lady in the other aspects of our lives. I had no idea I was not her only lover."

"She betrayed you?" Cressida could not prevent a tiny gasp from escaping her lips.

Lord Rotherham's lip curled. "Of course. She is a woman."

The curtain moved, brushing the back of her neck. A breeze sighed.

Kate bolted out of the window seat, holding her laptop like a shield. She snatched up her computer case on the way out of the room. Once in the hall, she clicked 'save' and thrust the laptop into the padded case. She had to find another place to write.

She almost collided into Kayla at the top of the stairs. "Kate, I've been looking for you everywhere. I want to show you the North Tower."

"Aren't you supposed to be in durance vile?"

Kayla wrinkled her nose. "What's durance vile?"

"Playroom arrest."

"Mam didn't say I had to stay there." Kayla sighed dramatically. "The nursery took hours to clean. The twins are pigs. But I'm free now. Let's go."

Tempting. But . . . "I really should be writing."

"The tower is a great place to write. Come on, I'll even help you. Mam always says I have lots of good ideas."

Why was it so easy to use any excuse to stop writing? "Why not? I'm sure I can fit a tower into the story somewhere."

Kayla led her around the corner into another long corridor. Portraits lined the wall interspersed with suits of armor which must have come from different periods in history because they didn't resemble each other. Someone had prudently removed the swords. At the far end, there was a pointed arch, inset with an iron-bound wooden door.

Kayla turned the knob. The door groaned open. She flicked a switch on the inner wall. The single lightbulb gave off a yellowish glow, barely illuminating a flight of spiral stone steps.

"I'm surprised there's not a key to keep you out."

"There was, but Mam and Dad kept locking it, so I took it away." Kayla pointed to the suit of armor closest to the door. "I dropped it down the Wicked Baron. They will never find it there. Come on."

Kate used the narrow walls as support, trying to ignore the reek of ancient dampness. Curving steps twisted upward to a square tower room with a wide-planked floor. Most of it was covered with a frayed turkey-red carpet.

The stone walls looked to be about twelve feet on each side. A high-backed chair and an ancient wooden desk occupied one corner. A second high back chair stood directly under a tall narrow window. A trunk heavily carved with birds and flowers sat against the opposite wall. Between the two narrow windows slits was a bookcase, lower shelves filled with picture books. A narrow stand held an ancient globe. An iron chandelier hung from the center of the room, its original candle sockets replaced with small flame shaped bulbs. Someone, Kayla surely, had dragged up three fat red cushions. They were scattered on the carpet like stray gumdrops.

"See? There's a desk and everything." Kayla plopped down on one of the cushions. "There used to be a bed, but it broke. Dad said it died of being jumped on."

Kate's imagination went into overdrive. Cressida and Lord Rotherham were definitely going to end up in a tower.

Standing on tiptoe, she peered out the window. Michael, Connor and Patrick were walking down the driveway carrying fishing poles. She spared a brief moment of pity for Michael.

From her glimpses of the twins in action he was in for a rough time. Never mind. He deserved it.

MICHAEL BELIEVED fishing was the perfect antidote to stress. He hadn't reckoned on Connor and Patrick. "The idea is to be quiet and lull the fish into thinking nothing's around but the worm."

Connor held up the worm from the can Jem, the stableman had given them. "I wouldn't eat this." He dropped it down his brother's shirt.

Patrick screamed. "Get it out! Get it out."

While Michael de-wormed Patrick, Connor waded into the stream. "You don't need worms to catch fish. You're supposed to guddle them." He bent over, staring into the water. "There's one. He grabbed a flash of silver. It leaped out of his hands. Connor fell backward into the stream.

Michael hauled the sputtering boy out by his shoulders. Connor grinned up at him. "I almost had him. You try."

He was not going to be beaten by a six-year-old. He removed his shoes and socks. His pants were already soaked from Connor's splashing.

Michael bit back words unfit for a child's ears. The water felt like it had come straight from an iceberg. He bent over, studying the tumbling flow. Flashes of silver were everywhere. "I've never seen so many fish." He lowered his hands into the ice bath. Instant numbness. The fish seemed to swim in slow motion. They probably had hypothermia.

Patrick slid into the water next to him. "It's easy. I'll show you." He cupped his hands together leaving just enough room for a fish to swim through. When one did, he slammed them shut against the fish. "See, Connor? I got one. I win!" He threw it on the bank. It flopped wildly.

"That's a mother fish," Connor shouted. He threw it back in the stream.

"That was my fish." Patrick splashed back to shore and tackled Connor. The whirlwind of rolling yelling boy slid downhill toward the stream. Michael felt a cold heavy fish slide through his hands. He grabbed for it. The fish had to weigh three pounds. It squirmed frantically, trying to get away. "Incoming," Michael yelled. He tossed the fish at the boys. It landed right between them.

They broke apart, staring at it. "That's a really big fish." They watched it flop back and forth.

"You need to finish it off," Patrick looked sick.

Connor closed his eyes. "I don't want to look."

Michael waded out of the water. His feet felt like rubber blocks of ice. He surveyed his twitching silver trophy and sighed. There was no way he could cosh a fish in front of two six-year-olds. He picked it up and tossed it back into the water.

The three of them watched it swim downstream.

So much for fishing. On the plus side, it kept his mind off Kate. "Let's go dry off."

25

"DO YOU SEE HIM, KATE?" KAYLA'S VOICE SOUNDED AS IF SHE were pointing out a butterfly, instead of a ghost.

"Yes," Kate whispered. The shadow hovered at the window emanating a feeling of incredible sadness. The weight of it pressed into her chest.

The outline of a man thickened. He wore a white shirt open at the throat. His dark red vest matched his knee britches. A sound rippled the air. It could have been a voice, or the sigh of the wind.

"He's rather boring. He never talks to me. Maybe he'll talk to you." Kayla raised her voice. "Sir Michael? I brought you some company."

The form turned. Kate could feel him staring at her. His mouth opened. A sound drifted out like a curl of smoke. "Elisssse . . ."

Kate's breath locked up.

Footsteps clattered up the stairs.

"I'm first."

"No, me."

"You never let me go first."

"I'm the oldest. I have to protect you from the ghost." Connor popped through the doorway followed by a red faced Patrick.

They skidded to a stop when they saw Kayla. "Let's get her."

Kayla backed away slowly till she hit the wall.

Michael appeared at the top of the stairs. "Bad idea, men. Never start a war with women. They're meaner and trickier than you can ever hope to be." When his eyes lit on Kate, his amused expression turned to distant politeness. "Gentlemen, the heights are occupied. Let's find another fortress."

Kate watched in fascinated disbelief as the ghost followed him out.

The children looked at each other open-mouthed.

"It's never done that before," Connor said.

Kayla looked at her brothers. "Let's see what he does. Hurry." The children jostled for position at the narrow entry way and exploded down the stairs.

The weight of sorrow was gone. The room just felt . . . empty. Kate had a very good idea of where the ghost wanted to go. Shouldering her computer case, she followed them.

Michael had an arm slung about each of the twins. "What about the secret passage?"

Kayla skipped ahead of them. "You have a ghost behind you."

Michael didn't bother to turn around. "We're not playing ghosts today."

Idiot. Kate stayed well back of the ghost. "It's no use warning him, Kayla. Men only see what they want to see. They ignore everything else."

Michael's shoulders tensed. Connor and Patrick turned to look behind them. "The Ghost is getting thicker." Breaking free of Michael, they grabbed Kayla's hands. "Run!"

Michael finally turned around. His eyes widened. "Bloody Hell." He backed away as the ghost advanced. "Kate. Run."

"It's not me he's after. Keep walking."

Michael backed around the corner.

Kate followed. She knew it was mean to enjoy his petrified expression, but after last night, it felt like justice.

A blue and gold ice whirl of color spun down the corridor. *"Michaelllll."*

"Elisssse!"

The wide-eyed children huddled against the wall.

A sound like a great bell tolling filled the corridor. The two ghosts merged, spiraled upward and vanished.

The hall was quiet except for the hum of a vacuum cleaner coming from downstairs.

Brad poked his head out of the yellow room. "What's all the commotion? It sounded like a wail of Banshees out here."

"The ghosts exploded," Connor said.

Patrick pointed at Michael. "He mixed them together."

"Well done, Michael." Brad clapped him on the back. "No ghostly intruders tonight then, Kate. Where would you like to sleep?"

Michael didn't wait to hear her answer.

Kayla looked up at Kate tragically. "Now who do I play with?"

"Maybe they'll come back," Kate said encouragingly. But please, God, not until I've left.

She rounded on Brad. "You did it again. Why are you trying to convince Michael there's something between us?"

Brad's smile was choir boy sweet. "Your hair's standing out like a halo. Anger? Or ghost residue?" He reached out to touch it. It crackled and clung to his finger. "You've got a bit of magic of your own, my Kate."

Kate brushed his hand away. "I am not your Kate. I am not anyone's Kate. I belong to myself. And that's the way it's going to stay."

26

Lunch was a family affair with the conversation centered on the children's' account of the exorcism.

"The ghosts just popped?" Hugh asked.

"Looked more like a chemistry experiment with a celestial vacuum cleaner." Michael didn't think he'd come off well in his first ghostly encounter. Kate had done much better. Of course, she'd had experience. No wonder she was so terrified last night.

Sheila sighed. "I suppose I'll have to rethink my views on ghosts since two rational humans actually saw them. I hope the popping was the end of them."

"Not all of them," Hugh said. "There's still the other knight, and did I ever mention the weeping kitchen maid?"

"No. And please don't." Sheila smiled at Kate. "You've probably had enough of spirits and fairy hunts. Yes. I heard about this morning. Would you like to go to my book club meeting today? They'd be pleased to meet another published author."

"Bunny, I was going to take them to the Aillwee Cave," Hugh protested. He turned to Michael. "My grandfather Jack discovered it when he followed his dog on a rabbit chase.

Granddad was a rather silent chap. He didn't mention the discovery for thirty years."

"If you and your brother were anything like our brood, I don't blame him. He probably wanted you to survive long enough to sire progeny," Sheila said. "Aillwee Cave's a major tourist stop these days. Would you prefer to explore the caves, Kate?"

Kayla bounced out of her chair and wrapped her arms around Kate. "Please say yes. It's got real bear bones inside and a waterfall."

"Caving is not the best exercise for a strained ankle," Michael said. "Too many uneven surfaces. You'd be better off with the book club."

Kate ignored him. "I'd love to explore a bear cave." She turned to Sheila. "But I would also love to attend your book club. Is there any way we could do both?"

"Of course. The book club meeting's not till six."

Treysa stood up. "If you're going to Aillwee, mind you stop at the dairy and pick up some cheese for the Craic."

"This particular Craic is a women-only meeting," Hugh said. "No men or children allowed."

"Does you good to care for the chislers on your own. Makes you appreciate us more." Treysa stacked plates onto the tea cart.

"And while they are gone, we can have our Cowboys and Indians game," Connor whispered to Patrick.

Connor needed to work on his whisper. They could have heard him in the stable.

Sheila exchanged glances with Hugh and sighed. She turned to the twins. "No tying anyone to the stake and absolutely no fires."

∽

THE LOW WALLED cave echoed with the sound of dripping water. Michael had to duck to enter the next tunnel. It broadened into a cavern hung with wet stalactites. They looked like pieces of dissected intestines. The yellowish lighting made it look like a scene out of—

"This looks like the cave in *The Goonies*," Kate said.

Michael nodded his agreement. "One of my favorite movies."

"What are Goonies?" Kayla asked, trying to pry her hand out of her mother's grasp.

"A film you won't be allowed to see till you are grown up," Sheila said.

Brad had a firm grip on a squirming Connor. "A sad example of parental censorship."

Hugh had an equally firm grip on Patrick. "We narrowed their access to films after we let them watch *The Lion, the Witch, and the Wardrobe*. We also put all the wardrobe keys in the safe. We didn't find the boys for five hours."

Their guide raised her voice to be heard over the sound of the waterfall. "The stalactites are over eight thousand years old. Bears came in here to hibernate because the temperature stayed the same in here all year long."

The children broke free of restraining hands when they reach the bear cave. "Bones," Connor yelled.

All three children reached through the gate protecting the fossils, trying to get their hands on them.

The guide smiled. "It's all right. They aren't the first curious children who've tried to touch the bones. They'd have to grow arms like Plastic Man to be able to do it."

"I wouldn't put it past them," Brad said.

Michael glanced at Kate. The amusement he saw in her eyes echoed his own. He turned away. Every time he looked at her he wanted to take her in his arms. And he wasn't going to let that happen. He knelt beside the children, scrutinizing the bone fragments.

"The last brown bears in Ireland died over a thousand years ago," the guide said. "This is all we have left of them."

Kayla peered at the bones. "I wish they were still alive. Maybe they'd be like the talking bears of Narnia and I'd make friends with them. I need someone to play with." She looked at Michael reproachfully.

The child still blamed him for the disappearance of the ghosts. "I'm sorry," he said, not knowing what else to say. "I didn't mean to do it."

Brad came to his rescue. "Kayla, Michael had nothing to do with the ghosts disappearing. When Elise and her Michael found each other, they completed what they had to do on earth and moved on to—"

"I know. They live happily ever after. I really, really hate that part."

"You'll like it when you grow up." Hugh put his arm around his wife and smiled down at his children. "It's—"

"—really, really quite wonderful," Sheila finished.

KATE TOOK a deep breath of fresh air. Would anyone ever look at her the way Hugh looked at Sheila? Unlikely.

The cave had been fascinating, but a little claustrophobic for her tastes. She reached for her notepad, needing to write down every nuance.

Connor tugged on her sleeve. "We're going to see the Raptors next."

"Bird show," Hugh said. "Lots of flying. They've got a vulture wandering round. The children are quite fond of it."

Sheila removed Connor's clutching hand from Kate's arm

and turned him toward his father. "You men take the children to the bird show. Kate and I are going cheese shopping."

Sheila led Kate to a tall building faced in round stones, divided into two rooms. The first room was a combination café and gift shop. Kate wanted to browse the open counter filled with home-made fudge, but Sheila kept walking. The second room was . . . Kate stopped in the doorway overwhelmed by the mingling scents. Rich strong milky cheese, with overtones of garlic, cumin, and a fascinating smell she couldn't identify.

"Irish gold." Sheila pointed at the floor-to-ceiling wooden shelves filled with round golden-waxed cheeses. This will do you far better than the Leprechaun sort." She walked up to the counter. "Hello, dear. I'll take four plain, and two each of Cumin, Nettle, and Piri-Piri."

"Planning a party, are you?" The smiling clerk had a face as round as the cheeses she sold.

"Between the Book Club and the family, it feels more like provisioning for a siege." Sheila took a tooth-picked sample from the platter on the counter and offered it to Kate. "Piri-Piri's a bit spicy. Try and see, if you like it. I know Brad could eat an entire round by himself. You're not serious about Brad are you?"

Kate choked on the chili infused bite of cheese. "No. We're friends. That's all."

"Just as well. His relatives are a difficult sort. I'm not sure Brad is ready to settle yet." Sheila speared a second cheese sample. "It's a very important decision for a man in his position."

In his position? What an odd way of putting it. Kate lifted her chin. "I don't feel like I'm in a position to consider a relationship. I have to concentrate on my career." She felt embarrassment flaming her cheeks. She sounded so priggish.

Kate waited until she and Sheila were settled in the café with a pot of tea and sample plate of bread, cheese and, praise be, squares of rich creamy fudge. "I have an idea for my next book if I managed to live through this revision. What can you tell me about Cluhalaugh?"

Sheila blinked. "Ah, the Matchmaking Festival. There used to be a great deal of magic in Cluhalaugh. It's said the Lady of Cluhalaugh got her gift from the Fair Folk. I don't recall the why of it. But when the Lady made a match, the marriage was a true joining. My own mother and father swore by the Lady. They wanted me and Hugh to go to Cluhalaugh at the Summer Solstice, just to be sure, you know."

"And did you go?"

Sheila's eyes twinkled. "We couldn't wait for the festival. I'd already begun to show. And I didn't need a matchmaker to tell me what I already knew. Hugh was the only man for me. But Kate, the last Lady died a few years ago. I've heard the festival is simply an excuse for a grand party. Brings in the tourists and the town could certainly use the money."

Kate bit into a piece of fudge, letting the dark chocolate taste console her. Nothing about this trip was going according to plan. She still wanted to see Cluhalaugh. She'd set her story there and make her own magic. Nothing wrong with weaving a bit of Hugh and Sheila into her heroes. The bond between them almost made her believe true love was possible.

"Are you planning to go to the festival, then?"

"Yes."

"Michael seems like a lovely young man. Perhaps . . ."

"No."

27

KATE WAS SORRY TO SEE THE LAST OF THE DRUMLOGIE FAMILY. They crowded round the car, to say goodbye. Kayla threw her arms around Kate. "You're more fun than Tinkerbell. I think you are a real fairy."

Kate glanced at Michael. From his expression, his belief in fairies, and in her was nil.

She hugged the children and ignored the door Michael opened for her. "You take the front, Brad. I want to make notes on the castle so I don't forget."

Brad slipped into the front seat. "I would think you wouldn't have any trouble remembering since you had such a memorable encounter with . . ."

Kate reached forward and pinched his ear.

"Ow." Brad turned to her. "You didn't have to do that. I was talking about the ghost."

Michael fitted himself into the driver's seat. "When I was a kid, I wanted to be a Ghostbuster. They were a lot less scary in the movies."

Kate closed her ears to the conversation in the front and

scribbled down her impressions of the castle. She'd braved the Queen's room last night. Revised three more chapters. Slept without disturbances. No ghosts. No Brad. No Michael. So why did she feel so unsettled?

They passed through small towns with stone churches and more pastures. After an hour, the road began winding upward.

"We're getting close," Brad said. "You'll see Galway Bay soon."

Kate pressed her nose to the window. The shining expanse of gray water lit by shafts of sunlight lifted her spirits. "It's gorgeous. When I am rich and famous I'm going to have a house on Galway Bay."

"I thought you were planning a small castle in The Lake District," Michael said.

"I've changed my mind," Kate said shortly.

The road turned into the city streets of Galway.

"Where shall I drop you?" Michael asked.

An obvious non-invitation for them to stay wherever he was staying. Fine. As if she'd want to. "My hostel book recommends the Kinley Eyre. If you'd drop us at Eyre Square, we'll make our way from there."

A short few blocks brought them to the center of town.

Michael unlocked the back and handed them their suitcases. "Enjoy your stay."

Kate lifted her chin. "Thank you. You've been very kind. I hope you have a wonderful time with your Essie and her family." She pulled up the telescoping handle on her suitcase. It broke off in her hand. She closed her lips tightly. Minor setback. Nothing to cry over. She grasped the leather handle on the side and hefted it into her arms.

Michael tried to take it from her. "That's too heavy for you. Let me drive you to where you're going."

Kate turned away from him. "I can manage. Have fun." She

strode toward the far corner of the square, where the Kinley Eyre Hostel was barely visible.

Brad gave Michael a what-can-you-do shrug and followed her. "Wait up." He took her suitcase from her and handed her his unbroken one. "You know what this is, don't you? It's a sign."

"Sign of what?"

"It's a sign it's time for you to buy a new suitcase. There's a mall over on the right side of the square. I'm betting they have a luggage shop."

Kate sighed. There went her budget. "Not the souvenir I'd planned to bring home." She knew to the penny how many Euros she had on her. "I hope they take credit cards."

MICHAEL WATCHED Kate's stick-straight back march away from him. He had to get his libido under control. Turning away, he pulled out his phone and found Declan's number.

"Ah, Michael. Essie was beginning to think you might have had some car trouble. Where are you?"

"Eyre Square. Can you give me directions?"

"I'll do better than that, dear boy. You stay where you are and I'll come find you and lead you here."

Declan pulled up beside him. Brenna jumped out and knocked on Michael's passenger door. "Da thought I'd better accompany you in case you lost him."

Brenna's chatter filled the short drive, requiring only a few nods and smiles from him. After some tricky twists and turns, Declan pulled up in front of twin two-story houses, each faced in brick and creamy plaster. The black-framed windows were cross-hatched in an Elizabethan pattern. Brick-paved front walks bordered by pink and white flowers led up to the front doors. One front door had a glass framed porch with teal-blue pots filled with familiar looking red flowers. Essie grew a lot of those at home. The other door had two guardian china dogs.

Brenna rested her hand on his sleeve. "Aunty Maire's house is the one with the geraniums. Park around back, right next to Da."

Michael waited for Declan. "Are you sure there's enough room for me? I can always book in at a hotel."

"Essie said you might feel that way so you're staying next door. It's a B&B too, but the owner's away and they'll be no other guests. You'll have the place to yourself."

Essie and Shauna waited in the small living room. Essie jumped up and hugged him. "Ah, you're here at last. Where have you been and what did you see?"

"I ran into the couple we met at the airport at Trinity College. They couldn't find a car for hire, so I offered them a ride to Galway. We visited Blarney Castle, Cork City, the Burren and Aillwee Cave. We spent the last two nights at a castle."

"A castle? And where would that have been?" Essie's eyes twinkled up at him.

He could see she thought he was teasing her. "A few miles from the Burren. It was called Drumlogie."

Brenna's mouth dropped open. "Drumlogie Castle? But it isn't open to the public."

"Brad went to school with the lord of the castle—Hugh. I never did get his last name or his title. Very nice man." Michael sat on the sofa, taking Essie's hand into his. "How was your visit with cousin Padraic?" He felt her pulse jump."

"It was grand. Of course, he's changed since I last saw him. Fifty years will do that to a body." Essie's smile came and went like a like a flash of sunshine. "I'd forgotten how the man could make me laugh."

Michael looked to Shauna.

Shauna answered his unspoken question. "Padraic took one look at Essie and decided to attend the festival."

Essie's blush didn't match the frown she sent Shauna's way. "Go on with you, then. He simply decided it was time to be getting on with his life. We'll find him the right person."

And maybe Essie had decided it was time to be getting on with hers. Michael dropped the subject. "Where's your sister?"

"She's away next door making up a room for you," Essie said.

"I don't want to put her to any trouble. I can make up a bed."

"She doesn't mind at all. Her best friend owns the B&B next door, and Maire often looks after it for her. Maire's never happy unless she's doing three or four tasks at once."

The front door banged open. "Is he here then?"

Maire didn't look like Essie, except for the blue eyes. His mom would have loved her attire. A knobby blue sweater came down over a gauzy skirt which stopped just above her skinny ankles. Her feet were shod in rubber-soled purple slippers.

"Yes," Essie said. "This is my Michael."

Maire looked him up and down as if he were an item she was going to buy. "Fine strong lad. He'll make wonderful babies for some lucky girl."

Michael was surprised she didn't check his teeth.

"I've put fresh towels out on your bed. I've another couple coming in at the last moment. I made up their room too. Yours is the blue room. Go up the stairs. Then right at the end of the hall. Here's the key to the house. No need to lock your room. If you need to do laundry, there's a machine in the utility room."

Maire bustled into the small kitchen, calling out behind her. "I'm off to the altar guild and then I'll pick up the couple. It's fair hard to find the way here. Essie's made the tea. I'll see you tonight unless you go out to explore the town, and if you do, I'll see you in the morning. I serve a full Irish breakfast. Do you like tomatoes then? Some Yanks don't."

She came out of the kitchen, her skinny arms weighed down with bulging string bags.

Michael sprang up to help her.

"Oh don't bother, dear, I can manage. If you'd just open the door, that would be grand."

He relieved Maire of her packages. "Why don't you open the door and I'll put these in the car for you?"

Maire patted his arm. "It's a sweet boy you are. Brenna, you take Michael out and show him Shop Street. That's the favorite place for the tourists."

Brenna beamed "That's a fine idea."

No, it wasn't. The last thing he wanted was to be shown the sights by the sweet and talkative Brenna. He needed some alone time. "Could you tell me if there's a good place to run near here?"

Brenna's face fell. "Are you sure you wouldn't rather go to a pub? I know some great ones."

"I've been doing too much driving lately. I need to stretch out."

"Well, I don't do any running myself," Declan said, "but I've heard they do a marathon here every year. I believe the route is down by the bay and over to Salt Hill."

"Thanks." He'd look up the route on his phone. "I'll take my gear over to the other house, then come back after my run."

"We'll have tea ready for you," Essie said.

"I've a better idea," Declan said. "There's a wonderful fish and chips place at the bottom of Maiden Lane. Why don't we eat there tonight?"

Essie's face lit up. "I've a longing for fish and chips."

"Sounds good," Michael agreed. "I'll come back in time for dinner."

Michael unlocked the front door, nodding courteously to

the two china dogs guarding the entrance. Mom made a game of waving at statues when he and John were young. "It's the friendly thing to do," she used to say. He no longer waved, but he generally managed the odd unobtrusive nod.

There was no mistaking the blue room. The bright blue bedspreads imprinted with small red flowers gave it away. He unzipped his bag. The sweatshirt he'd worn the other night fell out. Kate's fragrance clung to it. Damn. He tossed it aside and pulled out his only other sweatshirt and his last pair of clean socks. He'd packed the way he did when he was a teenager, backpacking through Europe. Laundry was now a priority. He repacked his duffle and took it downstairs.

The controls on the small stacked washer and dryer looked simple enough. He found the soap and selected a cycle. With luck, the other guests wouldn't want to be doing laundry. He'd change it over to the dryer after his run.

The skies threatened rain. Michael jammed a baseball cap on. He didn't care if he got wet. Starting out slow, he picked up the pace till the only sounds in his ears were the slap of his running shoes on the pavement and the sound of his heartbeat. Trees and houses flowed by. He reached the river and let the sight of the shore birds soothe him.

"Would you mind kissing me?" Kate's words looped endlessly in his brain. Would he mind? Nothing could have stopped him.

Michael brushed away the sweat dripping down his face, wishing he could as easily erase the memory of their lovemaking. The connection between them had felt all consuming. He could have gone on forever. He could have sworn she felt the same way. Was every woman faithless or did he just attract them?

And what kind of person was he to fall so hard and fast for a lovely face? "Give yourself a little credit, Michael. She's far more than a face. Kate is intelligent, funny, and she can beat the pants off you at Mario Kart. And she's taken. So think about something else."

His disobedient brain brought up the image of Kate's lovely face, her lips parted in laughter, begging to be kissed. He turned back toward the B and B increasing his pace. Maybe he could run off the memory.

28

THE KINLEY EYRE WAS FULL. THE FRIENDLY YOUNG MAN AT THE desk called several B and B's for them. "You're in luck." He beamed. "Betty's B and B had a room open. You'll like the owner. She said she'd come round for you in an hour, because while it's close, it's a wee bit hard to find. Do you mind waiting? There's a shopping mall two blocks down if you want some lunch."

"We don't mind waiting," Brad said. "Do you happen to know if there's a store in the mall which sells suitcases? My friend's case lost the handle."

"I'm sure there are a couple at least." The receptionist smiled at Kate. "You can leave your luggage here while you shop."

THE MALL WAS small in comparison with an American one. Kate scanned the map. "Oh, great. Burger King, Claire's Accessories, JC Penney. I am not coming home with a suitcase from JC Penney. There has to be something else."

"Let's just walk and see, shall we? Also, I'm hungry."

Kate sniffed. "Big surprise."

"I'm a growing boy. Let's find some place we can't find on every street corner in America."

They passed by Healing Earth and Claire's Accessories.

"Aha. La Croissanterie." Brad peered in the window. "Doesn't sound Irish, but at least, I haven't seen one in New York."

Kate looked at the menu and shook her head. "I'll pass."

"Fine. You can have a cup of tea while I eat." Brad ordered a cup of soup, a ham sandwich and a meringue covered tart."

The enticing aroma of the French Onion soup reminded Kate it had been a long time since breakfast. One bowl of soup wouldn't kill her budget. She paid for the soup, resolutely keeping her eyes off the chocolate.

Brad went back to the counter and returned with an éclair on a doily-covered plate. "I saw what you weren't looking at. Eat. You're too skinny."

She didn't need a lover. Not when she had a man who called her skinny and bought her dessert. "Thank you." Kate pushed away thoughts of Michael and picked up a fork.

Bag and Baggage displayed a range of suitcases in all sizes. Brad pulled down a Tinkerbell backpack. "I know you'd like this for yourself."

"Funny." Kate marched over to a carry-on size bag in basic black. "This will do." She turned over the tag and did a rapid calculation from euro to dollar. It was more than she wanted to spend. "No. I think I'll look further."

"You missed this one." Brad wheeled over an emerald green suitcase with a darker pattern of shamrocks. "It's on sale."

Kate fell in instant lust. It was larger than the one she had now and so pretty. The original price of 100 Euros was marked out. Below it was a squiggle she couldn't decipher. "Brad, can you read the price?

"Of course, I can." He bent down and put his eye to the tag. "Twenty-three Euros. Can't beat that."

Kate looked at Brad suspiciously. "Twenty-three Euros would be more than seventy percent off."

"You don't believe me? Go ask the salesgirl."

"I will."

The girl examined the tag. "You're in luck. That's the floor model piece. We can't get any more of them, so Mr. Griffin's letting it go cheap. Cash only I'm afraid."

Brad handed her a hundred Euro note. "Don't use all your cash. You might need it. You can pay me after we get home."

The salesgirl counted out the change and snipped the tag for her. "Enjoy your trip."

"Oh, I will. I am." Her luck was turning. This was her perfect souvenir and a sign that the rest of the trip would be just as she'd imagined. She couldn't be happier.

They took the escalator back to the street level. Kate looked across the green and saw a statue she couldn't quite make out. "I'm a sucker for statues. Let's go see who it is."

Kate studied the figure of a middle-aged man seated on a rock with his feet toed in together, one foot on top of the other. He was writing something on a paper in his lap. "He must be an author. How odd. The statue looks like you, twenty years older. Do you think you could be related?"

"Perhaps." Brad found the plaque. "His name is Padraic O'Conaire. He's a storyteller."

"He looks like he could be one of the fair folk. Is he supposed to be a leprechaun?"

"Says here he was a fluent Gaelic speaker. Born in Galway, but spent many years in London. "When he returned to his native land," Brad read, "he bought a small donkey and cart and became a familiar character traveling the roads collecting material for his stories, teaching and telling stories as he did so."

"Stand next to him." Kate snapped a picture of Brad and the statue. She saw a hint of sculpted curls beneath the writer's broad-brimmed hat. He and Brad were extraordinarily alike. Perhaps it was the expression. "Why would an Irish storyteller voluntarily leave his own country? Do you suppose he was banned?"

"I don't know. Perhaps he had a geas put on him. Perhaps he had to perform a task before he was allowed to follow his heart. That's often the way of things." Brad's smile didn't reach his eyes. "Let's get back to the Hostel. We don't want to miss our driver."

Their driver looked like an elderly Mary Poppins. In lieu of Mary's signature hat, she sported a black tam trimmed with red poppies on her straw-brown crimped hair.

"Sorry to be so long but I had to stop by the church for a meeting of the Altar Guild." She swung Kate's suitcase into the boot; then grabbed Brad's. "I'm not Betty, ye ken. She's away in Connemara visiting her new granddaughter. It's her seventeenth grandchild and I don't believe she's ever missed a birth except for the time when she had the heart surgery. I manage the house when she's away. I've a guest house of my own next door, but I'm full up at the moment. I'm afraid you'll have to pay cash for the room. Betty doesn't take credit cards. Will that be all right? It's sixty Euros for the two of you."

Brad nodded. "I can give you . . ."

By this time she'd zipped around a couple of curves. "I made up your beds. There's a blue room and a yellow room. You're in the yellow room at the top of the stairs to your left. I've keys to the front door for you. There's only one other guest, so I'm sure you'll have a nice quiet time. It's a bit tricky finding your way here, but once you walk back down to Eyre Square, you'll know the way back." She pulled up in front of a double house flanked by brick walks. "My house is number twenty-five. You are in number twenty-four. I'll just take your cases up the walkway and you can go on from there. My family's visiting and I don't like to be gone too long. We're all going out to dinner tonight. McDonagh's Fish and Chips. It's the best in town. You ought to try it."

During this flow of words, Brad managed to take the suitcases from her and receive the keys.

"You can pay me in the morning. I do a full Irish breakfast from seven to nine. Just knock on the door in the morning and I'll do your fry up. Enjoy your stay." She unlocked the glass-enclosed porch and hurried inside.

Kate and Brad looked at each other and laughed. Brad unlocked the door. "I feel like I've been talking to a gale force wind."

"I want to have that much energy when I'm old," Kate said.

"When I'm her age, I want to be in front of the Telly with my pipe and slippers, asking my wife what's for supper."

"Wife?"

"A figure of speech, Kate. A figure of speech. Nice little place. Let's go upstairs and see where she's put us."

There were three doors at the top of the stairs. "What room did she say?" Brad asked. "I got lost in the word storm."

"So did I. I'm pretty sure I heard yellow and blue." Kate opened a door. "Well, this one's yellow, but it's only got one bed. I'm not sleeping with you." She opened the other door. "This one's blue and it's got twin beds. It must be ours."

"What if you're wrong? She did say there was another guest, didn't she?"

Kate scanned both rooms for suitcases. "There's no sign the

guest is here yet. We'll leave the yellow door open. The guest can move in there. Maybe she'll like having a bigger bed."

"Fine." Brad slung her case onto the bed. "I like to sleep on the left side. You can have this one."

Kate opened the third door. "Looks like the two rooms share a bathroom." The sink was spotless and the shower, dry. "I wonder where Betty sleeps when she's at home?"

"Do you want to transfer everything to your new case?"

"Yeah. I need to wash out a few things. I'm running out of fresh undies."

"Want to do mine while you're at it?"

"No. I should have brought more clothes with me. Wonder if this place has a washing machine?"

"Let's take a look."

They found a pantry with a stacked washing machine. Kate opened the washer. "Drat there's laundry in here."

Brad shrugged. "At least, we know there's a machine." He shook the box of laundry soap. "Bit low. Let's go exploring. We can pick up some soap, and find a place to eat."

Laundry soap shopping? "Tell you what, Brad. You go shopping and find a place to eat. I'm going to explore the town."

"Nothing to prevent us from doing both. We'll wend our way through the crooked streets and get back to the main square. Guide book says there's an ancient church and a ruin near Shop Street."

"Yes. Ruins. Let's go."

"And right after that, we'll find the fish and chips place our landlady was talking about."

"Do you ever think about anything, but your stomach?"

"Occasionally. This isn't one of those times."

29

Michael's head felt more in place after the exercise and a quick shower. He rang Maire's doorbell.

Essie answered it. "How was your run?"

"Great. Funny thing, though. When I came back, there was a green suitcase on one of the beds. Did your sister rent out the room to someone else?"

Maire pattered to the front door. "Ah, it's that young couple. They must have misheard me about the room. I told them to take the yellow one. That's got a nice big bed."

"Maybe they are the kind of couple who requires separate beds," Essie said. "Although I can't imagine it meself. I always wanted to cuddle after a good roll."

"Essie, consider my ears. That's more than I wanted to know about you."

"Ah, Michael, you young people think you invented sex."

"My brother used to tell me our parents had sex. I thought he was lying to gross me out."

Essie love-tapped his ear. "You're a disrespectful one. No doubt about it. You'll run your wife a terrible race."

Michael had a quick flash of running after Kate and catching her. "I'm not getting married, Essie. I told you that."

Essie motioned him to bend down. "It's because you haven't met the right one yet," she whispered. "Brenna's not the lass for you. It'll all come right in Cluhalaugh."

Declan came out, followed by Shauna and Brenna. "We won't all fit in the car. Michael, why don't you take Brenna and she can show you the way?"

Brenna clamped her crimson-tipped fingers around his hand. "We'll meet you there in half an hour. The man deserves a Guinness before sitting down with the whole passel of us"

Michael smiled down at the girl. "I'll pass on the Guinness. I'm starving. Lead me to the fish and chips."

Brenna belted into the passenger seat. "Perhaps we could do the pubs after dinner." Her voice lowered to a sexy purr. "I could show you a very good time."

In spite of her vamp lashes and siren red mouth, Brenna still looked like the Catholic schoolgirl she'd probably been a couple of years ago. Michael had a feeling she bruised easily. "Brenna, you're a lovely girl, but I have a girl already waiting for me back home. I couldn't be unfaithful to Lola." His GPS wouldn't mind standing in as his girlfriend.

Brenna looked like a disconsolate kitten. "Aunt Essie said you were unattached. She's taking you to Cluhalaugh."

"Essie doesn't know about Lola. They haven't met yet. Lola and I have been keeping our relationship quiet, because . . . ah, because she has an old boyfriend who's a very possessive man. He works for the Mafia and she's afraid of what he'll do when he finds out about us." Maybe he ought to take up writing.

Brenna looked enthralled. "What does Lola look like?"

"She's . . ." *Made of black plastic; about three inches by four inches and has a Marilyn Monroe tattoo on her upper plate?* Think of someone else.

"She's tall for a girl, about five foot nine. She got amazing green eyes and her eyebrows wing up at the corners and her smile is . . ." Michael swallowed. What was he doing? "Her smile invites you into her world, and you know that's where you want to stay for the rest your life."

Brenna looked at him as if he were some kind of god. "That is beautiful. I want someone who feels like that about me. I hope Essie can find him."

Brenna directed him to the underground car park in Eyre Square. They rode the escalator back to the square, crossed Abbeygate, and turned down Shop Street.

The two and three story buildings all looked like they were built in the 1800's. No cars. The street belonged to the pedestrians. A girl in a long dress sat at a harp singing a song of lost love. People moved slowly, pausing to study the shop windows.

Brenna halted in front of a window featuring three elegantly dressed mannequins. "Will you look at that?" She pointed at a black, wide-brimmed straw hat with a complicated decoration on the side. "It looks like something Kate would wear. She'd look lovely in it."

Michael felt a blip of disorientation. "You know Kate?"

Brenna laughed. "Don't I wish. I'd love to know Kate. She's so lucky. She found her prince."

Princess Kate. Of course. He'd forgotten there were other Kates in the world.

The cobbled street wound around to a view of the river. Michael spotted a large white sign McDonagh's.

Declan stood up from an outdoor table sheltered by a red awning. "Over here, Michael. We've got a fine table, big enough for all of us. Go ahead in and order."

Brenna and Michael joined the long lines weaving up to the service counters. The menu was simple. Fried fish. Fried chips. Fried onion rings.

"Order me some fish with a side of onion rings, Brad." Kate's clear voice rang out. "I'll find us a place to sit."

It couldn't be. Michael looked down the line toward the front. But it was.

"Onion rings?" Brad said. "No one will want to kiss you."

"Well, there's no one I plan to kiss, so that's fine." Kate turned and headed for the door.

Michael tapped Brenna. "Would you mind holding our place? I'll be right back." He followed Kate.

Kate stepped back from the door to let in another customer and bumped into Michael. He heard her murmur "Excuse me."

Then she looked up. "No. This isn't possible."

Michael shrugged, enjoying her deer-in-headlights look. "What can I say? It's a small town."

"Yes, it is."

He wished she looked a little happier about their encounter. "Did you find your hostel all right?"

"We found a place," Kate said shortly.

Brenna waved at Michael. "Hurry up, we're almost at the front."

Kate stared at Brenna. "She's lovely. Has she graduated high school yet?"

"Cute." Michael steered Kate over to Brenna. "Brenna, meet Kate. She and her friend Brad are the people I gave a lift to." He turned back to Kate. "Brenna is Essie's niece. You and Brad are welcome to sit with us. Essie and her family are holding a table."

Brad came up to them, his arms full of paper bags and drinks. "We meet again, I see. I'm beginning to think it's fate."

"Yeah," Kate said expressionlessly. "Fate." She relieved Brad of some of the bags. "I thought we could take these down by the river. It's a lovely evening for a picnic." She smiled at Brenna. "Goodbye. Nice to meet you." She hooked her arm through Brad's and cooed up at him. "Come on, darling, let's go."

Michael suppressed a grin. Darling, indeed. His heart lightened the moment he heard what Kate said about not kissing anyone. Why had she let him think she and Brad were involved?

He thrust forty euros at Brenna. "I forgot to ask them where they were staying. Could you order me a fish and chips and some onion rings? I'll be right back to help with the carry."

Outside, he turned past McDonagh's and went toward the river. The breeze had freshened. No one sat on the quay. His high spirits took a nosedive. He returned to the café and joined Brenna in line.

She handed him his change. "Did you catch them, then?"

"No. They must have found a sheltered spot." He took the bags from Brenna. They edged onto a bench at the plank table with the rest of the family.

"Smells grand, doesn't it? Take a bite," Declan urged. "You'll think you've died and gone to live with the angels."

Michael took a bite of the light crispy fried fish. "Best I've ever tasted."

Conversations sprung up around him. Maire's recounting of the priest who wanted the church to start a tea shop to fund the church faded into background noise. Kate *had* tried to tell him Brad wasn't her boyfriend, but he'd cut her off. He'd acted like a jealous idiot. Why had he been so sure she was like Tracy? He pushed his plate away, no longer hungry. What was the name of the hostel Kate planned to stay at? Kinley something? He had to find it.

30

KATE SHIVERED IN THE CHILL BREEZE BLOWING IN OFF THE RIVER. "It's too cold to picnic. Let's go back to the chocolate café we saw near the church. If we order drinks, they might not mind us bringing in outside food,"

"How about a pub instead?" Brad gave her his best choir boy smile.

"Chocolate beats out a beer any day in my opinion."

"Chocolate's full of caffeine," Brad grumbled. "A Guinness is relaxing."

"Chocolate."

The sign above Butler's Chocolate Café had a slogan, *Purveyors of Happiness*. Excellent. Chocolate happiness. That should take her mind off Michael

They took their paper sacks to a back table.

Kate returned to the counter and ordered herself a tall hot chocolate. "Is it all right if we sit here?" she asked the smiling server. "McDonagh's was full up."

"You're more than welcome." The server slid a frothy cup toward Kate. "Enjoy it."

"Thank you. It smells divine." The image of a heart swirled

into the whipped cream brought her thoughts back to Michael. Wishful thinking gifted her with a picture of Michael standing close to her, holding her hand and smiling down at her. Walking down by the river together and then going home to . . . "Stop it!"

Brad looked up. "Stop what? I wasn't snitching your onion rings. Although if you'd care to offer one, I wouldn't say no."

"Help yourself." Kate unwrapped her paper boat of fish and took a bite. "Incredible. This has to be the best I ever tasted."

"We must thank our landlady at breakfast tomorrow for recommending McDonagh's." Brad took a sip of the mineral water he'd ordered at the fish and chips cafe. "Wish they'd had something a bit stronger."

"You went through the church for me. I absolve you for the rest of the evening. Go have a pint at that pub you were looking at so longingly. Give me the keys. I'll walk back to the B&B."

"I could walk you back to the room first and then go to the pub. It's rugby tonight. Ireland's playing the New Zealand Blacks. I really want to see it."

"I don't want to go back to the B&B yet. I want to do a little more exploring."

He took the keys out of his pocket. "You won't get lost?"

"Relax. I have a GPS in my head. See you back at the room. Call me and I'll come down and let you in"

"All right, then. If you change your mind, come join me at O'Connell's. I'll save you a seat." He patted her shoulder and took off.

Kate finished her chocolate, cleared their table, and stepped back onto Shop Street.

A misty rain left the cobblestones gleaming in the light from the store windows. Couples strolled arm in arm. The sound of music drew her around the corner.

A man seated on a wooden box played a small accordion. No. There was another name for it. A Concertina.

In front of him danced a girl with long black hair. Her hands hung loosely at her sides. Her smile was easy and carefree, a sharp contrast to the crisp tapping of her shoes. Her feet pointed and flexed in a beautiful precise rhythm. Kate lost herself in the magic of the moment. When the music stopped there was a smattering of applause. Cameras clicked. Coins tinkled into the music case beside the concertina player. Couples resumed strolling. She joined them.

The mixture of old brick, and medieval stone buildings—all faced with brightly painted storefronts fascinated her. It felt like a street from a storyteller's imagination, dropped in place from another time. She paused at the display of whimsical teapots in shop aptly named Treasure Chest. The sign was partially obscured by vines trailing from a second story window box. Kate craned her neck to see past the third story bow windows. An almost full moon looked pinned to the roof.

The sound of a harp and a plaintive voice drew her to another clustered crowd. The ballad sounded like music from *Lord of the Rings*. Michael would have—

Kate turned away. Drat Michael anyway. He was stuck in her head like a song that wouldn't stop. "Think about something useful. Like how you are going to get to Cluhalaugh?"

She walked down to Eyre Park and sat on a bench in front of the Browne Family Door Monument. Odd thing to put in a park. A freestanding ancient door with a Tudor window above it lit in golden light. Rather magical, actually. Her story mind started plotting. What if you could step through it into another time?

Lord Rotherham's velvety voice soothed her frayed nerves. "Cressida, if you follow me through the door, your world will change forever."

A loud rumble interrupted her train of thought. A bus. Bus Eireann was operating again. Kate hurried to the bus station at the far corner of the square. It was lit and open.

The long room was full of doors to bus bays and a few rows of molded plastic chairs. The cashier window at one end had an actual human behind it. "Are all the buses running? I want to go to Cluhalaugh."

"Aye. We're back right enough and the Cluhalaugh bus leaves at nine am. Would you like a ticket?"

"Two please." She handed her credit card to the man, resisting the impulse to high five him. He'd probably chalk it up to crazy American ways. At last, one part of her plan was going right. She had to tell Brad.

She raced across Eyre Square to O'Connell's. She shouted above the din of the crowded pub. "The buses are operating again. I got our tickets to Cluhalaugh."

"Great," Brad said. He joined the groan the rest of the patrons voiced.

Kate looked up at the screen. She had no idea what was going on. American football was bad enough. This sport looked a lot more dangerous. "The bus leaves at nine. I'll set an alarm."

Brad stayed glued to the screen. She punched him on the shoulder. "Pay attention."

He looked at her, startled. "What did you say?"

"We're leaving at nine in the morning. Are you sure you can find the way back?"

"Course I can. I have a brilliant sense of navigation . . . er, direction . . . of not getting lost."

Wonderful. He was drunk. She couldn't leave him here.

The bartender put another Guinness in front of Brad and smiled at Kate. "One for you as well?"

One of them ought to stay sober. "No, a coke, please. How much longer is this game going on?"

"'Bout another twenty minutes."

She could bear it for twenty minutes, and then, like it or not, Brad was coming home with her.

31

"WUUNERFUL GAME RUGBY. I ALWAYS WANTED TO PLAY AT university, but I wasn't big enough. I went to all the games, though. Beauful night." Brad slung a heavy arm around her shoulders. "Moon's almost full. Doan need the street lights."

Kate supported him up the steps. "Come on, Brad, we're almost there."

Brad patted his pockets. "Lost the keys."

"No, you didn't." Kate unlocked the door. How was she ever going to get him up the stairs?

Brad staggered into the living room. "Nice sofa. I think I'll sit here for a minute. Tired."

He flopped onto the flowered sofa. "Kiss me goo night." His smile was sweet and enticing. Kate bent down to kiss his forehead. His face turned up and she kissed his lips instead. "Nice," Brad slurred. His eyes closed.

That solved the stair problem. She looked for something to cover him. The armchair had a crocheted throw. She draped it over him, removed his shoes and lifted his feet onto the sofa. "Sleep well."

In the soft yellow light from the ceiling fixture, the hall

wallpaper looked like a faded flower garden. Pictures climbed the wall next to the staircase banister. Groupings. Five different wedding pictures. The first was from the fifties. A young man in a gray suit with a rose in his buttonhole. The bride looked all of seventeen. They seemed gloriously happy. Probably the absent Betty and her husband. Then came four more wedding pictures. Those had to be their children. In the first two, a middle-aged Betty and her husband stood to the side of the bride and groom. In the last two, Betty was alone. She still looked proud and happy, hand outstretched, as if holding on to an invisible person. Sometimes, maybe, love didn't go away.

Kate's eyes filled. "That's the kind of love I want," she whispered.

Ethel, the Critic, chipped in. "*Then you'd better get back to writing about love because that's the only way you're going to get it. You want to be loveless and editorless?*"

Ethel was right. Forever love wasn't in her cards. Kate fired up her laptop, propped herself up against the headboard, and stared at the wall. Where was inspiration when she needed it?

"Butt on bed, Kate. Hands on keyboard. Write." She set her phone timer for an hour and started typing. The only rule was *don't stop.*

The memory of the lit door in Eyre Park sparked an idea. She sent them through a time gate into a mysterious island paradise. Under a full moon, with a waterfall playing in the background, Cressida surrendered to Lord Rotherham's passionate embrace. She was just getting to the good stuff when Parsley followed them through the time gate. He nipped Lord Rotherham's trouser leg, destroying the mood with his yapping.

Kate slapped the keyboard, creating a new word in the process. "That was not the way it was supposed to go," she complained to the screen. "I wanted a beautiful romantic scene."

Maybe she could send them to a castle with a resident ghost instead?

The timer dinged. Had she written a single word she could keep? Kate hit save and closed the laptop. Morning was time enough to look again.

Her Tinkerbell pajamas were in the laundry bag next to the washer. They'd never started the laundry. She took a T-shirt and her shower bag into the bathroom and turned on the taps.

She craved a bath with bubbles and candles and soft music. The kind of bath she rarely had time for. But she'd settle for the comfort of hot water and her lavender thyme shampoo. Humming a waltz, she pulled her hair out of its twist tie and sank into the tub.

She massaged a capful of shampoo into her hair. The bar of soap the absent Betty had provided smelled of spearmint and lemon. She stroked it over her body; then sank down till only her face was above water, letting her thoughts drift away to the sound of her heartbeat.

A rap on the bathroom door startled her.

There goes my long bath. "I'll be out in a minute."

A tentative voice came from the other side of the door. "Kate?"

"Michael?" This could not be happening. Kate stood up and grabbed the towel. "What are you doing here?"

"I'm staying here. You're in my room."

Kate secured the towel around her, stalked to the door, and flung it open. "I thought you were going to stay with Essie's sister."

"She's next door. Maire's B&B was full and she looks after this one as a favor to Betty." Michael stood in the doorway, eyes full of wonder. He took a deep breath. "You smell of lemons." He smoothed away the frown between her eyebrows with a gentle finger. "Do you know your eyes glow green when you're angry? They remind me of Kryptonite."

Kate shivered at his touch. Her anger dissolved into need. "I feel like I'm in a movie. 'Of all the gin joints in all the towns'—"

"'in all the world,'" Michael continued, "'she walks into mine.'" He bent down and touched his lips to hers. She couldn't think past his lips. He tasted of rain and fresh air and a dark honey promise. And she wanted him.

He broke the kiss, his breath ragged. "Kate, you're not involved with Brad, are you?"

"No. I tried to tell you that, but you wouldn't listen."

"I'm sorry. I should have listened. I . . . I need to tell you what happened between me and Tracy."

Kate pulled away. "No, you don't."

"Yes. I do. I had my proposal to Tracy all planned. I had been holding onto the ring for a week. When she said she had to work late, I decided to go to her apartment and surprise her. I brought food, flowers, and Champagne. I thought I'd get a meal ready, light a few candles. Put on some music. Make it romantic. When I let myself in, the music was already playing. And so was she. With her co-star."

Michael's lopsided smile made her ache for him. "Oh, Michael."

"Looking back, I think my pride was hurt worse than my heart. When Brad walked in on you and me in the kitchen, all I could think was I was doing to someone else what had been done to me. And I blamed you for it. Forgive me?"

Kate wrapped her arms around him. Her lips parted to welcome him in. Her world narrowed to the feel of her body against his.

"You're shivering." He swung her up into his arms and carried her to the yellow bedroom. "You need a blanket." He placed her on the bed and covered her body with his own.

The warmest sexiest blanket in the world. "You have too many clothes on." Kate slipped her hands under his sweater.

Her fingers molded themselves to the ridges of muscle on his abdomen. She tried to slip the sweater over his head.

He obliged by stripping it off. He parted her towel.

She lay there looking up at him, her wet hair streaming over the pillow.

"I always wanted my own personal mermaid." He ran a slow lingering trail of kisses down to her breasts, tugging and teasing the shell-pink nipples with his lips, tongue, and teeth till they stood up in sharp peaks.

The raging desire she felt in the castle swirled through her. And there was no ghost to blame. Her fingers struggled with his belt buckle, seeking to free him.

He unbuckled it for her and stripped off his clothes with super speed. His body gleamed golden in the lamplight. There was no question he wanted her. And she wanted him with a need beyond reason.

He knelt beside her, pinning her hands above her head. "I forgot where I was. I have to start over." He started a new line of kisses at her hairline, feathering her eyelashes, moving past her lips to her throat.

She arched into him, trying to put his shaft where it belonged.

"Wait," he whispered. He continued the trail of kisses downward lingering on her thighs, moving down to her feet.

Kate's attention focused on his hands forging trails of heat down her body. Who would have thought the insoles of her feet were erotic? Her fingers forged their own path down his back as far as she could reach. She felt the explosion building. "Now, Michael. Please."

He eased two fingers inside, massaging her pulsing center.

"Michael!"

Michael entered her while she was still trembling from the throes. He took her higher and higher till all that existed were the sensations they created together. He muffled their cries with a kiss.

Still joined, he rested his weight on his hands to keep from crushing her. He eased out slowly and cradled her in his arms.

She nestled in, reveling in his quick warm breaths against her skin.

"It has to mean something, Kate. You keep appearing in my life and I want you so damn much."

"Coincidence," Kate whispered. Her eyes closed. She didn't really believe that. When you have too many coincidences, that's the universe telling you to pay attention.

"Will you come with me to Cluhalaugh?"

Kate rolled away and sat up. "What?"

"It's a small village, famous for their—"

"I know what they're famous for. It's why I came."

"You came to Ireland to go to a matchmaking festival? Why?" Michael's incredulous look was like a spritz of cold water.

Kate looked away. There was no way to explain this and not feel like an idiot. "For my book. It's research. Cluhalaugh's matchmaker is supposed to have some kind of magic. Not that I believe in that sort of thing."

"Of course not." Michael's straight face didn't match the amused gleam in his eyes.

She wasn't lying. She didn't believe in it. If she wished it was true, that was her secret. "I have to see it for myself. Hundreds of people show up to this festival. Can you imagine that?"

Michael pulled her down beside him. "I suppose they come because they believe there's a magical way of finding the perfect partner. I don't need to go to Cluhalaugh for that. I've already found her."

His words shivered a chord in her. She fought it. "No. You don't know anything about me. I don't believe in love at first sight."

"Hardly first sight. Had to be at least third."

Michael's lips pioneering a new path of kisses down her throat made it hard to think.

"All right, I'm attracted to you," she said. "You have an amazing body and the sex is off the charts."

"It's a start. Kate, we click. Do you know how rare that is?"

Everything she felt for Michael was rare. And terrifying. "Not rare at all. It's sexual attraction. It gives the natural human urge to mate a blessing. A feeling of destiny. But when the sex wears off? When the newness is gone, it's just an obligation."

"What are you talking about? What I feel for you goes way beyond sexual attraction. I want to get inside you. I want to make love to your mind."

His words were a drug. She wanted to let go, drink them in, but she couldn't. Some people weren't made for happy endings. She didn't have the genes for it. Her parents proved that. Eric proved that. "Michael, I don't believe in that kind of love. It's a fairytale."

Michael eyed her narrowly. "You write love stories and you don't believe in love?"

"No." She believed in love between the covers of a book. Book love didn't betray you and leave you broken. "Romances are fairy tales for grownups. We don't live in a fairytale, Michael, so I know what's between us can't be true."

"Who hurt you so much you can't believe in possibilities?" His fingertips brushed her cheek.

Kate jerked away from the comfort of his touch. "I'm not hurt. I'm realistic." And right now she wanted to breathe into a paper bag. "I have five stepmothers and three stepfathers. My parents always thought they found the perfect person and they were always disappointed. There is no perfect one. It's a game and I don't want to play."

Except she did want to play. She wanted to give in and believe that Michael was the one. But she didn't dare. She worked to keep the panic out of her voice. "I'm attracted to you, Michael, and I like the way you make me feel. Could we leave it without any fairytale icing? Let's enjoy what we have."

"So fairy rings and a matchmaker who has the gift are out of your picture?"

Kate rolled her eyes. "I wish. Duh. I'm going to Cluhalaugh to see the show. Not believe in it."

Michael curled his hand around hers. "Will you go with me to see it?"

Her fingers tightened on his. "Brad's downstairs sleeping off the Rugby game. He'd have to come too."

"Wonderful. How could I have forgotten Brad? I'm booked to take Maire and Essie. Five will be a tight fit."

"Never mind. Brad and I have bus tickets for the morning." Was it too soon for a second time? She rolled over on top of him. "Maybe we could meet up."

Michael's indrawn breath sounded like sweet agony. He put his arms around her, fitting them together. "Given the way this trip is going. I'd say it was a sure thing."

She glided up and down loving the slow building pressure.

He brought her mouth down to his, his breath warm against her lips. "Kate I'm going to change your mind."

"Mmmm." She barely heard his words. All her attention was on the friction they were creating. Only with him. Only with him did she feel a pleasure so intense it was almost pain.

He captured her hands, holding them over his head. "Look at me, Kate."

Kate forced her eyes to open. *Oh.* Michael's eyes. Dark. Intense. Filled with a need that matched her own.

"You are my magic," Michael whispered. "Only you."

32

THE KNOCKING WOULDN'T STOP. "GO WAY." KATE REACHED FOR Michael and found a pillow.

Brad's head peeked around the door. "Kate. It's eight-fifteen. Did you want to make the bus?"

Kate sat, pulling the covers around her. Where were her sweats? She eyed the towel folded neatly at the end of the bed and remembered exactly where they were. Her eyes met Brad's amused ones. She could feel the blush starting on her chest. Wait. Eight-fifteen? "Oh, no! I set my alarm."

"Yeah, you did, but it's in the other room. I heard it when I got out of the shower."

Kate wrapped the bedspread around her and edged past Brad making a supreme effort to look casual. She grabbed her jeans, clean shirt, and fresh undies from the blue bedroom. "I'll be ready in a minute. Did you go next door for breakfast?"

"No, I just woke up."

"Too late now. Maybe we can get something at the station." Kate headed for the bathroom and her shower bag. She looked at herself in the mirror. Her hair was a tangle of curls. Her lips, beard-stung. Her eyes, heavy lidded. She looked like an ad for sex. "Bad", she scolded herself. Her lips curled into a cat-ate-the-cream smile. She dragged a wet brush through her hair and braided it in a tail.

Had Michael left her a note? She ran into the yellow room. Nothing visible. He must have left something. She shook out the covers.

"Kate. Hurry up."

"All right, I'm coming." She grabbed her jacket and started down the stairs.

Brad looked at her and shook his head. "Umbrella? Purse? Phone? Any of those ring a bell?"

"Right." Kate ran upstairs and unplugged her phone from the charger. She checked her purse to see if her emergency umbrella was there. She started out and turned around. Unzipping the shower bag, she took out her small makeup kit and added it to her purse. It was a matchmaking festival after all.

"Kate?"

"I'm ready. I'm ready." Kate dashed down the stairs and ran past Brad. She gained the curb and turned around to see him locking the door. "You're such a slowpoke," she teased. "Why are you always so late?"

"Just for that, you can buy your own coffee."

The bus station was rumbling with buses ready to start. Kate found a coffee machine and bought them each a latte. No breakfast pastries, so she bought them each a packet of chips and a chocolate bar. "Lovely healthy breakfast," she caroled.

"My favorite kind, Miss Sunshine. You're looking remark-ably," Brad paused, "healthy. Can I assume your sleep was uninterrupted?"

She looked at him coolly. "At least, I found a bed. How was your sofa?"

"Fine, thank you, until I rolled off it at three in the morning. I got up, had a couple of aspirin and sought my own downy nest. I did happen to notice your bed was unoccupied. Leaving me desolate. I was looking forward to trying to crawl in with you. I hope your new accommodations were friendly. Who was he?"

Kate's cheeks flamed. How dare he assume she'd sleep around. "The King of Siam," Kate snapped. "Not that it's any of your business."

The loudspeaker crackled. "Cluhalaugh bus now boarding at gate sixteen."

The bus driver took their tickets. Kate marched up the steps and took the front seat. She pointedly put her purse on the adjoining seat.

Brad looked at the purse, shrugged and took the seat behind her.

He leaned between the seats and whispered. "Sorry. I know I was out of line. Sometimes the devil takes hold of my tongue and wags it."

Kate ignored his overture and sipped her coffee. She wasn't ready to let go of her mad.

She stared out the window at the bus bay. Her morning high seeped out the bus's floorboards. First Michael left her without a word and then Brad accused her of sleeping around.

The bus lumbered into the street. The front windscreen was a picture window. They drove past plaster and brick faced cottages, past an ancient church with moss-covered grave-stones. Kate unlocked her phone for a picture and realized the message light was flashing. **Didn't want to wake you. I had to leave at six to pick up Essie's brother-in-law. What time does your bus leave?**

How had he gotten her number? Brad. She turned and looked at him through the seats. "You knew I was with Michael last night. You gave him my number."

Brad rose with a murmured excuse me to the burly farmer next to him and slipped into the seat next to Kate. "I might have happened to see him when I passed him in the hall this morning."

"What did he say to you?"

"He said he was in love with you and asked me for your hand. I told him it wasn't mine to bestow, so he asked for your number instead."

Kate pinched him.

"Ow!"

"That's for implying I would sleep with a stranger." She handed him a chocolate bar. "And that's for giving him my number."

"Well, well, well." Brad unwrapped the chocolate bar and handed her a piece. He broke off a bigger one for himself. "You've found your one true love?"

"No!"

"When you lie, your nose grows. Did you know that?"

Kate automatically felt her nose. "It's not love. It's lust. I am definitely in lust with Michael."

Brad looked as if she'd said there was no Santa Claus. She needed to fill his silence. "Did you know he was going to Cluhalaugh too? He talked as if the matchmaking was real. He believes in true love. I don't."

"Then why in the name of Finn did you agree to come to a matchmaking festival?" Brad spit out the words as if they were bullets.

Why was he so angry? She wanted to look away, but his eyes pinned her. How could she tell him, tell anyone a secret place inside her hoped the magic in Cluhalaugh was real. "I want to hear Irish music and take part in a tradition. I want to meet the matchmaker. It's all fuel for my book."

Brad's tone was steel wrapped in velvet. "And what book are you speaking of? Not the one you're writing now surely?"

"It's for my next book. *Perfect Match*."

"You never mentioned another book."

"I don't talk about a book until I have a first draft on paper."

Brad's disbelieving stare goaded her into saying more. "The plot revolves around a middle-aged woman who's been married one too many times. Despite everything, she still believes there is a happy ending waiting for her. She hears about this festival and decides she has to come. So she sells her car and buys a ticket to Ireland. Her kids try to prevent her going, but she's convinced Ireland is full of rainbows anchored to the ground with pots of gold. She's sure one of the pots has her name on it. So she gets on a bus and starts to see the real Ireland."

"What happens to the woman?"

Mom's still looking. She will look till she dies. Kate pasted on a bright smile. "What do you think happens? She meets the man of her dreams. The one who'd always been meant for her and she lives happily ever after."

Brad unfolded her fisted hands, massaging her cramped fingers. "But you don't believe it, do you? You don't believe your own ending. How can you write romances and not believe in happy endings?"

She needed more chocolate. "I believe in them in books. I love happy endings. I read my favorites over and over. That's why I wanted to write romance in the first place. To give back some of what was given to me. But real life doesn't work that way. There's no such thing as love forever. It's only in fairytales."

"Don't you know fairytales are based on truth? Kate, you had no damn business making a wish if you didn't believe it could come true."

Kate's eyebrows winged up. "What are you talking about?"

"You don't understand. Humans never do. You blew a heart wish onto a clover. That's a serious business."

There it was again. A flash of disorientation. The night they met. Surely she hadn't been tipsy enough to blab her four leaf clover moment. Wishing was a private addiction. "I wished for a hero. For my book."

"The heart of your wish was for your own Happy-Ever-After. You can't lie to a clover." Brad's eyes probed hers. "I think you're lying to yourself about what's in your heart."

Was she? Just because she melted every time she remembered Michael's smile didn't mean she was in love. "Like I said, I am in lust with Michael and I think he's in lust with me. He just wants to call it something else."

"Kate, you are wrong about magic and you are wrong about true love. They both exist."

"Right. Well, I can believe in magic sooner than I can in true love. Stop talking. I'm missing too much scenery." Kate turned back to the window.

BRAD SAW his future slipping away. He stared out the window. An old stone ruin flashed by. A manor house. Another gray stone church thrust its tower in the sky. Then sheep and more sheep.

If she denied her own heart wish, he'd lose everything he'd built. Ireland was a grand place, but the fire and thunder of New York fed his heart. He'd no desire to spend the next seven years in Ballyban tied to his Omaeara kin. There had to be a way to make her see.

The bus pulled into a town with a short main street of three buildings. A gnarled old man in a green wool vest leaned up against a building. An unfiltered cigarette dangled between his fingers. A woman with one hand on a stroller and the other holding the hand of a little girl waited for the doors to open.

The driver got out and helped her with the stroller. The child dashed back to the old man and hugged him. The woman cradling the sleeping baby urged the child up the steps ahead of her. The girl looked around with bright curiosity at the passengers.

Brad tapped Kate's shoulder. "Did you notice the child? Her eyes are full of smiles. You can tell she believes in magic."

"She believes in it now and it's lovely to see. But soon she'll learn it doesn't exist." Kate grimaced. "I still remember the vinegar tang of finding out there was no Santa. Why on earth do we tell children things like leprechauns and Santa Claus are true? Then they find out grownups are nothing but liars."

Brad handed her back the rest of her chocolate bar. "You need this more than I do. Kate, I understand your parents didn't do well by you, but don't measure your world and your possibilities by their lack."

Kate looked surprised. "I don't really. I know there are nice parents out there. It's . . . I think my possibilities are limited by what they couldn't give me. I think there's a gene for Happy-Ever-After. How could they give me what they didn't have?"

There was no moving her. He leaned back and pulled his cap over his eyes. "I'm going to take a nap. Wake me when we get there."

Tonight was the harvest equinox. When light and dark were equal. A night of truest magic. A magic he wasn't allowed to use. He'd have to depend on the matchmaker.

33

THE BUS GROANED TO A STOP BY A SMALL STONE CHURCH WITH arched plain-glass windows and a slate roof in need of repair.

The driver turned around and smiled at Kate. "Cluhalaugh. Return bus leaves at seven o'clock. Enjoy your stay."

Kate nudged Brad. "Wake up."

"Coffee first," he said blearily

She watched the other passengers file off the bus. How many of them were here for the festival? None of them looked like they were going to a party. That's what the festival was, wasn't it?

She wouldn't allow herself to hope there would be love. Kate felt a smile starting inside her. But there would be good Irish music and maybe some dancing. She wanted to dance with Michael.

Brad followed Kate off the bus onto a street lined with billowing yellow and blue bunting. "Wonder what the bunting's in aid of?" He flicked up his sleeve to look at his watch. "Eleven. Bit early for festivity, I imagine. Let's find some breakfast."

The street curved into a main square. The gray stone-slabbed center of the square looked like a dance floor. To one side was a statue of a dancing couple. A couple of older men, with beers in their hands, lounged on a long curved bench. A sculpture of a fiddler and a man tapping on a round, narrow drum rose from the flower bed behind them. There were only a few people in the square. None of them were Michael.

Three sides of the square had brightly painted two-story buildings. Salmon and green for The Irish Arms Bar, White with red trim for Nellie's Bar. The Ritz was barn-red building with a peaked roof and large white framed windows. It looked like all of them served drinks. No one was going thirsty in Cluhalaugh.

Brad pointed to the sign in front of the Ritz. "Food served all day. Come on."

Kate pulled back. "I'm not hungry. I want to look around."

"That shouldn't take long. Cluhalaugh's a very small town. I'll get us a table."

Kate nodded and walked past the square. Still no Michael

The sidewalk was as wide as a car-traffic lane. Tinkling Irish music lured her past a tented canvas stand featuring handmade jewelry.

A gaily costumed mechanical band with paper Mache faces played a tinny Irish tune. Their arms were operated by some kind of machine. It looked like a Disney exhibit. Behind them in the doorway, a tall bearded man wearing a loose brown jacket and a black hat banded with a gold buckle played a fiddle. Next to him a short white-bearded man wearing a gaudy vest and a similar hat played a penny whistle.

In front of the band was a musician's case with coins and paper money scattered across the brown interior. On either side of the exhibit were two framed pictures. One had two cartoon Leprechaun figures, the other had two cartoon fairies. The figures had holes where their faces ought to be. Kate whipped out her phone.

"Remarkable isn't it?" An older man holding a smoke-darkened pipe smiled at her. "There is no end to man's ingenuity trying to find an easier way to make a living."

"Don't give them any money. It just encourages them." The speaker, a tidy woman dressed in a twinset and a tweed skirt, looked like she'd breakfasted on lemons.

Kate smiled at the fiddler and his companion, hoping their feelings weren't hurt by Lemon Lady. "I think it's very inventive."

A short man wearing a green shirt strode up to the fiddler, blocking her view. "If you don't take that green shirt off the monkey, Seamus O'Toole, you're going to be meeting the end of my fist. I won't let you make a mockery of leprechauns."

The man holding the fiddle grinned down at the newcomer. "Eamon Flynn, you're the last person I expected to see today. I'll remove the monkey's shirt, if you'll take a turn on the fiddle."

"You'll remove it in any case, Seamus. The green-shirted man took the fiddle. "But I'll take a turn just to spare these people's ears." He tucked it under his chin.

The tinny sound of the paper Mache band was overlaid with magic. The man's bow rollicked across the strings in a tune that made Kate itch to dance. The penny whistle played a perfect counterpoint. The older man put his pipe in his pocket, linked hands with Lemon Lady, and began to jig. Seamus offered Kate an arm. "Let's have a go, love." Her feet found a rhythm she didn't know they had. Other passersby joined them. Their dance became a patterned reel. Kate lost track of time, her mind and body filled with the music.

"*Stop.*"

The music ended in the middle of a phrase. Kate felt an emptiness that ached.

A woman with hands fisted on her hips glared up at the fiddler. "Eamon Ó Baird, have you no sense at all? To be playing *that* tune on a choosing day in front of *them?*"

Kate blinked. Surely that was Brad's cousin Piri?

Eamon scowled at the woman. "What are you doing in Cluhalaugh?"

"Saving you from yourself, apparently. Do you have any idea of what they'd do to you if they found out?" She snatched the penny whistle from the white bearded man. "You need a keeper. Let's unwind it." She started a tune with the whistle.

Eamon tucked the fiddle back under his chin, playing a counterpoint to the stream of notes.

The tune was spritely. Toe tapping. But it didn't have the wild enchantment of Eamon's first melody. The emptiness inside her faded. The people around her began to clap in tempo. Lemony Lady blinked as if she'd just woken up. Her face pruned up again, but her head nodded in time to the music. The older man reached for her hand. She didn't draw away.

The music ended on a pretty trill. People applauded. Several dropped coins in the musician case before they continued on down the street.

Piri handed the penny whistle back to the white bearded man.

Seamus took the fiddle from Eamon. "Thanks to you, both. You increased our takings considerable."

Piri snarled. "I didn't do it for you, Seamus O'Toole. And I'll thank you to take down that ridiculous fairy picture." She pointed at the board with two gossamer winged figures with cut out faces.

"Hah!" Eamon pointed a finger at her. "One minute you're whinging about fairies getting equal time. And the next minute you want them taken down. Make up your mind, woman!"

Piri slapped away his finger. "And you'd complain too if those leprechauns over there looked like Betty Boop and Peter Pan."

She had a point. Those were very odd looking fairies,

although why Piri cared was beyond her. Kate fished a two euro coin out of her purse. "Thank you for the entertainment."

Piri turned to Kate. Her lips curved slowly into a scary smile. "Ah, it's the American. I might have known you'd find your way to Cluhalaugh. Where's that beautiful man you were traveling with. I've a yen to know him better."

"I've no idea." Kate walked away, her spine stiff. *What a horrible woman.*

She stopped in front of a mustard colored building with a huge mural. The building trim had red hearts and cupids running down it. Talk about overkill. The silver-haired man pictured on the mural looked like he ought to be the host of a talent show. All smiling and genial and totally false. Behind his head, two plump cupid angels sat on a cloud and made out. Red letters proclaimed *Some matches are made in heaven . . . But the best ones are made in Cluhalaugh. Most people meet in the Matchmaker Bar.*

Meet what? Their maker? Sheesh. If that Kenny Rogers wannabe was a matchmaker, she'd eat her notebook. Page by page. Her tiny secret hope of a magical matchmaker dissolved into I knew it couldn't be true ashes.

Kate stepped inside and looked around. The walls were salmon colored and full of framed pictures. A scarred wooden bar extended the length of one wall. Black and white checked linoleum covered the dance floor area. A live band played on the raised dais behind the dance floor. She couldn't identify the song, but she knew it was country western. So much for Irish music.

A few people sat on the faded red banquet to the side of the dance floor. One seemed to be working a crossword. The younger man sipped a beer from a tall glass and stared at the flat screen TV to the right of the band. A woman hung over him, but she looked bored to death. Kate couldn't figure out if they were early arrivals or left overs from the night before.

The band finished the song they'd been playing and struck up *Waltz Across Texas*.

Kate left and walked back to the square. Where was Michael? She checked her phone for a message. Nothing. She tapped out a quick text. **I'm at the Ritz on the square. Come find me**, and went to join Brad.

"Dig in," Brad said. "I ordered you the Full Irish."

The bacon and eggs and grilled mushrooms looked delicious, but . . . "What's this?" She pointed at the horrible looking black square of something which was definitely not a brownie.

"Blood pudding. Try it. It's an Irish delicacy."

Kate forked up the unwholesome-looking thing and put it on his plate. "Help yourself."

He dug into to it with evident enjoyment.

Kate averted her eyes. He probably liked snails too.

"I gather you didn't find Michael. Did you find the matchmaker?"

"He doesn't come in till six." She described the bar to Brad. "The whole thing's a horrible fraud. They're not even trying. How could a whole festival be built around such an obvious fake?"

Brad smiled. "It's not built around a person. It's built around hope, don't you think?"

"Huh?"

"Unlike you, most people want to believe there is an absolutely right person for them and that they have a hope of finding her or him. It's a lonely world out there, Kate. It's easier if you are holding someone's hand."

Kate's throat constricted. She wished she could believe. "Well, this whole setup is a trick. I bet the matchmaker charges a hefty fee."

Brad opened his mouth to speak. Then shut it. "What do you want to do now?"

"Explore the town I guess. The festival looks like a bust."

She hadn't really expected anything, had she? Why the letdown?

Kate pushed her plate away. She knew she was lying to herself. Inside must have been some kind of hope of something. After last night, she thought that she'd be sharing the fun of the festival with Michael. But no Michael. No matchmaker. And no fun.

She looked around the restaurant. The family from the bus was there. The mother spooned food into the baby's open mouth, ignoring the little girl's excited bouncing. Two older couples talked quietly. They looked neither happy or sad. They were just . . . there. Most of their patrons had their eyes glued to the flat screen TV.

Brad's eyes followed the TV too. "County Clare is in All Ireland Hurling Final. That's what all the bunting's for. Hurling's the national sport of Ireland. This match is a very big deal."

Was that where Michael was? Inside a bar with his eyes glued to a TV? "I don't want to interrupt your love affair with the television. I'll go look around by myself."

Brad tore his eyes away from the screen. "It's okay. The match hasn't started yet." He dropped some money on the table. "Come on. Let's explore."

The square was filling up with people. Country music blared from the Irish Arms Bar. A fortunetellers van had parked in front of the bar, and a long line snaked to one side waiting to avail themselves of her services.

The sun shone on the flowers and faces alike. The square's curving benches were crowded. Most of the men and quite a few of the women clutched long-necked bottles of beer.

"Look at those two." Brad motioned to a couple in their sixties who radiated contentment. "That's what they're all after. Come on, let's go talk to them."

Kate followed him, scanning the faces for a glimpse of Michael.

Brad sat down next to the older man. "You two don't look like you need the services of a matchmaker."

"We don't." The man twined his fingers with his wife's hand turning them to display matching gold bands carved with Celtic knots. "We've been married fifty years tomorrow. And you? Are you looking?"

Brad shook his head. "Fifty years. That's a marvel. You look like you've a happy marriage."

His wife's hair was gray, cut short in a wavy style. She wore no makeup and she didn't need it. She was lit from the inside. Kate couldn't resist the shine in the woman's eyes. "How did you meet?"

"We were matched by the matchmaker fifty years ago today."

"How lovely," Kate said, trying to project enthusiasm.

The woman's eyes twinkled. "Don't be fooled by the Matchmaker Bar and that gormless James O'Halloran. Jimmy's not a real matchmaker. He's set himself up as one for the tourist trade and it's a shame."

Hope flickered. "Was there another matchmaker?"

"Aye. The real one had a gift. She could see. But Essie moved to America a long time ago. Her cousin Iona became the next matchmaker. Iona matched our Jimmy and our Essie both." She held out her hand to Kate. "I'm Mary O'Mara and this is Daniel."

Daniel and Brad were talking up a storm. Kate sat down next to Mary. "Was it all happy?"

Mary shook her head. "We've has some fine stramashes and some fine making-up to follow. You can't always be agreeing with each other. But we've been happy enough to stay in love. We made three children together and they're all doing well."

Mary spoke of her children and Kate smiled and nodded in

the appropriate places. So there *had* been a real matchmaker here once.

"And we named our daughter in honor of Essie O'Callaghan. The finest matchmaker this town has ever known."

Michael's Essie? Wasn't her last name O'Callaghan? No. Not possible. "How did they do it in the old days? Did you come and register with her?"

"'Twas more of a ceremony." Mary's voice had a *Once Upon a Time* cadence. "At the four quarters of the seasons, seekers came to The Dancing Hart in hopes of finding the perfect mate. I came at the Summer Solstice. I was a bit skeptical, but my best friend dared me to go and I was never one to refuse a dare. The men lined up on one side of the room and the women on the other. Essie chanted something in a language I didn't under-stand and air filled with—"

"Magic?" Brad interrupted. His smile to Mary looked like he was sharing her memory. Kate's spine prickled.

"Aye. That's how it felt. Then Essie presented me to Daniel and told him to take me to the Ring. And I knew." The glance she gave her Daniel was like a kiss blown in the wind.

"I'd known him before, of course. We'd met and talked and I thought he was a fine young man. But so was Sean, the grocer and Peter, the clerk." Her eyes grew dreamy. "But this night when I looked at Daniel, I knew."

Daniel took her hand. "She glowed. There was a light around her and I knew this was the one for me. I'd only come as a joke. My mate Eric said he needed support. But when I stood in the ring, I saw Mary and only Mary."

Kate's heart twisted at the way they looked at each other in remembrance. She couldn't imagine such a thing for herself. She looked around at the few couples dancing in the square. They didn't look like they were in love. She smiled at Daniel and Mary. "I hope you have another fifty years of marriage."

Mary patted Kate's hand. "I wish the same for you. She pulled Kate's face to hers and whispered in her ear. "Go to the real matchmaker. If one is here, she'll be at the Dancing Hart. Take your young man and stand in the ring tonight."

"He's not my young man."

"Well then, who's to say there'll not be another standing there waiting for you?"

"Yeah," Brad said. "Who's to say?"

They said their goodbyes and strolled down the street. "Don't they make you believe in true love?"

Kate tried for a sniff, but her heart wasn't in it. "There's always the exception."

"You're a hard case, Kate Carnahan. Come on. Let's go find the Dancing Hart."

34

MICHAEL PUT AWAY HIS DEAD PHONE. WHY HADN'T HE WRITTEN Kate's number on a piece of paper instead of entrusting it to his contact list?

"Too bad you left your charger," Declan said. "Mine won't help you at all."

"Do you good to be without one," Catriona boomed. "There's too much cell phone these days. Young people always on the phone or the tablets, tapping away, never looking at each other. How can a body have a decent conversation?"

Michael surveyed the group sitting around the farmhouse dining table. Essie's younger brother, Sean, was regaling Maire and Shauna with the doings of the local priest.

Cousin Padraic hadn't taken his eyes off Essie since they sat down to breakfast. He looked like a mastiff guarding a beloved toy.

Two of Sean and Catriona's children, Moira, and Danny, engaged in a lively argument with Brenna about the latest pop band. Thea, their youngest watched Padraic and Essie with thoughtful eyes.

Essie rose from her place and took Thea by the hand. "We're off now. We have things to do before the night."

Sean nodded. "I always thought it would be Thea," He leaned across the table to Michael. "You can see the look in their eyes, you know. It was the same with Essie when she was young. Fairy touched, both of them. It will be a grand time tonight."

Michael smiled. "I think I'll leave you and have a look around the town."

"There's not much to see." Moira lifted her heavily pierced eyebrows. "A few streets and a river."

"That's why they all leave," Catriona said. "Nothing for them here. The matchmaking festival attracts a crowd, but there's no work. The only reason Danny stays is because of the farm. But if he wants company, he's got to drive to Inchmore or Galway. We're hoping tonight he'll find the other half of his heart. Moira, now. She's no interest in courting. She thinks of nothing but her band."

Moira looked up. "Wait till we're on *Ireland's Got Talent*. Then we'll go to America with a record contract." She studied Michael. "You're from California. Do you know any record producers?"

Michael knew that look. He'd seen cats look at mice in just the same way. "Sorry. I don't know anything about modern music. My mother tells me I have a tin ear."

Moira immediately lost all interest in him and turned back to Brenna.

Michael strode down the farmhouse driveway toward the main road. The driveway forked next to a grass bordered brook. One path led across a small arched bridge to a white building with diamond paned windows and a peaked roof. Red wooden shields hung above each window. He could just make out the golden figure embossed on each one. A deer on his hind legs, forefeet lifted. Ivy climbed over a signpost near the red front door. A row of trees lined a dirt path to the main street.

It looked like someone's dream of a pub. Kate would love it. Where was she?

He walked down the main street looking in the Rathbone Hotel and the Matchmaker Bar.. He searched for her bright head in the crowd around the fortune teller's van. No Kate.

Maybe they stopped for something to eat? Michael walked through the Ritz and the other two buildings surrounding the square. Still no Kate. "Ridiculous. I bump into her all over Ireland and in this town with one main street, she's invisible?"

Maybe her bus hadn't gotten here yet. He turned the corner past the Spar market and stopped at the huge red Bus Eireann sign. The schedule showed the bus from Galway arrived an hour ago. Maybe she'd missed it.

Michael thrust his fists in his pockets and stared unseeingly at the church. He wouldn't believe she wasn't coming.

"She's got to be here." He turned and went back up the street. Cluhalaugh was laid out like a Halloween tree with a wide center street and a few, a very few forked branches. He followed each fork. No Kate.

The main street was now crowded with people trying to get into the hotels. Women in tight spandex tops and short fluffy net skirts stood outside Matchmaker Bar, smoking cigarettes, clutching their drinks of choice. They eyed the passing men like owls looking for prey.

The sound of Garth Brooks blasted from the main square.

Someone tapped him on the shoulder. He turned and looked into Declan's grinning face. "You'll no find anyone in this crowd. Come on over to the Rathbone. The match starting in a couple of minutes. I'll buy you a draft."

"I need to look for Kate. We were supposed to meet."

"If it's supposed to be, she'll find you. In the meantime there's a grand match on the telly. Come on."

He followed Declan reluctantly. He'd searched the whole

blasted town. Disappointment felt like a lead weight in his stomach. She had to have missed the bus. Where was she?

35

"Now there's a place that looks like magic should happen," Kate said.

"Really?" Brad's eyes invited her to share his amusement.

"If magic existed," Kate qualified, "which it doesn't." She leaned on the bridge studying the red trimmed square white building at the bottom of the hill. "It looks like a doll house that got into an enlarging machine. I wonder what its story is?"

A woman with short cropped white hair stopped next to them. "Beautiful, isn't it?"

Kate smiled back at her, admiring the woman's purple sweater knitted in a complicated pattern. What looked like Celtic runes bordered the collar.

"There's more magic down there than in all the rest of Ireland put together." The woman lit a cigarette. "Are ye here for the matchmaking then?"

"I read about it and I wanted to see what it looked like. I'm not here to be matched," Kate qualified. "I'm a writer."

The woman nodded. "A writer are ye? Well, write about that Jimmy O'Halloran then. He's a scandal and a disgrace. Setting himself up and pretending he's a matchmaker."

A woman after her own heart. "Did he try to match you?"

"No. The real matchmaker, Essie O'Callaghan matched me many years ago and a darlin' man he was. He's gone now, rest his heart."

"Don't you want to try again?"

"And if I did, which I wouldn't, where would I go? To the fool of a Jimmy?" The woman sucked in a drag of smoke. "Me best friend was a nurse in London. She wanted to find a good Irish husband and move back here. I warned her, but she paid Jimmy sixty quid. And he introduced her to an eighty-year-old man from Texas." Her expression invited Kate to share her outrage.

Kate nodded her sympathy. "I saw his picture on a poster. He doesn't look like the kind of man you'd want to trust with your future. "

"No indeed. Mind you, if I were in the market for a husband, I'd be down there." She pointed at the giant doll house.

"It looks like a private residence."

"See the shields over the window? That's the Dancing Hart. It's only open for special occasions. For a sing or a ceremony. You're here on a special day. Tonight there be a grand sing in honor of the Autumn Equinox."

"Real Irish music?" Kate asked. "We've stopped at every pub in town and all the music is country western."

"Ah well, it attracts the tourists and it's fine music to dance to." The woman nodded her head toward the building. "They open at five down there. You should go."

"Thank you."

"American are you?" She turned to Brad. "You've the look of Ireland in your face. Who are your people?"

Brad's eyes crinkled at the corners. "I don't know. I was adopted."

The woman eyed him narrowly. "I'll be guessing who your

people are. They don't often give up one of their own. You'll be there tonight." She turned and abruptly walked away.

Kate studied Brad's face. "Do you know what she was talking about? About your people?"

"I know. It's not important." He grabbed her hand. "Come on. Let's get back to the pubs. I want to dance."

Brad's ears were a bit pointed. Why hadn't she noticed before? The penny dropped. "She's saying you're related to a leprechaun. That's derogatory. Just because you are short and have red hair and pointy ears."

He touched the top of his ear. "They do seem a bit pointier than usual. Tends to happen around the Equinox. Kate, the only thing that matters about who or what I am, is I'm your friend. I'd never do anything to hurt you. You believe that, don't you?"

Kate felt her sense of reality tilt. "There is no such thing as a leprechaun," she choked out. "So you can't be one."

"Good," Brad said. "All sorted out. I need a drink. Let's go find some Kenny Rogers. I wonder if you can do a reel to Kenny Rogers?"

36

MICHAEL DRAINED HIS GLASS. HE COULDN'T KEEP HIS MIND ON the Hurling match. "I'm going to walk around again. See if I can spot her."

Declan nodded. "You do that." He added his voice to the roar of disapproval echoing round the bar.

Michael eased around the engrossed watchers. The door opened, nearly hitting him in the nose. Brad walked in.

"Sorry," Brad said. "Oh, there you are. Kate's been looking for you."

The lead weight in Michael's stomach vanished. "Where is she?"

Brad shrugged. "Don't know. I got waylaid by a gaggle of women in puffy skirts and high heeled boots. They wanted to buy me a drink. I ducked in here to escape. Bunch of harpies, that lot. Kate ran."

"Did you see which way she went?"

"To the square, I think."

Another roar went up from the crowd. Brad turned to the TV. "If you see Kate, tell her to meet me back here." He shouldered his way to the bar, eyes glued to the screen.

Michael strode through the crowd in the square. He found her watching two children playing hide and seek around the fiddler statue. He turned her into his arms. "Kate."

* * *

Kate's world righted. "I couldn't find you." She reached up and brought his head down to hers. The shouts of the children were a faraway echo. The world narrowed to the warmth of his lips and the beating of his heart.

They broke for air. The strains of The Tennessee Waltz blared out from the loudspeakers of the Irish Arms pub. Michael took her hand, resting his other hand on the small of her back. They revolved slowly to the music, never taking their eyes off each other.

"I tried to call you, but my phone died and no one had a charger I could use. I looked in every pub. I've been to the square twice."

"Me too." It felt so good to be held in his arms. She rested her head on his shoulder, rubbing her cheek against his jacket's warmth. "I thought Fate was finished with us."

The music changed to something loud and obnoxious. Michael stopped dancing. "Let's get out of here. I want to show you something."

Kate left her hand in his. They strolled past The Match-maker Bar. The harpies were in full glare. Kate smiled at them dreamily. A roar went up from every bar on the street.

"Our side must be winning." Michael pointed at the Rath-bone Hotel. "Brad said to meet him there. I think he'll be fully occupied for the next couple of hours."

The sounds of voices faded to bird song and a rustle of leaves. Michael stopped before the bridge and led her down the path to the Dancing Hart.

Kate pulled back. "We're trespassing, I think."

"It's okay. It belongs to Essie's brother, Sean." Michael pointed at the huge white house beyond the red trimmed building. "Surprised the heck out of me when we drove up. He's got a farm beyond the house."

Kate looked at the huge house. "It's almost a mansion. What's he farming? Gold?"

"Cattle, maybe. I don't know. Maybe he's got a private leprechaun with a never-empty pot."

Kate peered into the window of the pub. The lathe and plaster walls were studded by wooden beams blackened by years of wood smoke. A huge stone fireplace filled one end of the room.

Michael gave a low whistle. "Big enough to roast a cow."

Kate swung round, her eyes wide. Her beautiful cows? "They don't do that do they? Cow roasts aren't part of the festival?"

"I doubt it." Michael ran his fingers through her hair. "These cows are cherished for their butter and cream."

"Oh." Kate leaned back against his hand, trying not to purr. "That's good. Let's go round to the other side."

The other end of the room held a heavily carved, dark wood bar. Rays of sunlight winked off the glasses hung above it. A few chairs and tables were scattered in front of a raised dais. Kate drew back hastily. "There's someone in there."

Michael put his nose to the window. "Essie and Thea. Thea is Essie's niece." Michael's eyes crinkled. "It seems she may have the gift."

"The gift of what?" she asked. More to hear Michael's voice than any curiosity about the answer.

"Matchmaking. Seeing. Essie's come to train her."

So Essie *was* the matchmaker Mary and Daniel had been talking about. A shaft of sunlight haloed Michael's head. She let her hand follow the sunlight. His hair wrapped around her fingers. Soft. Warm. It would be so easy to be lured into the promise of believing. "What are they doing?"

"Probably a simple witch's spell to set the stage for tonight's festivities. Do you know your eyes are sea-siren green?"

Kate stepped back. "Witch's spell?"

"Relax, I'm joking. Want to meet them?"

Kate shook her head.

"Come on. They aren't witches. You've met Essie. Does she look like a witch? And if she is?" Smiling, he quoted, "'*There are good witches and bad witches. I am a good witch.*'"

Kate took one more look inside and saw Essie hold out a hand to Thea. A blue light flashed between them. Someone or something moved in the shadows. Her skin prickled. "I don't think we should go in. Let's leave them alone."

"You're right. Let's follow the stream."

37

BRAD SIPPED HIS BEER. WHEN ESSIE SAW HIM SLIP IN FROM THE Fae door, she'd said nothing. She probably didn't want to make her protégé nervous. The darkened pub smelled of sage and whatever other herbs Essie and her pupil used to cleanse the place. The flames from the candles they'd set around their circle burned straight and true.

Essie joined hands with the girl and began to chant. Some of the words were familiar to him but they were set in a magical working he didn't recognize. "*Ó mé a thabhairt duit, ó tú dom. Mar Beidh mé, mar sin Mote dó a bheith.*"

A blue light sprung up around their joined hands. Together they chanted, "From I to you, From you to me. As I will, so mote it be."

Brad looked with interest at Essie's companion. Slender, long unbound wheat colored hair. And that dreaming look in her eyes? She was fairy-touched all right.

He waited for them to finish before stepping out of the shadows. "A fine day to you both and the luck of the Solstice."

Her companion stifled a scream. Essie frowned at him. "If I hadn't known you were here, you'd have scared years off my life. And I haven't many to lose. Thea, this is the culprit who summoned me home, Bradley Flynn. Bradley, this is my niece, Thea O'Callaghan, the new Lady of Cluhalaugh. Bradley belongs to both worlds."

Brad bowed to Thea. "And pleased I am to meet you. Have you been to the hill yet?

Thea blushed scarlet.

"I take it you have. You needn't be afraid. You are their Lady as well as the human's Lady. As it happens, I know at least two will show up tonight."

Essie's eyes twinkled. "Have you been matchmaking then, Brad? You know you should leave that to the professionals."

"I have every intention of doing so. My mission was to get them here in the first place. Cast your mind back to your own time in the Hill. "Do you remember meeting my two friends?"

Essie gazed inward. "I do. A boy who was my age. A little taller than you. He didn't say much. It seemed to me he never took his eyes off the young girl. I thought then they would be a good match. Did they marry?"

"No."

"What a pity. They would have made beautiful children."

"And therein lies the problem. Piri is ashamed of her human half and doesn't want to pass those genes on to a next generation. Eamon feels a stranger in both of the worlds. Neither of them believes there is a match for them."

Essie chuckled. "And that's what you've been up to. Persuading the two of them to come tonight?"

Thea looked nervous. "I thought my first time would be only humans. It would be a terrible thing to make a mistake with those who would be matched for centuries."

"It would indeed," Essie said. "Tonight, you and I will both look. But I know you'll do fine." She reached out her hand to Thea. "You were born for this, *mo chroi.*

Brad could see the faint blue light shimmer between them.

Also the love. Why had she never had children of her own? Was that the price of her gift? "You should have grandchildren to spoil, Essie."

"Aunt Essie has a suitor who would gladly gift her with his." Thea's smile held a touch of mischief. "He had five children and they've done well by him in that department."

"Ah, no. I'm too old for all of that." When Essie turned away, a shaft of sunlight highlighted the red color flooding her cheeks.

"No one's too old for love." Thea's eyes had a distant look. "You have many years ahead of you."

Essie picked up the bundle of fresh herbs and flowers from the counter. "I'll get started on the wreaths."

Brad watched as Essie deftly twisted together sprigs of rosemary, bay laurel, and a stem with star shaped leaves and tiny flowers he didn't't recognize. "What's that one then?"

Essie bound her handiwork with green ribbons. "Ladies Mantle. It strengthens all the magic of the other herbs. Bay Laurel for seeing and Rosemary for love and protection, and of course, clover. The red, the four leafed and the two leafed kind."

Brad winced at the mention of clover. "Don't make any wishes. Please."

"And how are Kate and my Michael getting along?" Essie asked.

Brad felt the rise of temper. "She wished for a hero and now she says she doesn't believe in true love. She says she only wanted a hero for her book."

"But that can't be true," Thea said. "A clover only answers a heart wish."

"I told her that, but she doesn't believe me. A very contradictory woman is my Kate."

Essie looked up. "*Your* Kate?"

Brad retreated. "A figure of speech only. I'd better be off to find Eamon and Piri. I don't want them to kill each other before the choosing."

Essie looked at him sternly. "Bradley Flynn, you will stand in the line tonight. I must see her choices."

"I know." He turned to Thea. "I don't suppose you could give me a charm that would keep me from being chosen?"

Thea shook her head.

"I was afraid you'd say that. I'll see you both tonight."

38

Kate and Michael followed the path bordering the stream. It wound back toward the Dancing Hart through a stand of trees and ended in fairyland.

A glade carpeted in velvety grass starred with tiny white flowers. The shafts of sunlight slanting in through the trees lit the air with gold dust. A butterfly rose up from a bush of pink flowers and spiraled through the sunlight past the trees. An unseen bird filled the air with liquid notes.

The largest hare Kate had ever seen poked its head out from under a bush of white flowers. It looked in their direction; turned around and fled. "This is a scene from a Disney movie," Kate joked. "We'd better leave before we get transformed into cartoon characters."

Michael picked her up effortlessly, and carried her to the center of the glade. "The only magic I want is you." He feathered a kiss across her lips.

She closed her eyes and let the butterfly kisses steal across her senses.

He stood her on her feet. She put her arms around him to steady herself.

"Look at me, Kate. I want to see you when I kiss you."

She opened her eyes and tilted her mouth to fit against his lips. The kiss felt like a covenant. His eyes, a solemn oath. If she could believe in magic, then this was it.

She freed her lips, but not her hands. His warm strong grasp steadied her. "Do you believe in magic, Michael?"

"Of course. Look at us."

Kate shivered and pulled away. "It's too easy, Michael." She wrapped her arms around herself for protection. "Love's a word that's used too easily. I could say it. You could say it. People say it all the time."

"I love you, Kate."

"There, you said it. Don't, please." She looked at him, willing him to understand. "Don't love me. Let's just say we're in lust. Isn't that easier to deal with?"

Michael shook his head. "I love you, Kate. You are the one I've been looking for my whole life."

His face was full of such trust. How could he do that? How could a sane, rational, perfectly glorious man not see the pitfalls in front of him? "If you say 'you complete me', I'm going to brain you."

"You're like the rabbit we saw. Ready to run." Michael held out his hand to her cautiously, as if she were said rabbit. "Why don't you believe I love you?"

"If you do, you're making a mistake." Why couldn't he take what she was offering? No ties. No strings. Wasn't that every man's dream? "Michael. I don't have the happy-ever-after gene. I've seen too many marriages go to hell to believe I can make one work."

He separated her fingers, kissing away the tension in them. "Do you love me?"

How could she think when he was doing that? "You're missing the point. Yes, I love you."

She had not just said it out loud. It was so much safer when the words were inside where she couldn't see them. Panic raced her heart. "But it won't last. Love doesn't last, Michael." She withdrew her hand. "I should go find Brad." She couldn't trust herself not to cry if she opened her mouth again. She wanted to believe. She wanted this man more than she'd wanted anything in her whole life, but saying yes felt like jumping out of a plane without a parachute.

Michael took a deep breath. "I'm sorry. I'm pushing, I know it. My mother always said I was the impatient one. Take your time, Kate. Take all the time you want."

They walked out through the trees. The air was cooler. Clouds drifted in.

"It looks like rain," Kate offered lamely.

Michael put his arm around her shoulder. "I'm trying for brotherly, Kate, but I'm not sure how long I can keep it up. Come on. I'll buy you lunch. You can tell me three things I should know about you and I'll tell you mine."

"You first." Kate leaned into his embrace in a way which wasn't sisterly at all. He didn't seem to mind.

BRAD WATCHED them walk up the path toward the main road. If Kate thought Michael was simply in lust with her, she'd badly misread the situation.

He turned back to the ring. A large white hare peeked out from a clump of ferns, whiskers twitching. "Change back, Piri," Brad said. "I know it's you."

The rabbit poofed back into a frowning Piri. "What does he see in her? Clumsy clod of a human. I wanted to play with him."

"I think she's quite attractive," said a voice from behind the giant oak."

Eamon. Lurking. Well at least he had them both in the same place. "Show yourself, Eamon."

Eamon stepped into the clearing. "I was having a wee gander at the woman," he said sheepishly. "I think she'll make a fine wife."

Piri looked at Eamon in shock. "You're going to wed a human?"

"Why would you care?" Eamon glared at Piri. "You've made it plain what you think of me."

A world of hurt flashed across Piri's face. Her fists clenched. "You great *clod*. I came to Dublin to work for you, didn't I? And all you did was make fun of everything I suggested."

"You didn't see my dream," he shouted back.

"You ignored mine." A swarm of butterflies attacked Eamon, beating at his face with their wings.

"Stop it, Piri" Brad said sharply. "This is a bad place to have an argument. Come away, both of you. I'll treat you both to a pint."

Eamon and Piri turned on Brad. "You stay out of this," they said in unison.

Brad held up his hands in surrender. "You're going to attract attention you don't want. The last thing you want is . . ." Brad's phone blared *The Wearing of the Green.*

McPhee's face materialized. "Someone's using magic in the ring. If it's you, you're going to be here for a very long time."

Piri stepped away from Brad, her eyes begging him not to tell.

Eamon expelled a breath, straightened his shoulders and took the phone from Brad. "T'was me, sir. I was playing a prank on Pirikit Mac Cionaoith."

The McPhee's voice went from ground glass to sweet whiskey. He'd always had a soft spot for Eamon. "Aren't you a bit old to be pranking a woman to get her attention? You've been nutty on Pirikit since you were a wee lad. Why don't you stop larking about and ask her to wed?"

Eamon mumbled something into the phone and handed it back to Brad. He looked everywhere but in Piri's direction. "You're safe now. Go chase your American."

"What did you say, to him?" Piri asked, all animosity gone from her voice

"I said you wouldn't have me." Eamon turned to go.

Piri caught his hand and spun him around to face her. "Did it ever occur to you that you might do well to *ask* what I want instead of assuming you know it all, you grand gobshite?" She stomped up the path without a backward look.

"Daft contrary woman," Eamon shouted after her. He turned to Brad. "What did she mean by that? I saved her from the McPhee. What did I do wrong now?"

Brad enunciated each word very clearly. "She wants you to ask her to marry you."

"Why? So she can beat me with a stick of my own making? I've a little pride left, thank you."

Brad looked at his cousin standing with shoulders stiff, mouth set in a stubborn line, his eyes a misery of longing. "You really *are* a great clod. You need a course in courting. Lesson one. Never assume you know what a woman's thinking. You're bound to be wrong. Do you love her?"

"I've always loved her," Eamon muttered.

"Then tell her. Lesson two. Women need to hear the words. Words are their treasure."

Eamon shook his head. "I'll wait for the choosing tonight. If the lady says we're a match, then I'll have her."

Lovers. Idjits, all of them. "No. You won't. Because Piri will never be sure you loved her enough to ask her without the Lady's seal of approval." He gave Eamon an affectionate shove. "Go ahead. I dare you to ask her now. What have you got to lose but pride? Pride's a mighty cold bedfellow."

Eamon rubbed his shoulder. "I'm going. But only because I've never backed down from a dare." He walked up the path Piri had taken.

"Open your heart to her, Eamon. Give her the words."

Eamon didn't look back. "And if she rips it out of my body, it's on your head."

The glade was still. Brad looked around. He'd done what he could. Tonight between the hour when sunlight left and moonlight took its place, the glade would fill with magic. And the Fae from the hill would let themselves be seen by the Lady's chosen ones.

There was time for a pint or two before the ceremony. He could use one to settle his nerves. Surely the Lady would match Kate and Michael? He wasn't ready to choose. His heart belonged in New York.

* * *

Eamon caught up with Pirikit at the bridge. Pebbles flew up beside her and flung themselves into the stream. "Don't you ever think?" he grumbled, "you're still too close to the glade. Do you want the McPhee down on us?"

The rain of pebbles stopped. Piri stomped away, her back stiff with that damnable pride of hers.

And who was he to talk? How many years had he gone alone because he was afraid to speak? Their pride was well matched.

He followed her down the road. He cleared his throat willing her to turn around. She didn't. Step, step, step, away from him. "I'm sorry."

She stopped and turned to him. "What did you say?"

"I said I'm sorry, dammit. Isn't that enough?"

Piri looked at him as if he were a toad in the road. "No." She turned and stomped on.

Brad's admonition echoed in his head. *Give her the words.* Have some courage, man. Eamon took a deep breath. "I love you." The words almost sounded like a croak. Had she bewitched him?

Piri turned around slowly. "What did you say?"

He cleared his throat. This time the words came out stronger. "I love you, Pirikit Mac Cionaoith."

She folded her arms. "Well, you've a fine way of showing it." But her tone didn't match her words. It was almost soft.

He stopped in front of her. "Words don't come easy for me, but I am trying. I have loved you as long as I can remember in spite of your crossed grained ways and your terrible temper."

He knew immediately he'd said the wrong thing by the spark in her eye.

She opened her mouth to speak. He blocked her by pressing his lips to hers. He let the love and longing he'd always kept in check flow from his breath to hers.

Piri's lips softened. Her arms stole around his neck, pulling them closer together.

Here was magic. He let the wonder of it flow through him. Above them a lark sang in the branches of the alder tree.

He broke the kiss. "I have more words for you. To me you are more beautiful than a sunset, more necessary than salt. I would promise to care for you all of my days if you will have me. I can think of no greater joy than having you to wife."

"What about my terrible temper and cross grained ways?"

Eamon shrugged, empowered by the fact that she hadn't said no. "I'm thinking we're a match in that. We might have a few bitty stramashes. But the making up would be grand."

Piri's eyes lit with humor. "Bitty indeed. What are a few thrown objects between friends?"

"Between lovers," Eamon corrected. "Will you have me then?"

Piri's hands dropped to her side. "And what of children? Would you be wanting them?"

Eamon knew her thought because he shared it. What if they produced a child more human than Fae? Could they come to terms with the possibility? "I believe that whatever we make together will be a blessing in our lives."

"I want to believe that. But what if we're wrong? I don't want for our child the kind of pain I suffered."

Eamon cursed the human father who caused Piri to feel less than she was. "Our child will have both parents. And I believe we will find the wisdom to raise her better that you were raised?"

"*Her*?" She fisted her hands on her hips, argument written all over her. "And what if it's a *him*? A great giant *him* taller than both of us put together?"

Eamon kissed her again. She opened her mouth to his. Heat rose through his body. He had to have her. "Come with me," he said hoarsely.

Piri caressed his cheek. "Aye. It's time we were together. But as to marriage? We'll let the Lady decide."

39

Kate and Michael had tea and apple tart with cream in a windowed porch at Nellie's Bar. She told him about Eric and the perils of using an ex-boyfriend as a role model for a protagonist. He told her about growing up in Hollywood and the perils of being a single doctor.

They talked of books and ideals and the crazy things they'd done as teenagers. Every story, every piece of her life she gave up to him was a tribute, binding her closer to his soul. Every story he gave her was a gift.

Kate could feel her resolution weaken. She had to be strong. For both of them. "This can't work you know. I live in New York. You live in California. Too long a commute."

Michael's lazy smile did unlawful things to her innards. "I know how to get to New York." In a perfect imitation of Bill Hader on the *Saturday Night Live, Californians* skit he drawled. "You take the I-5 to the I-405 to the I-10 and you get off at the Lincoln Tunnel."

Kate fought to keep her face straight. She couldn't do Kirsten Wig, but her Captain Kirk wasn't bad. "Or you could invent a matter transporter? Beam me to California, Scotty."

"Not my forte. I think we should take the easier route. Like a plane."

The sound of cheering erupted in the streets. Horns honked. Passers-by waved yellow and blue checked flags.

"Looks like County Clare won the match." Michael glanced at his watch. "I told Ness I'd be there by five-thirty. The moon rises early tonight. You'll come." He said it as a statement, but there was a question in his eyes.

"Yes." She didn't want to let this time go.

Michael read her mind. "This is just the beginning, Kate. We're going to have lots more time."

Kate winced. She wished she could believe it. "I'm only coming to watch, mind you."

They wandered back through the crowds like fish swimming upstream. Michael's hand in hers felt like a lifeline.

Brad caught up with them in front of the Matchmaker Bar. "Ah, Michael, don't you look like the cat who's gotten the cream." He turned to Kate. "How are you, kitten?"

"Don't call me that." Kate pulled away and stalked ahead of them.

Brad looked sympathetic. "Tough sailing?"

Michael's eyes followed Kate. "She'll come round. She has to."

"She came here for you," Brad said. "She doesn't know that. But she did."

"What are you talking about?"

"Nothing at all, dear boy. We'd better be on our way. The moon is rising."

They caught up with Kate. Michael and Brad both slipped an arm inside hers.

She looked from one to the other and slid out of their grasp. "I'll go quietly, gentlemen. Please don't shoot."

By the time they reached the bridge, the sun was setting in

great sheets of orange and red. The lilting sound of a fiddle and the ripple of a penny flute wafted up to them.

"Finally! Irish music." Kate almost ran down the hill.

The burly figure at the door barred her way. "I'm sorry, ma'am, this is a private event."

Michael caught up to Kate. "It's all right, Sean, She's with me. Kate, this is Sean O'Callaghan, Essie's brother. Sean, this is my friend Kate."

Sean eyed Brad narrowly. "And who's this? Will you be speaking for him?"

"I will." Essie stood in the doorway. She was a tiny regal creature in her green flowing-sleeved gown. "I know him. He has the right to be here."

Sean stepped aside. "A grand celebration to you all."

The room smelled of sage and other herbs Kate couldn't put a name to. It was crowded with people. The chairs she'd seen through the window had been put away. Rough wooden benches lined two sides of the room.

Essie joined hands with a lovely young woman dressed in a green gown like her own.

"That's Thea," Michael whispered. "Essie's niece."

With their unbound hair encircled with flowers, they looked like medieval high priestesses. There was something in their expressions which shivered Kate. Here was power. She could feel it. So could everyone else. Despite the number of people, there was silence except for the music. The hearth fire danced, shooting dragon lengths of flames up the chimney.

Essie and Thea crossed to Kate. "Have ye come to be mated?"

Kate stepped back. "I came for the music." The tune changed to a slow haunting tune which felt like a drug to her senses.

Michael's hand squeezed hers. "Please, Kate. Give it a chance."

The music circled and danced around his words, impelling her to believe in the power she felt swirling around her. But she couldn't. Kate started to shake her head, and found herself nodding agreement instead.

Brad patted her arm. "At last, you're showing some sense. We'll let the matchmaker decide it."

"What's wrong with you?" Kate whispered. "You're wearing the guillotine look again?"

"With any luck, nothing at all. Look inside your heart, Kate. You can't be matched against your will."

Thea spoke. "If you're matched, you must promise to be true to one another always, for you've been given a gift and it's a mortal sin to waste it."

Heads bobbed yes all around her, so she bobbed hers.

"Women to the left. Men to the right," Essie commanded. "Be seated."

They formed two lines like a giant reel, marched to the benches and sat.

Essie walked down the row of women, looking into each one's eyes. To each one she said, "Your true mate is in this room, but he may not be the one you came with. Are you willing to be shown?"

Thea did the same for the men.

Kate wanted to get up and run. She looked across to the line of men. What on earth was Brad doing in the line? Surely he wasn't planning to be matched. She turned back to Essie, but Essie had moved on.

The door banged open. Two figures stood silhouetted against the sunset sky. The woman spoke. "We've come to see the Lady, as is our right." The music stopped.

Kate recognized the voice. Brad's cousin Piri. The firelight flared up. She was hand in hand with the man who played the magical fiddle.

Essie beckoned them in. "You are most welcome. I

remember you both. We are blessed that you have come on my last night of choosing and the first night of our new Lady. We will look together for you." She held out her hand to Piri.

"No. I will not sit. Look now. Do we belong together?"

Thea stepped forward and curtsied. "I am the new Lady. Will you honor me with your names?"

"Pirikit Mac Cionaoith and Eamon Ó Baird." The man put his arm around Pirikit. Piri jerked away. "And she will not have me until you tell us yea."

Kate looked across at Brad. He was grinning from ear to ear.

Thea joined hands with Essie. She offered her free hand to Piri.

Piri took it. "Go ahead and look." Her voice vibrated like a too tight fiddle string.

Essie offered her free hand to Eamon.

Thea closed her eyes, whispering a sigh of words under her breath. Her eyes blinked open. "Why have you waited so long to claim what has always been yours?"

Essie joined Piri's and Eamon's hands. "Your fates are twined together. And your children will be a beannú to Ireland."

"Children?" Piri sounded terrified.

Kate winced in sympathy. The thought of bringing children with her genes into the world made her shiver.

Eamon raised Piri's hand to his lips. "Hush, *machushla*. We won't have children if you are unwilling. You are more important to me than anything the fates decree." He looked toward the men's bench. "Cousin, thank you for the dare. I'll tell the McPhee t'was your doing. No doubt we will be seeing you later, matched or unmatched."

Kate watched them bow to Thea and Essie, who waved them out a door she hadn't seen before.

The woman sitting next to her leaned over and whispered.

"Fae born. Both of them. And the Ladies matched them. Tis a lucky night."

Thea beckoned to the girl sitting to Kate's left. "Karin Hanrahan, come forward."

The girl jumped up, eyes wide, whispering something under her breath. A prayer, probably.

Essie walked her to the men's bench and stopped in front of a man with hands too large for his body. He stood up almost knocking himself over in the process. "David O'Shea, take Karin Hanrahan and walk her to the ring. She is your true future."

David looked like he'd just been given the world. He held out his hand. Karin took it and, as they turned to go out, Kate could see the wonder on her face.

Kate turned to the woman who'd whispered to her. "Did they know each other before tonight?"

"Karin and David have been walking out for a year now, but she wanted the matchmaker's blessing before she said yes. Her sister eloped and it turned out very badly." The woman's hands were clasped together so hard her knuckles were white. "You want to be sure in a thing like this."

"But there no guarantees for marriage," Kate protested.

The woman turned incredulous eyes on her. "Of course, there are. Why do you think we're here?"

The next girl rose happily and almost dragged Essie with her to a tall man with close-cropped brown hair.

He sprang up, ready to be presented.

Essie shook her head and moved further down the line. "Colum Trachie, Take Deidre O'Connor and walk her to the ring."

Colum's face lit up. Deirdre looked shell-shocked, but she took his arm.

Kate wanted to run for the door. What if Essie presented her to a stranger? No way was she going to trust her life to an

Irish superstition. She started to rise and felt an arrow of heat in her mind. *Trust. Believe.*

She sank back down and stared straight ahead. Why had she said yes, when Essie asked for her consent? Her heart pounded so loud it competed with the music. She struggled to take a calming breath.

Couple after couple were matched. Essie offered her hand to the girl Michael had been with at the fish and chips shop in Galway. Even made-up to the nines, she didn't look more than eighteen. "Brenna O'Callaghan, are you ready to be promised?"

Brenna jumped up. "I am." Under the false eyelashes, Kate saw eyes filled with hope and trepidation.

Essie walked her to the man with the close-cropped brown hair. The one the girl called Diedre had thought to be matched to.

"Quinn Riley. Brenna O'Callaghan. You loved each other as children and allowed yourself to forget. Remember now." Essie joined their hands.

The benches on either side of her were empty. On the men's' side were three men left. Michael, Brad, and an elderly man who had to be in his seventies. He looked strong and fit despite the white hair. He never took his eyes off Essie.

Essie took Kate's arm. "You'll be my last match. And the best of them, I think."

The other side of the room felt a mile away. She couldn't go through with this. What if Essie presented her to . . . Essie stopped at Brad. *No.*

Michael was half out of his seat. Brad rose and bowed to Essie.

"Bradley Flynn, son of the Omaeara, thank you for bringing her. Your work is done and you are free."

Brad stepped up to Kate and kissed her. "Be happy, Katherine." His skin shone with a golden light. "Time to believe, Kate. You've been a grand companion." He walked away and disappeared in thin air. No one else seemed to notice.

Essie walked Kate to Michael who looked as stunned as she felt.

"Michael Walshe, will you take Kate Carnahan and walk her to the ring?"

Michael took Kate's hand. "With all my heart."

"My turn." Thea took Essie's hand and led her to the older man. "Padraic Ferguson, will you walk Aisling O'Callaghan O'Brian to the ring?"

Padraic stood up so fast he almost knocked the bench over. "Essie, are you willing to take a second chance with me?"

Essie put her hand in his. "I trust the matchmaker." She smiled at Thea. "I know she has the true sight. I'll walk with you, Padraic Ferguson and feel blessed to find you."

Kate and Michael followed Essie and Padraic over the bridge.

Kate gripped his warm hand, her only anchor to reality. "Brad—"

"Disappeared. I know. I saw it."

"Nobody else did."

"Essie did. I think Thea did too." Michael grinned. "Essie called him a leprechaun at the airport. I thought she had gone a tad mental from being back on the old sod."

"He's CEO of a public relations company. How can he possibly be a . . ."

Michael's fingers tightened around hers. "Look around," he whispered. "What do you see?

In moonlight, the glade was the heart of fairyland. Creatures of wing and light landed in the trees. A band of small men in green caps played reed flutes and wind harps, weaving wild, achingly sweet tunes.

The music picked up tempo. Couples around them whirled

and stomped. Essie danced hand in hand with her Padraic. Lightly. Agelessly.

Kate caught a glimpse of Piri and Eamon spiraling above the ground. "Put us down, you daft woman," Eamon bellowed.

Piri's laughter sounded like wind chime crystals. They disappeared through a door made of light.

Here was true magic. The kind she'd always wanted to believe in. And if magic was real, then . . . She wound her arms around Michael's neck. "I surrender. I'm ready to take a chance on happy-ever-after."

Michael grinned down at her. "Oh, my love, if you could see your face. You look torn between trust and terror." He smoothed away the tension she felt between her eyebrows. "Don't worry. We were meant to walk through life together. The matchmaker and the leprechaun guarantee it."

The compelling tune intensified. He encircled her waist and offered his other hand. "Shall we join the dance?"

Kate felt a weight she hadn't been aware of carrying drift upward, toward the door of light. *You don't need that anymore, love.* The voiceless whisper sounded like Brad. A joyful certainty filled her. *Of course there is a happy ever after. The matchmaker guaranteed it.* She placed her hand in Michael's. "We shall."

40

CRESSIDA GAZED OUT THE TOWER WINDOW DOWN ON GREEN FIELDS *illumined with the gold of a perfect sunrise. Long tapered fingers encircled her waist. She leaned back against her lover, marveling at the feel of his body against hers. "I never knew it could be like this."*

"It would have been very improper of you to know, my love." Lord Rotherham's voice held a thread of amusement.

"I'm a fallen woman, now."

"No. I am a fallen man." He turned her in to his arms, assaulting her senses with strategically placed kisses. Her breath quickened. Her body sang to the tune he played on it.

"We will be married by special license." Lord Rotherham carried her to the bed where once a queen had slept. "I cannot have the ton gossiping about my wife."

How dictatorial he sounded. He couldn't be allowed to have it all his own way. That would never do. She sighed, putting on her most pensive expression. "I've always dreamed of a wedding at Saint Paul's with two bishops in attendance—"

Lord Rotherham pulled away, eyes chilled.

"And Parley as my maid of honor." Cressida put her arms around

his neck and drew him down to cover her body. "But perhaps that would give rise to too much comment?"

Lord Rotherham gave a crack of laughter. "I am sure Father Thomas can be persuaded that Parsley is a proper attendant."

Michael dropped a kiss on her head. "Who's Parsley?"

"No peeking. I'm not finished." Kate closed the laptop.

Kate and Michael had returned to Betty's Bed and Breakfast in the wee hours of the morning. Sean and his wife Catriona pressed them to stay at the farmhouse. But they refused claiming lack of clothes and in Kate's case, lack of computer. The truth was they wanted to be alone. They'd promised to be back in Cluhalaugh this afternoon for Essie's and Padraic's wedding.

Essie's sister, Maire, had urged the couple to wait the three month's Ireland's laws required for a church wedding, so her priest could officiate.

Essie said, at their age, they'd waited long enough. She and Padraic decided to have Thea perform a joining. It was Thea's right as Lady to do so.

Michael changed the target for his kisses to the back of her neck. They were playing havoc with her senses. "Are you ready for a wedding?"

Kate's phone danced a jig on the nightstand. "I thought I turned it off."

"I'll grab it for you." Michael handed her the lit-up phone. "It's a text from Brad."

Staying to see my cousins wed. I'll see you back in New York. There's a contract waiting for entitling you to free publicity for you next three books. After three, we'll talk about payment.

"That's ominously vague. Do you want to sign a contract with a possible leprechaun? What if he asks for our first born child?"

Kate drew Michael's arms around her. Children? Weddings? "I'm a little uncomfortable here. This feels too much like *happy ever after*."

"You're wrong, my love. This is just the beginning." Michael drew her toward the bed. "I think we should review Chapter 1."

EPILOGUE

Kate woke to a sticky kiss. "Happy Anniversary, Mommy." Her five-year-old son's red hair stood up in sleep spikes. "I maded you toast and eggs. All by myself." Ethan's gap tooth smile shot an arrow of love to her heart.

"You need to share those eggs. It's my anniversary too." Michael set a tray bearing two cups of fresh-brewed coffee and a vase of dew-kissed lilacs on the nightstand and sat down next to her. Barefoot, sleep tangled hair, beard-scruffy, and a smile the made her long to strip him of his faded blue T-shirt and Superman lounge pants and have her wicked way with him. But that would have to wait.

Kate rescued the plate Ethan held out to her before the eggs slid sunny-side-up onto the quilt. "My favorite breakfast in the world. You are the best son ever."

"Happy Birthsary, Mommy." Three-year-old Abigail bounced onto the bed. "I helped. I did the jelly." Her Cinderella nightgown bore sticky witness to her efforts. As did her rosebud mouth.

"Thank you my love bugs. I have the most wonderful children in the world." She glanced up at Michael. *Thank you.*

There's more.

After ten years they didn't need words.

"Kids, go clean up," Michael said aloud. "Grandma and Grandpa will be here any minute."

Ethan flung his arms around her neck. "We're going to Disneyland," he whispered. "Abby doesn't know."

Two strawberry-flavored kisses later the room was silent.

Michael reached over and speared one of the rock-hard eggs. "Pretty good for five. He'll make some woman very happy."

"Bite your tongue. You made Abby put her X on a promise not to marry till she was thirty. I'm holding Ethan to the same thing." Kate sipped her coffee. "This is bliss. Coffee in bed and . . ." She stroked a finger along Michael's prickly jawline. "Disneyland, huh? How long before they leave?"

Michael's indrawn breath told her she'd started something they both wanted to finish. "Not soon enough. I'll go hurry things along."

Kate leaned back and enjoyed the anticipation. She took a bite of gooey toast made with cold butter, strawberry jam and love, and sent up a prayer of gratitude to God for not listening to her. The children she'd been terrified of having were her greatest blessings.

It was hard to believe it had been more than ten years since she'd turned in *Chasing Cressida* and told her agent she was moving to California.

Ten years since they'd promise to love honor and cherish each other using the traditional words her mother had said so many times. She giggled at the memory. She'd recited her vows through lips stiff with terror. Michael had to pry their joined fingers apart to slip on the ring.

Kate sipped the last of the coffee. There was never a time when she hadn't felt loved. Sure, there were times when they fought. Not too many. Just enough to result in some spectacular making up.

Her office had a shelf for her three RITA awards. It also held Ethan's and Abigail's birth certificates, her very proudest works of art. Writing with young children was complete insanity, but Michael made sure she had the time to do it, which given his own insane schedule, was some kind of miracle.

"All clear." Michael joined her in bed. "Mom and Jeremy picked up the kids. We're supposed to retrieve them Sunday night."

Kate rubbed her cheek against his face. "Two whole days with no children? There can be no greater gift."

"There's one more gift. Brad sent us four tickets to Ireland. Cluhalaugh's holding a special celebration for Essie and Padraic's tenth anniversary. And there's a celebration at the hill for Pirikit and Eamon's tenth. He says we're invited to that too."

Kate drew back. "No. Tell him the children have small pox. The last time we visited the hill, their twins magicked wings onto Ethan. Can you imagine what Abby could do with a pair of wings?"

"It will be all right," Michael soothed. "Essie says there's a spell to magic-proof human children. And Brad told the twins that if they were very good, they could come to America. "

"Ha. According to Piri, pigs would fly before they'd make that journey. Eamon hates America. They would never—"

"Who said anything about Piri and Eamon? Brad's planning to escort the children to California to visit us."

"No," Kate moaned. "Stress the smallpox. Add some other disease."

"It won't work. Brad's a completely besotted uncle. He thinks that Kiera and Kiernan can do no wrong, aside from an odd magic trick or so and he's sure he's got that under control with bribery."

Kate shuddered at the thought of Kiera and Kiernan putting their heads together with Ethan and Abby. "Our kids do not need any help at inventing new ways to get into mischief. What are we going to do?"

"We'll think of something." Michael began a journey from her lips down her body. "You've got too many clothes on."

"So do you."

They remedied the situation and went back to doing what they did best, loving each other with soft sweet touches and rivers of fire-hot passion.

When it was over they snuggled into each other, reveling in the unusual silence.

Michael sighed. A deep sigh of masculine satisfaction. "Forty-eight grownup hours. Want to drive to the coast?"

She threaded her fingers through his. "I like it just where we are."

"I was thinking of dinner and a movie which doesn't involve cartoon characters, and—"

Kate silenced him with a kiss. "Yes to everything, especially the *and* part. Let's do that now."

"Woman, you wore me out. I hope I don't disappoint you."

She stroked her hands down the body of her husband, lover, friend. "You could never do that. You're my hero."

FROM THE AUTHOR

The hero of this book is Michael Walshe who is mentioned in Time and Forever and has a key role in Maybe This Time. I wanted his Happy-ever-after.But this book has no time travel so should I mention it as part of a series? Maybe, but it's definitely a stand alone.

I wrote this book after I visited Ireland's famous match-making festival. It was charming, but I wanted a wee bit more magic. What if there was a matchmaker who inherited the power to know your true love? What if there was such a thing as leprechuans or half leprechauns - a bit more human sized - who were under geas to fulfill wishes. I love 'what if's.' Do you?

ABOUT THE AUTHOR

Susan Berger writes second chance romances with a touch of magic as Susan B. James and children's books as Susan J. Berger. She writes older heroines because she is chronologically gifted and enjoys creating characters who remember that change is only on the outside. Inside our older shells is a much younger psyche.

In her debut romance, Time and Forever, two women in their sixties inadvertently travel back to London in 1969. Maybe This Time, winner of UnCaged Books 2019 Raven Award for contemporary romance and the 2019 Reader's Favorite Gold Medal for Time Travel, is the companion book. Her third book, Irish Magic released in August 2019.

Susan's other career is acting. More on IMDB

FOLLOW SUSAN ON SOCIAL MEDIA:

Blog: susanbjames.blogspot.com
   Twitter: @susanjberger
   Facebook: facebook.com/SusanJames/
   BookBub: bookbub.com/authors/susan-b-james
   Instagram: instagram.com/bergersusanjames/
   Goodreads:
   goodreads.com/author/show/7791397.Susan_B_James
   goodreads.com/author/show/3027649.Susan_J_Berger
   Acting: SusanBergerActor.com

www.ingramcontent.com/pod-product-compliance
Lightning Source LLC
Chambersburg PA
CBHW070652180626
46817CB00006B/2335